PRAISE FOR
JOANNA TROLLOPE

Next of Kin

"An involving and insightful domestic drama." —*Chicago Tribune*

"Trollope does an excellent job of describing the dynamics of farm life . . . an absorbing narrative." —*Publishers Weekly*

The Choir

"Compelling." —*The Boston Globe*

"Remarkably good at catching the small details . . . whether it is the chewed ends of a bishop's spectacles or the organist's instructions to the choir." —*Newsday*

"Sacred music . . . and delicious deadpan understatement create a uniquely rich soundtrack on the pages of this beautifully crafted tale." —*Publishers Weekly* (starred review)

The Best of Friends

"Entertaining, engaging, and literate."
—*Library Journal* (starred review)

"Joanna is as poised and intricate a portraitist as her famous novelist ancestor, Anthony Trollope. . . . The domestic tale takes on almost Shakespearean dimensions. . . . It is [the] intense focus on raw emotional issues in everyday lives that lies at the heart of Joanna Trollope's work and sets it apart from cozy village green tales."
—*The Washington Post Book World*

"Delicate nuance . . . a sly sense of humor."
—*Milwaukee Journal Sentinel*

continued on next page . . .

Other People's Children

"[Trollope] aims for the heart, and she hits it."   *—The New Yorker*

"Read Joanna Trollope's *Other People's Children*. . . . You won't be sorry."   *—USA Today*

"Deliciously addictive . . . a vivid chronicle of what can go wrong when a man and a woman fall in love and their respective dysfunctional families beget a series of stepfamilies."   *—Kansas City Star*

Marrying the Mistress

"This novel should easily vault onto the bestseller lists."

—Publishers Weekly (starred review)

"Just as one has forgotten the intense pleasure of reading Trollope, along comes another flawless novel."

—Library Journal (starred review)

A Passionate Man

"An elegant, witty, and deeply perceptive book."

—The Woman's Journal

A Spanish Lover

"Something we see all too rarely these days: a genuinely grown-up work of fiction, by, about, and for grown-ups." *—The Washington Post*

"Trollope is at her best analyzing the complex strands of DNA that bind families—and sometimes threaten to strangle them."   *—People*

The Rector's Wife

"Simply delicious."   *—The New Orleans Times-Picayune*

"[A] lively and entertaining novel." *—The New York Times Book Review*

By Joanna Trollope writing as
Caroline Harvey

A Second Legacy

"The Roman poet Horace once said that the exceptional writer was one who could wield ordinary words so skillfully that, in his hands, the ordinary was made new. But for the fact that Horace said it more than two thousand years ago, he might have been speaking of Joanna Trollope. Here is a writer who marshals simple prose and constructs stories around everyday people, but in her hands the humdrum is made strikingly fresh."   —*The Washington Post Book World*

Legacy of Love

"Three separate and beautifully realized historical settings."
—*The Cleveland Plain Dealer*

"Harvey brings a practiced hand to these nuanced narratives of young women's trials, sexual awakenings, and self-discoveries."
—*Publishers Weekly*

The Brass Dolphin

"Trollope explicates siege, faith, and passion with convincing force and detail . . . [a] rich account of wartime bravery and survival."
—*The New York Times*

"Malta is described so vividly that you can practically smell the white roses and feel the waves of sun-baked heat rising from the book."   —*The Seattle Times*

"Compelling and perfectly paced."   —*Publishers Weekly*

A Village
AFFAIR

Joanna Trollope

B
BERKLEY BOOKS, NEW YORK

𝓑

A Berkley Book
Published by The Berkley Publishing Group
A division of Penguin Putnam Inc.
375 Hudson Street
New York, New York 10014

PRINTING HISTORY
Bloomsbury edition / 1989
Black Swan edition / 1990
Berkley mass-market edition / October 1999
Berkley trade paperback edition / September 2002

Visit our website at
www.penguinputnam.com

Library of Congress Cataloging-in-Publication Data

Trollope, Joanna.
A village affair / Joanna Trollope.
p. cm.
ISBN 0-425-18605-9
1. Triangles (Interpersonal relations)—Fiction.   2. Depression, Mental—
Fiction.   3. Women painters—Fiction.   4. Married women—Fiction.
5. Villages—Fiction.   6. Lesbians—Fiction.   7. England—Fiction.
I. Title.

PR6070.R57 V55 2002
823'.914—dc21   2002066578

PRINTED IN THE UNITED STATES OF AMERICA

10   9   8   7   6   5   4   3   2   1

For Louise

ONE

On the day that contracts were exchanged on the house, Alice Jordan put all three children into the car and went to visit it. Natasha made her usual seven-year-old fuss about her seat-belt, and James was crying because he had lost the toy man who rode his toy stunt motorbike, but the baby lay peaceably in his carrycot and was pleased to be joggling gently along while a fascinating pattern of bare branches flickered through the slanting back window of the car on to his round upturned face. Natasha sang "Ten Green Bottles" to drown James and James amplified his crying to yelling. Alice switched on the car radio and a steady female voice from *Woman's Hour* explained calmly to her how to examine herself for any sinister lumps. Mud flew up from the winter lanes and made a gritty veil across the windscreen. James stopped yelling abruptly and put his thumb in his mouth.

"You are an utter baby," his sister said to him disdainfully. He began to cry again, messily, round his thumb.

Alice could see his smeary wet red face reflected in the driving mirror. The voice on the wireless said that if you disliked touching yourself, you should get someone else to feel for you. The interviewer said—perfectly reasonably, Alice thought—how would anyone else be able to feel what you could feel, not being, as it were, on the inside of yourself?

"Crying like that," Natasha said to James, "makes people think you are a girly."

James let out a wild squeal and flung his motorbike-clutching fist out sideways at his sister, just able to reach her cheek. Eyes wide with outrage and turned at once upon her mother, Natasha began to cry. In the very back, conscious of an atmosphere he didn't like, Charlie's soft round face gathered itself up in distress. He opened his mouth and screwed his eyes up tight. Alice stopped the car.

"The lymph nodes—" said the *Woman's Hour* woman into the racket.

Alice turned her off. She undid her seat-belt and twisted herself around.

"Be quiet!" she shouted. "You beastly, beastly children. I won't *have* this. You are not to quarrel in the car. How can I drive? Do you want me to drive you into a wall? Because that's what will happen."

Natasha stopped crying and looked out of the window for walls. There were none, only a hedge and a hilly field and some black and white cows.

She said, "There aren't any walls."

Alice ignored her.

"Where did I say we were going?"

"In the car," James said unsteadily.

His sister looked at him witheringly.

"To our new house."

"Yes. Don't you *want* to see it?"

"Yes," Natasha said.

James said nothing. At that moment he didn't want anything except to put his thumb back in, which he dared not do.

"Then," Alice said, "nobody will say one single word until

we get there. Otherwise you will have to stay in the car while I get out and look at everything. Is that clear?''

She buckled herself in again and started the car. Natasha watched her. She was the only mother Natasha knew who had a pigtail. It was very long. It started high up, almost on top of her head, and ended up half-way down her back. It was fat, too. Usually, she pulled it over one shoulder. Natasha wanted one like it, so did her friend Sophie. Sophie's mother had sort of ordinary hair you couldn't really remember, like mothers usually had. Looking at her mother's pigtail made Natasha suddenly feel affectionate, out of pride.

"I'm sorry," she said, in a minute voice, because of the ban.

Alice beamed at her quickly, flashing the smile over her shoulder.

"Nearly there."

Alice had always wanted to live in Pitcombe; everybody did, from miles around, and if a house there was photographed for sale, in *Country Life*, the caption always read, "In much sought-after village." It was the kind of village long-term expatriates might fantasise about, a stone village set on the side of a gentle hill, with the church at the top and the pub at the bottom, by a little river, and the big house—baroque—looking down on it all with feudal benevolence. Sir Ralph Unwin, who owned the big house, three thousand acres and two dozen cottages still, was tall and grey-haired and an admirable shot. He drove a Range Rover through the village and waved regally from the elevated driving seat. He allowed Pitcombe Park to be used constantly for functions to raise money for hospices and arthritis research and the church roof, though he drew the line at the local Conservatives. "I'm a natural cross-bencher,"

he would say, knowing he would be admiringly quoted. Alice had met him only once, introduced by John Murray-French from whom they were going to buy the house, and he had said, "You are more than welcome to Pitcombe, Mrs. Jordan, particularly if you have children."

She had wondered if he was well aware of how charming he was. Lady Unwin was charming too, in that capable, administrative way that women acquire after long practice on councils and committees. Lady Unwin chaired the county's St. John's Ambulance Brigade and the local hospice committee and saw it as her duty to attend PCC meetings and NADFAS outings and the village over-sixties jaunts. She had grasped Alice's hand in her own large and flexible one with its pink painted nails and peerless Georgian rings and said, "Oh my dear, hooray. Just what we need, some new young blood to liven us all up."

And Sir Ralph, taking his wife by the arm in one of those public displays of proud affection for which he was liked as much as for the independence of his politics, said with a warm smile, "Don't trust her an inch, Mrs. Jordan. She'll have you on every rota and committee in sight, within minutes."

Everyone round them had laughed. Alice had laughed too. She had liked it. She had felt welcomed and included, almost part of the life that she was quite certain she wanted to live in Pitcombe *for*. When they had heard, at a dinner party, that John Murray-French was selling up, privately, she and Martin had hardly slept for excitement. His was not just a house in Pitcombe, but one of *the* houses in Pitcombe, half-way down the hill, with the beeches of the Park above it and the river three fields below it, at the end of a little cul-de-sac which ran from the main street between pretty, low, haphazard rows of cottages. There was an orchard beyond it, and a paddock where the children could have a pony and, on top of the garage, a wonderful high beamed room with north light where

John Murray-French carved the ornamental decoy ducks for which he had become mildly famous and which Alice could use as a studio. She hadn't painted since James was born, more than four years ago. But she would be able to now, she knew it.

She swung the car in off the main street and drove carefully down between the cottages. It was early afternoon and the lane was quite empty except for a crumpled old face at a ground-floor window between a spider plant and a begging china dog in a large green hat. Alice waved and smiled. The face took no notice at all. A black cat on a garden wall didn't even stop washing to watch them go by. At the end of the lane were the two slender weathered stone pillars that announced the entrance to The Grey House. They had stone bobbles on top, smeared with ochre and greenish grey lichen. Beyond them, two clipped deep green rows of hornbeam marched towards the house. Alice stopped the car, suddenly exultant. Everything was going to be all right, it was, it *was*.

"Help yourselves," John Murray-French had said on the telephone that morning. "I'll be out but Gwen will be around somewhere supposedly packing books but probably swilling my gin in the broom cupboard. She knows you're coming." He paused. He was very fond of Alice. So had his son been, but too late, when she was already married. "I'm so pleased it's you," he said.

"Oh, John—"

"I've lived here for thirty-five years. Can't believe it. I'd hate it to go to a stranger."

"I promise we'll love it. I mean, we already do. In fact, I think it's the answer—"

"The answer? To what?"

There had been a tiny pause.

"Oh," she said, in a more matter of fact voice, "three children, more space, studio for me. You know."

She let the car creep between the hornbeams. The children, sensing the drama, began to give little squeals of excitement in the back. Natasha had already written, in all her books, partly from pride, partly to prevent James ever claiming them:

This book belongs to:
Natasha Jordan
The Grey House
Pitcombe
Wiltshire

And there it was. Long, low, grey, with its pretty sashed eighteenth-century windows reaching almost to the floors, its heavy panelled door with pediment and lion's-head knocker, its three brick chimneys, its terrace over the valley, sitting so beautifully in its pleasing sweeps of golden gravel and green grass. Sinuous grey arms of wisteria twined up over the pediment and along the façade, and either side of the front door a bay tree grew glossily in a Versailles tub. It was perfect.

Alice climbed out of the car and released the children. They raced down the lawn at once, still squealing, to climb the iron park railing that separated the lawn from the paddock below. Alice opened the back and picked up Charlie. He was very pleased and beat about in the air with his hands and crowed. She went up to the front door and rang the bell. John had said not to bother but she didn't want to alienate Gwen in any way, hoping she would stay and clean the house for her, as she had done for John for a decade.

Gwen opened the door after a very long time, clearly meaning to upstage Alice, but was undone in an instant by the sight of Charlie in his blue padded snowsuit.

"Ah. Bless him. Isn't he lovely? Come in, Mrs. Jordan. The Major said you'd be over."

Alice turned to shout for the children. They were still on the railings.

"I'd leave them," Gwen said. "Can't come to no harm. Who's a lovely boy, then?"

Charlie regarded her impassively.

"He's very good," Alice said, anxious to be friendly. "The best of the three, really. But he weighs a ton."

"Would he come to Gwen, then?"

She held out her arms. Charlie allowed himself to be transferred without protest. He examined Gwen's face solemnly for a while and then her pink blouse and her maroon cardigan. Finally, after long scrutiny, he put a single shrimp-like finger on her crystal beads.

"Aren't you gorgeous?" Gwen said to him, quite melted. "Aren't you and Gwen going to have a nice time, then?"

Alice felt a rush of gratitude towards Charlie.

"Actually, I was going to ask you—"

Gwen turned a beaming face on her.

"I thought you might be. Course I'll help." She turned her face back to Charlie. "Gwen's not going to turn down an old heart-throb like you, now, is she. I'll take him into the study, Mrs. Jordan, and you just poke about. The Major said to. I'll keep an eye out for the children. Now then," she said to Charlie, "I wonder if we could find a biccy?"

Alice said faintly, "He's only got two teeth. He's only eight months. Perhaps—"

"Who's a big boy?" Gwen said moving off rapidly. "Who'd have thought it? Eight months—"

The drawing room ran for twenty-five feet along the front of the house to the right of the door; the dining room rather less to the left. Behind them were a study for Martin, a room for a playroom, and a kitchen which opened with a stable door on to a wide brick path and then grass and then the eastward view. The stable door had seized upon Alice's imagination when she had first seen it; she had visualized a summer morning, with the sun streaming in through the opened top half, and herself up a ladder, singing while she stencilled designs her head was full of round the tops of the walls. She could *feel* how happy she would be. The kitchen was rather grim now because John was only concerned with it as a place to open tins in, but she had known the moment she saw it how lovely it could be. Looking at it now, darkly cream painted, shabby linoleum floored, with its scrubbed center table cluttered with half-empty marmalade jars, and corkscrews and newspapers and ripped-open brown envelopes, she suddenly had a tiny twinge.

It was very tiny, but it was there. It was like a sudden, faint, malicious little draught of cold air on a golden summer day, or a wrong note in a melody, very transient in itself but leaving something unnerving behind it. Alice shook herself, took hold of the comforting end of her plait, and looked sternly at the kitchen. Pale yellow walls, she had settled on that, white woodwork, strip, sand and polish the floor, scented geraniums along the windowsills, dried hops along the ceiling beams, jars of pulses and spices on the dresser, a rocking chair, patchwork cushions, a cat . . . She began, without warning, to cry. It was horrifying. Why was she crying? Huge sobs, like retching, were surging up brokenly inside her and these vast tears were spilling over and she couldn't see. She fumbled frantically for a handkerchief, scrabbling in the pockets of her coat and her skirt, up her sleeves, in her bag. She found a crumpled tissue and blew her nose violently. She *never* cried. Strong Alice who hadn't cried since after Charlie which was obviously postnatal. She sat down in one of John's scuffed kitchen chairs and bent her head. She was frightening herself.

Probably she was tired. It had been quite a strain wondering if they really *would* get The Grey House, and Martin wasn't good at this kind of thing and fussed a lot about money and surveys and things like that. She had said to him, trying to encourage him, "But the *right* things are right, aren't they? I mean, the house *feels* right so I can paint again and make a bit of money at last, and perhaps we could have a pony. It never matters with money in the long run, does it? We always manage. We will now."

He said crossly, "*I* manage you mean."

She tried not to feel furious. She tried not to remember that Martin had a private income, even if it wasn't huge, so that money never was a proper problem to them, as it was to other people. They weren't rich, but they weren't uncomfortable either. Martin hated her to talk about his private money; he was very secretive about it. She thought that his pride suffered from knowing he did not earn very much as a country solicitor and probably never would. She told herself he had to pretend he earned all their income, for his own self-esteem. So she waited, looking at his rough, fair head bent over the newspaper, and after a bit she said, "You see, I think we'll be so happy at The Grey House. That's the element I think is so important."

They had many such conversations. Sometimes Martin said, "Aren't you happy here, then?" and sometimes he said, "Oh I know, I know, I'm just being an ass, you know how I hate thinking about money," and once he said, "Thanks a bloody million," and stamped out. She began to follow him but stopped, and they went to bed that night hardly speaking. That kind of thing was, of course, terribly tiring, far more tiring than digging a whole cabbage patch or painting a ceiling or spending an entire day in London Christmas shopping in the rain. Alice blew her nose again now and stood up. She would go into the drawing room. Nobody could ever want to cry in the drawing room.

But she did. She stood by the fireplace in the lovely long low room with its bookcases, and windows to the terrace, and imagined decorating the Christmas tree in that corner, and doing a vast arrangement of dried flowers in that, and hanging up those marvelous miles of ivory moire curtain that Martin's mother had given her, at all the windows, and she felt worse than she had in the kitchen. She felt despair. At least, she thought it was despair, but she did not think she had ever had a feeling like this in her life with which to compare it. She fled from the drawing room to the dining room, confronted images of herself smiling down the candlelit length of the table across dishes of perfect food, and fled again, upstairs and into the first bedroom she came to.

It was John's. It would be hers and Martin's. It was the room she had dreamed of most, of lying in bed with the view of the valley surging in through those near floorlength windows. She knew where she would put her dressing table, and the little sofa her mother-in-law had given her, and where she would hang her collection of drawings of seated women, a collection she had begun when she was fourteen. She looked at the room now in panic. There was no malevolence in it, nothing in it but its usual graceful, placid charm. The panic was in her. She put her hands to her face. It was burning hot.

In the bathroom John's old pug was curled up in a basket in the bottom of the airing cupboard. The door was open so that he shouldn't feel claustrophobic. He grunted when Alice came in but didn't stir. It was a huge bathroom, with an armchair and a bookcase, ancient club scales, lots of magazines in ragged stacks, a lovely view and several friendly, doggy old dressing gowns hung in a mound on the back of the door. Alice shut the door behind her and locked it. She ran a basin of cool water and splashed her face, then she dried it on John's towel, which smelt attractively male, and sat down in the arm-chair. Deep breaths, one after the other. Close eyes. Idiotic Alice, mad Alice, *lucky* Alice. She was still holding John's towel. She buried her face in it. How good male things were when they were impersonal to you: the sound of a strange man's confident stride across a wooden floor, a man behind you at a newspaper kiosk rattling the change in his pocket, the contrast of wrist skin and shirt cuff and jacket sleeve on your neighbor at a dinner party, John's bald old bath towel. She felt better and stood up.

"Never a word of this to anyone," she said to the pug and went downstairs.

In what would be Martin's study, and was now a fuggy and welcoming burrow where John spent winter evenings, Alice found Charlie sitting on Gwen's knee with her beads round his neck, and Henry Dunne. Henry was Sir Ralph's agent, and although John Murray-French had bought The Grey House from the estate long before Henry's day, it was still regarded as being in the fold. Henry and John's son had been at Eton together and Henry often came in on his way here and there across the estate, to tell him this and that and to describe the hunting days which were his passion and which John, leisurely french-polishing his ducks, didn't seem to mind hearing about, over and over. John's patience meant that when Henry got home he didn't feel the urge to tell Juliet, his wife, all about hunting, which was just as well because it made her scream, literally, with boredom.

Henry thought Alice was wonderful. He thought her beautiful too, with her long dark blue eyes and her astonishing high-plaited hair, but he was rather afraid she might be quite clever. Last New Year's Eve he had hoped she thought him wonderful too because he had boldly kissed her, quite separately from all that lunatic midnight kissing which was always such chaos you might well end up kissing the furniture, and she had seemed to like it. He said, "Goodnight, my lovely," to her in a whisper when the party broke up at last and she gave him a long look. But when he saw her next it was in Salisbury, by chance, and she was pushing her baby in a little pram thing and although she smiled at him, she was absolutely composed and even said, "Wasn't that a lovely party, at the New Year?"

He said, "*You* made it lovely. For me."

And she smiled at him and shook her head.

"Do you mean, Alice, that you didn't—"

"I mean that—"

She stopped. He said, "What? What? *Tell* me."

She looked at him again. There was a flicker of fear in her face, he could see it, even a dope like him whom Juliet was always saying had the perceptiveness of a myopic buffalo.

"Please not," Alice said, and then she had kissed his cheek quickly and pushed her baby into Marks and Spencer.

She seemed only delighted to see him now. She kissed him, said, "How's Juliet?" and "Oh, you old ponce," to Charlie, and sat down beside Gwen.

"The house looks so nice," she said to Gwen, untruthfully, since she had hardly noticed.

"I do my best. Bit of a business, what with the Major's pipes and the carving and the dogs. But we struggle on, don't we gorgeous?"

Charlie made mewing noises in Alice's direction. She lifted him off Gwen's knee and returned the beads.

"Gwen says she's staying on," Henry said.

"I know. Isn't it marvellous of her?"

"Four mornings I'll do here. And a day to muck out the Major when he's in his cottage. You should see the place now, walls running with damp—"

Alice stood up, holding Charlie against her shoulder.

"Thank you so much for your kindness, Gwen. It's such a

weight off my mind, knowing you'll help me. I ought to go and round up the children now.''

"I'll come with you," Henry said. "I only came to leave John the surveyor's report on his cottage.''

Gwen opened the front door for them both. Alice put a hand on it. Her front door. She took her hand away quickly and put it back under Charlie's solidly padded bottom.

"Bye now," Gwen said. "Mind how you go. Bye-bye, you lovely boy.''

When the door had shut, Alice said, "Is she going to drive me mad?''

Henry looked mildly shocked.

"I don't think you'll find anyone else very easily. Everyone is crying out for help and I know for certain Elizabeth Pitt has her eye on Gwen, and so does Sarah Alleyne, except nobody can bear to work for her for more than a month.''

He opened the car boot so that Alice could stow Charlie away in his carrycot.

"We're all thrilled you have got this house, you know. It'll make such a difference to the village.''

Alice straightened up.

"We're so lucky.''

"I'll say. The hordes John has had to beat away don't bear thinking of. He said a chap appeared out of the blue driving a black BMW and offered him four hundred thousand.''

"What has a BMW got to do with it?''

Henry said, faintly nettled, "He must have come down from the City. That sort of money.''

Alice said nothing. She stood quite still and looked at the house. The light was beginning to fade and Gwen had switched on a lamp here and there, coral-coloured rectangles in the soft grey façade. It looked idyllic.

"I'm sick with envy," Henry said, watching her. "Me and half Wiltshire.''

Alice turned slowly to face him. She reached out and touched his hand for a second.

"The thing is," she said, quite calmly, "that now that I have it, I don't in the least want it."

And then she burst into tears.

⌘

"I don't know what it is," Martin said into the telephone, keeping his voice down even though Alice was upstairs in the bath. "She doesn't seem able to tell me. She thinks The Grey House is lovely, she doesn't want to stay here, but she says she is terrified of moving."

His mother, fifty miles away in Dorset, said, "Is it the moving itself?"

"Can't be," Martin said. "She never minds anything like that. I've never seen her like this."

"She was very upset for a while after Charlie—"

"That's all over," Martin said. "Pronounced A-one four months ago."

"Have you," Martin's mother said, "been quarreling?"

Too loudly Martin said, *"No."* Then he said, more ordinarily, "The odd bicker, I suppose, over what we ought to offer for The Grey House, but not *quarreling*."

"Can I speak to her?"

"She's in the bath. She doesn't know I'm ringing you."

Martin's mother, who loved her daughter-in-law dearly, said with some indignation, "Behind her back, as if she was unfit to hear? No wonder she cries."

Martin drooped. It was as it ever was. He couldn't remember a time when he hadn't longed to please his mother, to feel confidential with her, and then to know every time that he had failed. He knew she loved him—but he wasn't ever sure she liked him. It was rather the same with his elder brother Anthony, except that Anthony was tougher and ruder, so that they sparred together. He remembered with customary bewilderment his mother saying to Alice ten years ago, "I'm glad it's Martin you're marrying, not Anthony. I love Anthony but I know he is really a horrible boy."

And she meant it. It wasn't a doting mother's joke. Martin wondered uneasily what his mother had said to Alice about him; there was so much she had said to Alice that he would never know.

"Of course talk to her," he said now, stiffly, "if you think it'll do any good."

"Get her to ring me," Cecily Jordan said, "when she's out of the bath."

He sighed and put the receiver down. He was frightfully tired. He had got back from a long day, and everything looked entirely as usual, children in bed, supper ready, Alice in the low slipper chair by the fire in their tiny sitting room, stitching at some tapestry thing until she turned her face up for his greeting kiss and he saw she had been crying. She then cried on and off all through supper. She said, between crying and mouthfuls, that she had an awful feeling of foreboding that it just wasn't going to work. He had said, "The Grey House, you mean?"

"No—no—not the house exactly, just living there, us living there—"

"But it's the thing you have always wanted!"

"I know," she said, pushing her plate away half-full. "I know. That's why I am so afraid."

He tried to jolly her.

"You're not afraid of anything! You never have been. You terrify me, skiing."

"Oh," Alice said dismissively, "physical things. Easy. This is something much more alarming, a sort of utterly lost feeling, as if I'd staked everything on something that wasn't there at all.''

Martin began to finish the lasagne she had left.

"I don't understand you," he said.

He still didn't. Perhaps his mother was right and it was the remains of post-Charlie blues. He felt sorry for her, but at the same time faintly aggrieved that she couldn't behave normally about something she had said she desperately wanted and that he had really had to battle to achieve. He'd had to sell a lot of shares, a *lot,* for The Grey House. He looked round the room, tiny but full of fascinating things and bold stuffs and extraordinary paintings which he wouldn't have chosen himself in a million years but which he found he really liked, now he saw them. Very Alice. He looked into the fire. He felt she was failing him.

When she came down, in a yellow dressing gown with her plait pinned up on top with a comb, he said, trying not to sound surly, "Ma says would you ring her."

A kind of light came into Alice's eyes, a look of relief and hope.

"Oh yes," she said. "Did she ring?"

"I rang her."

"Martin, I'm not being deliberately neurotic. I detest feeling like this. If I could stop, I would."

He got out of his chair and went to kick a log in the fireplace. He thought of his mother's tone to him, on the telephone. He said to Alice, "Is it me? Is it something to do with me? Are you sick of me?"

Alice gave a little gasp.

"Oh no!"

He grunted.

"Just wondered."

The wrong note in the melody sang out again, tiny and harsh, in her mind. She went across the room and put her arms round him from behind, laying her cheek against his back.

"You know it isn't that. Haven't I kept telling you that I want The Grey House because I know we'll be happy there?"

"But that doesn't fit in with all this panic."

"Exactly. It's probably some hormone imbalance. That's what I've been thinking about in the bath."

He turned round and held her. He thought how much more often he needed to make love to her than she wanted to have it made to her. He took a deep breath.

"Go and ring Ma," he said.

TWO

Before Cecily Jordan had married, she had been, briefly, a Lieder singer. She had gone to Vienna, to train, in 1937, in the teeth of her parents' opposition, and had, at eighteen, fallen wildly in love with music, with Vienna, and with a young Jewish composer and political activist. It was he who introduced her to the pure and lovely solo songs of Schubert and who taught her to vary her performance from lyrical to intensely dramatic, as the Lied required. This he did partly by technical instruction, and partly by taking her to bed and awakening her to a consciousness of her own powers which she found quite natural to express in song.

In the winter of 1938 he made her promise, by threatening never to see her again if she wouldn't comply, to go home at once to England if anything should befall him. He made her write the promise down and sign it. In June 1939, he was arrested while crossing the Ringstrasse, in midday sunlight, and a note from him, containing the written promise, was brought to her while she stood in her sunny, dusty, cluttered room out by the Prater Park, doing her voice exercises.

"To break your promise will make everything infinitely

worse for both of us and I should despise, not admire you for it,'' her lover wrote. ''The best thing you can do for us now is to take that lovely voice we have made together back to England, and use it as a light in a dark world.''

He did not write that he loved her. Sitting in a series of hideous trains crawling home across Europe, Cecily reflected that he had never said it either. She hadn't noticed, so busy had she been doing the loving for both of them. She arrived in battened-down England in August, numb and almost speechless, and went out to Suffolk to her parents' house, where her mother was relishing the prospect of the privations of wartime, had already sold all her childhood books for salvage and had painted a red line round the bath, four inches from the bottom, as a peculiarly irritating kind of Plimsoll line.

Cecily tried to sing, but she couldn't. War was declared in September but it seemed to her that the news came from very far away and had no direct relevance to her. She slept badly and spent a greater part of each night lying awake reliving Vienna. By day she went for punishing walks and talked a good deal about joining up, which she did not do. Then suddenly, out of the blue, she announced she was going to Canada, to Toronto, to teach singing in a large girls' school. She went for six years. Her parents thought she might marry a Canadian, but she married no one. She returned to England in the grisly winter of 1946 and the following June she married Richard Jordan, whom she had met on the train that she had taken from Southampton after leaving her transatlantic ship.

Richard Jordan was an engineer. He had been in Southampton looking at a bombed site as a possible place for a factory to make drills for wells. He prospered. He and Cecily had two sons in five years and bought a manor house in a wooded valley a mile from the sea beyond Corfe in Dorset. Cecily, who found in due course that she could not naturally enjoy the company of any of the three men in her life, discovered some kind of recompense in the manor's garden. She became a gardener of imagination and then distinction. She wrote books on gardens and was invited to lecture all over England in the sixties and, as her fame spread, all over Eastern America in the seventies.

And then, in 1976, her younger son, Martin, brought Alice home. It was a September day of ripe perfection, the gardens at Dummeridge replete in the late warmth, bursting fallen plums lying stickily in the long grasses, fat things humming and buzzing in the borders. Cecily had been out by the eighteenth-century summerhouse she had discovered derelict in Essex and had transported to Dorset, tying up a heavy double white clematis that obligingly bloomed twice a year, when someone behind her said, quite easily, "You must be Martin's mother."

She turned. There was a tall girl standing six feet away. She wore jeans and a blue shirt and her abundant brown hair was tied up behind her head with an Indian scarf.

"I'm Alice Meadows," the girl said. "Martin wanted to catch up with the cricket but I said I couldn't bear not to come out here. I hope you don't mind."

"Mind," Cecily said, "I should think not."

She took off her gardening glove and held her hand out to Alice.

"More than welcome, Alice Meadows," she said.

She had put Alice to sleep in the little south bedroom that she privately thought she would use for herself when Richard was dead. It had a brass bedstead, polished floorboards with rough cream Greek rugs, blue and white toile de Jouy curtains, deep windowsills, and, in a corner, a huge china jardinière out of which a violently healthy plumbago cascaded in a riot of starry pale blue flowers.

"Do you like it?" Cecily said, unnecessarily.

"In every way."

"It's my favourite room. It has a very nice personality."
She glanced at Alice. "Are you and Martin serious?"

Alice returned her look, entirely unperturbed. The house and
the room and this fascinating, strong-looking woman with her
drill gardening shirt and trousers, her beautifully coiffed hair
and her ropes of pearls, made her feel that there was nothing
to fear or to be decided—it would all be done for her.

"No," Alice said. "We have known each other for two
weeks. Martin met my brother, playing squash, and my brother
brought him home. We have been to the cinema twice and to
the pub a bit. You know. And then he asked me here."

She ran her hand round the fat brass knob on the bed end.

"Do you think," she said to Cecily, "that I was wrong to
come if I don't mean to be serious?"

"No. Whatever you end up being, you were right to come."

They went down into the garden again together and Cecily
left Alice under a willow at the edge of the lawn while she
went to make tea. Alice lay back in an old cane chair whose
arms were unravelling in spiny strands, and looked up at the
strong blue sky through the fading blond-green fronds of willow and felt—she hunted about in her mind for a word.
Happy? Too thin. Content? Too sluggish. Gorgeous? Too self-
regarding. But all were right in their way, and so was replete
and sleek and blissful, and so was—

Would she, Alice wondered abruptly across her own
thoughts, tell Martin's mother about her family? Would she
say that to come to this ancient and lovely house, to drowse
in this romantic and sensual garden, was an answer to a prayer,
the antidote to her own home where the unlovely walls echoed,
day in, day out, with her mother's steady complaining? I am
ripe for this, Alice told herself, pushing off her shoes with her
toes and stretching her bare feet in the sun. I am an absolute
sucker for this paradise, I was a pushover even before Martin's
mother opened her mouth. She shut her eyes and let the willow

dapple its shadow softly across her eyelids. At home now, at 4 Lynford Road, Reading, her mother would be drinking Indian tea out of an ugly mug given away by a garage, while not listening to *Kaleidoscope* or the end of *Afternoon Theatre* on Radio 4, but instead storing up in her mind all the day's grievances which were, indeed, a lifetime's grievances, against her friendly, amiable philandering husband, Alice's father, who was probably, even now, taking a seminar on the Metaphysical Poets at the university and thinking about sex.

She wouldn't leave him. It was one of her complaints to Alice that she wouldn't because she loved him and look how she was treated, how her loyalty was abused. Alice had come to see that it was closer to tyranny than loyalty, even though her father's carryings-on disgusted her. She felt, as she got older, that even her friends weren't safe from him; they all thought him dishy and flirted with him when they came to collect Alice for the cinema or a disco. Alice's mother wanted her to take sides, to defend her, but Alice wouldn't. She thought they were both wrong, and she knew that the moment she had finished art school, she would leave Reading and the hideous house with its charmless contents and her mother's bitter laments and her father's self-indulgence and she would go, like her brothers had, and not come back.

One of her brothers had gone right away, to Los Angeles, where he was a tremendously successful taxi driver. The other had only gone to London, to live happily in a huge disordered flat with six others off Lavender Hill, and do his Law Society exams. It was he who had brought Martin Jordan home—well, not home exactly because passing through was all he could take—on their way to play squash in some tournament in Oxford, and because Alice had been upstairs painting in an absolute fury after the newest student conquest had telephoned quite openly to ask to speak to Professor Meadows, they had taken her to Oxford too. She wouldn't watch them play squash, but went to the Ashmolean instead and looked at the Caernavon marbles, and came away much soothed. Martin Jordan had come down from London four times in two weeks to take Alice out—the last time he had brought flowers for her mother which nobody had done, Alice thought, in twenty years—and then he had telephoned and said he was coming through Reading, on his way to Dummeridge, and that he would collect her. If she'd like to go.

Alice said Reading wasn't on the way to Dorset from London.

"It is," Martin said, "if I'm coming to collect you."

So he had, and they had driven away from Lynford Road and Alice would not look back to wave at her mother because she knew herself to be the cause of a new complaint for daring to go off to enjoy herself while her mother was forced to stay behind and suffer. And here she now was, as long and supple and warm as a stretched-out cat, lying under a willow in a place like heaven, while someone wonderful brought tea which would be, Alice knew, China, in pretty cups, with slices of lemon to float in it and perhaps almond biscuits.

"There," Cecily said, "what a contented looking girl." She put down the tray. "I hope you like China tea. And Dorothy, who helps me, has made some shortbread."

Alice said laughing, "I said almond biscuits in my mind."

"And China tea?"

"Oh yes—"

Cecily smiled broadly and sat down in a cane chair.

"Martin is still glued to the box."

"I don't mind. As long as he doesn't want me to be glued too."

"He says you paint."

"Yes."

"Things you see, or things you imagine?"

"Things I see coloured by things I imagine."

"Lemon?"

"Oh, please—" She swung herself upright and put her bare feet down on the brisk, warm, late summer grass.

"You don't know," she said to Cecily with some energy, "how heavenly this is."

"I do, you know. Don't forget that I have virtually made it, so I like to take all the credit."

She held out a shallow eggshelly cup painted with birds of paradise.

"Where I live," Alice said, taking it reverently, "everything is as ugly as possible. I think it's my mother's revenge on life for not making her happy."

"Almost nobody is happy," Cecily said. "It's rather that one must devise ways of cheating or eluding unhappiness. And of course, some people love unhappiness with a passion."

"My mother just loves it with a grim determination," said Alice and let out a burst of sudden laughter, "Oh, oh, I'm mean, *mean*—"

"Yes," Cecily said, looking at her with great liking, "you are. Now, you had better tell me all about her and your clever father. I fear you have come into a gravely illiterate household. I believe my husband reads nothing but newspapers and engineering periodicals, Martin reads nothing but colour supplements and his brother Anthony reads nothing at all. What about you?"

Alice put her cup down carefully and lay back again in the cane chair.

"Love stories. I'm mad on love. Do you think it's the answer?"

"Now that," Cecily said, thinking of her son Martin, "is something you will have to find out for yourself."

Even as a baby, a brand new baby, Martin had looked faintly anxious. He was a pretty baby and then a dear little boy and then an attractive bigger boy and finally he emerged as a sturdy, fair, good-looking man. But he still looked anxious. If you were in a good mood, Cecily always thought, you wanted to comfort that anxiety away, but if you were not, his expression resembled the silent reproachful pleading of a dog who has nothing to do all day but beseech you for a walk you haven't time to give it. She loved Martin very much but she didn't want him with her a great deal; she never had. He was undeniably rather dull, but she wouldn't have minded that. It was his want of boldness she found so discouraging, his unadventurousness, his lack of curiosity. Bringing this uncommon girl down was the most enterprising thing he had done in twenty-four years of life. Not only had he brought her down, but he was handling her beautifully. Cecily would have expected him to be too eager, too slavish, but he wasn't. He was quite challenging in fact, and even though Cecily suspected him of being besotted, he gave little hint of it. Alice had the same bold, free manner with him; there were no longing glances or furtive looks. When Anthony came home, later, for dinner the first evening, Alice took almost no notice of him at all even though he was dramatically rude in order to attract her attention. He was so rude that his father, roused from his inner world at the far end of the table, said suddenly, "Leave the room."

"Father—"

"Leave the room."

Anthony turned to his mother.

"Go on," she said.

"This is barbaric—"

"Leave the room," Richard Jordan said, and suddenly there was a bull-like threatening look on his face. Anthony got up.

"What will Alice—" He stopped. They were all watching him. He left.

Cecily seemed quite unmoved.

"I believe a Frenchwoman has written a book describing how she finally got rid of her five sons. I must buy a copy."

Martin did not try to come to Alice's room that night. She had thought he might and had rather hoped he wouldn't. She had been to bed twice with men before, once when she was seventeen to see what it was like and get the first time over with, and once six months before, driven by a simple physical longing to be made love to. She had, somewhat inevitably, preferred the second time, but neither had been what she was hoping for, which she put down to not being in love with either man. She was quite clear that she wasn't in love with Martin either, and so didn't want sex with him to become some litmus paper test. But she thought, lying there in linen sheets in her charming room while a disgracefully theatrical copper harvest moon hung outside, that she would very much like some good sex. She would like to be taken over by some huge physical force inside herself and feel every atom of her body as a *body*. One of the lecturers at the art school—rather a creep, in fact—had said that good sex made you a better painter. Alice had thought about this and finally had dismissed it as a very sixties view. What about Toulouse Lautrec and Van Gogh for starters? What Alice really wanted to know, she decided, her hands flat on her cotton nightie-clad belly, was what an orgasm really felt like, what it did to you. Then she could stop *wondering*.

She turned on her side, and slid both hands between her thighs. This was the most wonderful place she had ever been to. If Martin asked her to marry him tomorrow, standing perhaps in the creeper-clad stableyard while the white pigeons flew erratically about in the blue air above them, she would say yes. Then she could always come here and, best of all,

Cecily would be her mother-in-law. She began to giggle, help-lessly, out of happiness and excitement, and Martin, standing in the dark passage outside her door, was very nearly, but not quite, brave enough to come in and ask her what she was up to.

He knew he wanted to marry her. He knew it the moment her brother Josh had pushed open the back bedroom door in that grim house in Reading, and there was Alice in black-and-red striped tights and a vast blue smock smeared all over with paint and her hair screwed up on top with a paintbrush thrust through it, painting away in a terrible temper. He didn't even look at what she was painting, he was so busy looking at her. He had never seen anyone who looked so—so *vital*. She flung herself at Josh, who seemed equally pleased to see her. And then they had carried her off to Oxford and Martin had felt that his little Mini was absolutely pulsing with interest and life even though Alice didn't say much. She just sat in the back and *existed*, and occasionally he glanced in the driving mirror at her and felt his guts melt. This was *something*.

He found she gave him courage. He could dare with her, conversation with her was a kind of game. He realized, leaving a pub with her ten days later, that he didn't even feel dull or conventional, he felt brilliant. He grew afraid that if he didn't make her his, for ever, that brilliance would go, he would go back to being the dear, ordinary old Martin who fussed about train times and driving conditions and made his mother—how-ever she strove to conceal it—visibly sigh. Asking Alice down to Dummeridge was a brainwave, an absolute corker of an idea, and now here was Alice adoring the house and getting on with his mother like a house on fire. And even his father ... Anthony had once said, in a rage, that living with their father was like living in a house where the biggest and best room was always locked, and though Martin, by nature both conventional and loyal, was distressed by the image, he recognized the truth of it. His father wasn't exactly dull, he was just ruthlessly private, but he was watching Alice, Martin could see that, and what was more, he liked her. Being Alice— Martin felt himself dissolve at the thought—she didn't appear to notice that Richard was withdrawn. She talked to him, and so he talked back. He smiled at her. The only person she ignored was Anthony and that was Anthony's own stupid fault, all that capering and showing off to attract her attention, trying to impress her by bitching the parents. It was the first time, the first glorious time in Martin's life, that he had scored over Anthony, that he had something Anthony wanted that he couldn't have, that he had found something of real stupendous quality that his father and his mother applauded him for. He was ten feet tall. He was a new, a different man. If he could keep Alice, everything would fall into place from now on, there would be a goal, a future, he would work for *her.*

With stupendous self-control, and guided by a subtlety of instinct he had never experienced before but which he entirely trusted to, he did not propose to Alice for three months. They saw each other every week, and two weekends a month he arrived in Reading with russet or mauve chrysanthemums for Mrs. Meadows ("Only get her hideous flowers," Alice said. "She despises pretty ones.") and drove Alice down to Dummeridge. He had a half-gun in a local shoot, and sometimes Alice went with him, to beat, and sometimes she stayed at Dummeridge and painted and talked to Cecily. Cecily admired her paintings a good deal and persuaded her into both watercolours and painting pictures of corners of the house. Alice painted a cobwebby window at a turn of the cellar stairs, and a scattering of hens on the old stone mounting block and a corner of the drawing room where a battered little alabaster bust stood on a table shrouded in an Indian shawl against a faded, striped wall covered in miniatures.

At lunchtime they ate eggs and salad and home-made brown bread by the Aga, and Cecily always gave Alice wine—at home there was beer and whisky for her father and sherry for her mother which of course she wouldn't touch for fear of feeling better, but never wine—and they talked as Alice had never talked before. Cecily even—and it was thirty years since she had mentioned it to anyone—talked about Vienna. The story fired Alice with a yearning passion, not just the love story but the foreignness, and the powerful romance of the voice that blossomed and was then locked away in a box for ever when all the circumstances that had awakened it were wrenched away. Alice had never travelled, except on a school trip to Paris which was chiefly distinguished by interminable and sick-making hours shut up in a bus. The Jordans had all travelled; they took it as a matter of course. Richard travelled constantly, on business; the boys went skiing and both had been on safari in Kenya; Cecily went on her lecture tours and on her own to France and to Italy to look at things, she said, and to eat and drink both literally and metaphorically.

"You should go," she said to Alice. "It's criminal that you haven't been to Italy."

Alice began to think that indeed it was. As the autumn wore on, she became privately very angry when Sunday night came and she had to leave Dummeridge, glimmering away in the firelight in its wealth of old stuffs and books. Lynford Road looked worse on each return, the scuffed carpet tiles in the hall, the uncompromising, harshly shaded ceiling lights, the black and green tiles in the bathroom, the mean proportions that confronted her everywhere, too high, too narrow. She began to long for Martin's Monday call, regular as clockwork, telling her when he was coming down to take her out. His arrivals, invariably punctual, became events of real excitement. Every time she found him standing on the tiled doorstep in Lynford Road, in a tweed jacket she had last seen him wear in the drawing room at Dummeridge and the brogues she could still hear striking the stone flags of the kitchen passage, her feeling of being rescued grew greater and more glamorous.

In the first week of December he arrived to take her out to supper in Marlow. He was wearing a suit and Alice, convinced he would say *something* to her, put on the black dress she had made from a length of jersey from the market, piled her hair high on her head and added some enormous copper earrings a friend at art school had made for an Egyptian exhibition. The restaurant in Marlow had pink napkins and red-shaded lights. Martin made a face.

"Sorry," he said to Alice.

She wasn't entirely sure why he was apologizing; it looked to her just as she would expect a restaurant to look. In any case, she was far too full of anticipation to care if the panelling was phoney or Mantovani was being played whisperingly over the loudspeaker system. Martin ordered everything competently, told her about his week—she hardly listened to him— and then said he had something to tell her and something to ask her. She forced herself to look at him quite, quite straight.

"Tell first," she said.

"My mother has two commissions for you. Two friends of hers have seen the paintings you have done of Dummeridge, and they want you to paint in their houses. Ma said she has asked a hundred and fifty for you. Each."

"Each!" Alice said, and went scarlet.

"Well?" He was smiling hugely.

Alice clutched herself.

"It's—it's *wonderful*. So's she. Heavens. *Real* money—"

There was a sudden small hard lump in her throat. She supposed it to be amazement and delight.

"I rang her last night. She really wanted to tell you herself at Christmas, but I made her let me. That's the other thing. The thing I wanted to ask you."

Alice couldn't look straight this time; she didn't seem able to look anywhere. She looked down instead into her melon and parma ham and Martin said to her bent head, "Would you come for Christmas? To Dummeridge?"

There was a pause. Oh, Martin thought, you cool, cool customer, don't keep me dangling, don't, don't. Say yes, say yes, say . . .

"Love to," Alice said. Her voice was warm but not in the least eager. It betrayed nothing of what she was feeling, nothing of the sudden fury that had seized her, a fury against Martin. Ask me, she had screamed at him silently, ask me, *ask* me. And he had said, come for Christmas.

"That's great," he said. "They'll all be thrilled, I know it. What about—"

"My parents?"

"Yes—"

"I've spent twenty Christmases with them," Alice said with a fierceness for which Lynford Road could not be blamed, "and I think I deserve one off. Granny's coming, anyway."

They arrived at Dummeridge on Christmas Eve to a house garlanded in green, with pyramids of polished apples and candles and the smoky scent of burning wood.

"So lovely!" Cecily said. "To have a woman to do it all for."

From the moment she and Martin got to Dummeridge, Alice

was the star of Christmas. She could feel the atmosphere lifting as she entered rooms and knew that everything was being
done for her, with an eye on her. She had a fire in her bedroom, and a Christmas stocking of scarlet felt, and wherever
she went the eyes of the household were upon her and the
hearts of the household were hers. Even Anthony, she noticed,
was striving to please. She felt, moving through the lovely
rooms, taking the dogs out for windy walks high above the
grey winter sea, that this was what she was meant for, that
she had somehow come home.

So confident was she, so queenly, that when Martin did
propose she felt no elation, no sudden lurch of delight and
relief, just a warm acknowledgement of the inevitable. It was
Boxing Day and they were racing along Seacombe Cliff,
shouting into the wind, when he seized her suddenly, breathless and laughing, and said, "You will marry me, won't you?"

And she said, laughing back, "Certainly not!" and ran away
from him, and he knew she didn't mean it and chased her and
pulled her to the ground and pinned her there, on the cold
exciting turf under the racing wild clouds, and made her promise. Then he carried her home to Dummeridge and his father
opened champagne and whenever she looked across at Cecily,
Alice knew she could have made no other choice. She was
loved here.

That night, relaxed and warm and full of power and confidence, she had an orgasm in Martin's arms. He had one rather
later. She was a bit confused—the champagne perhaps—as to
why she had had one and how much it had to do with what
he was doing to her, which wasn't, actually, much at the time,
but she felt great triumph that her body had taken her over,
as she had been so anxious for it to do. It did occur to her
that the release that had happened to her body didn't seem to
have overwhelmed her mind at the same time, but she pushed
that thought aside, as clearly, if she had had an orgasm with

32

Martin she must be more in love than she thought, which meant in turn that it would, as a feeling, grow. She slept gratefully in Martin's arms until five, when he gently disentangled himself and went discreetly back to his own room. They met at breakfast in a mood of mutual, and visible, triumph, and Cecily, noting this with inexpressible relief, felt that thirty years of negative life had at last turned a corner.

THREE

They were married, in 1977, by unanimous agreement, at Dummeridge. Alice's mother, quite overwhelmed by Cecily, allowed all decisions to be made for her, including a shopping trip to Bournemouth for her wedding clothes. She returned, saying a little fretfully that she had never cared for green, but she was clearly elated, and refused to describe the trip in order to show her husband and her daughter that she too could have her lovely secrets. Alice didn't care. She went down to Dummeridge every weekend without fail, and made plans—where Martin should look for a job, what kind of house they should seek, where they should go for their honeymoon, what her dress should be made of, what she ought to put on her wedding present list.

"You mean I can actually ask outright for six cream bath sheets and a Spode blue Italian soufflé dish and a dozen wine glasses and a tin-opener?"

"I most certainly do. People expect it."

"Wowee! Now," Alice said. "Let's think what else—"

Martin was offered a job in Salisbury which he took with alacrity, and not long afterwards Alice and Cecily found a cottage on the edge of Wilton, with three bedrooms and a charming elevated fireplace made from an old bread oven, and an apple tree in the garden. It was May and the tree was luscious with blossom. In June, Alice left the art school, packed up her bedroom in Reading and moved down to Dorset. Her mother, truly wounded now, did not even try to stop her because it was so glaringly evident to everyone why she was doing it. Her father, however, did try.

"Are you sure," he said to her, propping his attractive bulk against the kitchen cupboards and cradling a glass of whisky against his chest, "that your head hasn't been turned?"

Alice said waspishly, "Well, that's certainly something *you* would know about."

He laughed. He had always been exasperatingly impossible to annoy.

"Come on, Al. You've only two months more to stick out here. It's a bit rough on us to be so publicly cast aside for the glamorous prosperity of the Jordans even *before* you're married. You look spoiled. We look inadequate."

"I don't mind how I look," Alice said, "and I can't help how you look. The boys have both gone, I've had three years here on my own. At Dummeridge there isn't a permanent atmosphere and I can paint." A tiny, proud pause. "I have three more commissions."

"You might perhaps," Sam Meadows said unwisely, suddenly struck by the vision of opening the Lynford Road front door to find nobody but his wife inside, "think of me."

Alice snorted.

"I see. You'd like me to stay so that there's some sort of buffer state here between you and Mum. Well, bad luck. That's one of the *reasons* I'm going now."

Sam took a gulp of his drink.

"Frankly, Al, I don't think I could take it on my own."

"Then you should understand exactly how I feel. Don't

whine,'' Alice said crossly. "And don't try and make me feel guilty. I'm going, and that's that.''

Her father levered himself upright and came round the kitchen table to put his arm around her and plant a competent, whisky-scented kiss on her head.

"I don't blame you,'' he said, "and you shouldn't blame me for having a go at making you stay.''

"Blame,'' Alice said, leaning against him and resentfully acknowledging how good he was at touching women. "Don't talk about blame. It's a word never used at Dummeridge, and nor is guilt or loyalty or betrayal or any other of the awful emotional claptrap words you and Mum use *all the time.*''

Her father had gone out then, and she had returned to her room to finish packing, and when she came down, her mother was sitting on the brown repp-covered, foam-filled sofa in the sitting room staring into space with her hands gripping one another in her lap. Alice squatted beside her.

"Martin's coming for me at five.''

"I know,'' her mother said.

"There's not much difference,'' Alice said with difficulty, "between going now and going when I'm married. Honestly, there isn't.''

Silence.

"It isn't—it isn't because I don't—well, it's not that I'm—I'm not fond of you and Dad, it's just the atmosphere here.''

"I see.''

"Nobody asks me to take sides there,'' Alice said, pleading. "I haven't got to think who I'm going to upset every time I open my mouth.''

Elizabeth Meadows continued to stare at nothing.

"I see.'' A little pause. "And is the Jordans' marriage a happy one?''

Alice was rather startled. She had never stopped to consider such a thing, and now that she did it came to her that perhaps it wasn't particularly companionable as a marriage but it was perfectly all *right,* and anyway, they both had their own lives, *that* was the difference.

"They don't want it to be everything in life to them, like you do," Alice said, making everything worse. "Cecily has her own career, Richard's very successful—"

"How perfect," her mother said, as if spitting out broken glass.

Alice sighed. She got up and went over to the French windows that opened into a sad little strip of garden that her mother tended with ferocious tidiness, filling the parallel beds with salvias and African marigolds in regimented rows.

"Look," she said, "whatever I do, I can't get it right. Either you're upset or Dad is. So I'm going only a little bit before marriage decently allows me to, where I get it right all the time without even trying."

Elizabeth said, "You protest too much. I am not attempting to prevent you," and then, blessedly, the doorbell rang and it was Martin.

Alice never slept at Lynford Road again. The two months at Dummeridge passed like a happy dream. Richard was away almost all the time, and Cecily was in America for three weeks, and as Martin, taking his final exams, could not be there except weekends, Alice had the house to herself, looked after by Dorothy and as free as air. She slept in a hammock in the garden at midday, and at night wandered about in the pale summer darkness and made herself voluptuous sandwiches filled with cream cheese and dried apricots and chopped walnuts, which she sometimes ate sitting quite naked on the moonlit lawn or in the unlit drawing room. She went down to the sea at midnight, with the surprised but politely acquiescent dogs, and swam in the glittering black water, and then walked home barefoot and sat on the Aga, wrapped in a blanket feeling her salty hair dry into long whispering snakes down her back. She meant to paint, but she didn't. She knew she would have to, when Cecily came back, so she spun out her time alone greedily, luxuriously, drifting through the hot hayfields beyond the house, leaning her cheek against walls and trees, lying on her stomach on the lawn with her arm plunged into the goldfish pool watching the light darting in the water and the bubbles of air pour upwards from the hairs on her arm.

She saw Martin off to London on Sunday nights without a pang; indeed, when the sound of the Mini's busy little engine had quite faded away she felt a bubbling up of her spirits, as if she were really free again. This made her go straight to the kitchen and sit down at the huge scrubbed table and write to him very lovingly, telling him how much she looked forward to Friday, and how carefully he must drive. She wrote these letters in all sincerity. When she had written them, she would go down to the sea and swim and swim and swim. Dorothy, finding wet towels on the Aga rail so many early mornings, wondered whether she should say something about the lack of sense in swimming alone in the sea in the middle of the night and decided, looking at Alice, not to. The moment she was married, that freedom would vanish, you never got it again, so even if it was risky, it was worth it, and after all, everything worth having was a risk, one way or another.

Alice had only two visitors besides Martin, while Cecily was away. One was Anthony who arrived unannounced for the night, drank copiously at dinner and tried, in a very practised way, to kiss her afterwards. She said, standing quite rigid in his arms. "But I don't fancy you at all. I don't find you in the least attractive."

"Try me," he said, bending his head.

She bent away.

"In any case," she said, "you are only having a go to score off Martin."

So Anthony dropped his arms and went to bed, and was gone when she woke in the morning.

The other visitor was her future father-in-law, at home for two nights, between journeys. He telephoned her to say he was coming. She said, wanting to be dutiful, "Is there anything I ought to do? I mean, anything you'd like or usually have—"

No, he said, nothing. She was to take no notice of him; Dorothy could do what had to be done. He would be there for dinner. So she went for a long, aimless, happy walk, spending a great deal of time in an unexpected stream building a dam, and came back about teatime to hear the sound of someone playing the piano. It could only be Cecily. Full of a sudden rush of pleased excitement, she burst into the drawing room crying, "Oh, I wasn't *expecting*—" and found that it was Richard.

He stopped and turned round.

"But," Alice said, "you don't *play* the piano!"

He smiled.

"I do."

"But Cecily—"

"I always have. I'm competent but uninspired, as you may imagine. I never play if I think there is anyone in the house."

She crossed the room slowly, and stood beside him. He had been playing Schubert, too.

"I've really thrown you," he said, "haven't I."

She felt her face grow hot.

"Yes. I thought—" she paused.

"I know," he said. "People do." He got up from the piano and brushed his hands briskly together as if he were shaking off the disconcerting unfamiliarity. He looked down at her and she wondered if he were very slightly laughing at her, but all he said was, "You look well. What have you been doing?"

And she said, looking back, "Absolutely *nothing*."

He had liked that. He wanted, later, to hear what absolutely nothing involved. She could tell him parts of it, though clearly to tell a man who is about to become your father-in-law that you had lain naked on his drawing room sofa eating sandwiches in the middle of the night was hardly one. She was, to her surprise, sorry when he went away, bound for Heathrow and then the Gulf of Mexico. He hadn't seemed, while he was at Dummeridge, either to take the house away from her—and after all, it *was* his—or to encroach upon her freedom. On the contrary, he seemed to have his own private freedom which tantalized her a little, made her want to know more about him. When he was gone, she found to her intense annoyance that she was just a little lonely, so that when Cecily returned three days later she had the same kind of thankful, over-excited welcome from Alice as from her dogs.

"I shouldn't have left you so long, but this wretched tour was fixed up almost a year ago. Never, never do I wish to have to explain again that it is not possible to make an English spring garden in Selma, Alabama."

Everything pulled itself together once Cecily had returned. Days and nights went back to their conventional roles, lists were made, letters were written, Alice's wedding dress—ivory chiffon over peach-coloured silk—was finally fitted. Presents arrived by every post, presents from complete strangers and from shops that had never been in Alice's orbit—the General Trading Company in Sloane Street, Harrods, Peter Jones, Thomas Goode, the White House. The dining room at Dummeridge slowly fitted up with sheets and china and saucepans and Chinese lamps, things that she, Alice, had chosen and asked for and was now being given. As the piles grew, she discovered that she did not like it, even though she liked the things.

It was not that she felt that she was being spoiled, but rather that these bales of towels and pairs of garden shears and boxes of brandy balloons were somehow buying *her*. She tried to say something of this to Cecily, and Cecily, believing her feeling to be the result of the material modesty of her upbringing, said she must simply lie back and lap it up.

"I promise you, people *want* to do this. They would think it most odd if you hadn't a list, and goodness knows you haven't been greedy."

So Alice wrote her letters obediently and tried to decide constructively about flowers and asparagus rolls and the colour of lining for the marquee which was to be very grand and have French windows in case the day was cool. At night, instead of lying languorously in her linen sheets, Alice lay and worried, worried about details and *little* things and felt that from somewhere a pressure had arisen that was now sitting on her chest and her brow and making it difficult for her to see or breathe.

When her wedding day came, she was in no mood for it. It happened, of course, the great machine being inexorably in motion, and she went up the aisle most decoratively on her father's manifestly pleased arm, but she felt lonely, all day, and by the end of it she was tearful and exhausted from the effort of seeming as she wished she were feeling.

"She's tired," Cecily said to Martin privately, tucking them into the car to go away while the guests, unnaturally jolly after champagne drunk unsuitably mid-afternoon, stood on the gravel and cheered. "Look after her."

He did his best. She slept most of the way to Athens next day and he was very solicitous and tucked blankets round her and motioned the air hostesses not to bother her with lunch and drinks and duty-free watches. A friend of Cecily's had lent them a villa on Patmos, and they were alone there except for the couple who were caretakers and who were so assiduous in both house and garden that they were quite difficult to elude. They swam and slept and lay in the sun, and Alice drew a bit, and at night Martin made love to her which she didn't mind but didn't seem able to look forward to much, either. What he felt about it she didn't know because they didn't talk about it. They were perfectly companionable and years later, when both of them, separately, tried to remember their honeymoon, neither could, in any detail.

"I think," Alice was to say to her father-in-law, trying to be truthful and fair, "I think I was simply asleep."

When they returned, wearing the tan and the faint, pleased air of achievement expected of honeymooners, Alice's parents took the final step of obliterating Lynford Road from her life. They had hardly been home two weeks, and Alice was still in the state of early nesting, where to find the perfect place to hang a washing line gives the keenest pleasure, when her father arrived, quite unannounced. He looked absolutely normal; it was Alice who was astonished. She took him proudly into her little sitting room, sat him down in the only proper armchair they possessed and pointed out various aspects of the room he might admire while she went to make coffee. He said he would rather have a brandy.

"Brandy?" Alice said.

"Yes, brandy."

"We haven't got any brandy."

Sam Meadows closed his eyes.

"What have you got?"

"A wine box."

"Then a glass of wine box, please."

Alice went out to her kitchen and took one of her new glasses out of her newly painted cupboards and filled it from the wine box. The wine, she noticed irrelevantly, appeared to be being sold by a mustard company. She took the glass back into the sitting room and Sam said, before he even had it in his hand, "You see, I've come to tell you that I have left your mother."

Alice, distanced by Apple Tree Cottage and Greece and Dummeridge from her parents' ancient torments, said only, "For whom?"

"For nobody," Sam Meadows said. "For my sanity."

Alice put the glass of wine in his hand. She said, "Did you plan this?"

"Oh yes. I'd been planning it for years. I knew I couldn't stay once you were all gone, but on the other hand if I had gone before you might never have been able to leave yourself." He took a swallow. "I left the night of your wedding day."

"You *what*—"

"We drove home from Dummeridge in complete silence. I think the only word either of us uttered was when she said 'Mind' passing a bicycle somewhere near Andover. When we got home, she began. Nothing new, just all the usual things, over and over. So I went upstairs and packed a bag—silly really, just like some melodramatic telly thing—and I drove to a university residence where I knew there was an empty room destined for an American postgraduate who had never turned up. I'm still there."

"But I've *spoken* to you," Alice said. "And to Mum. And neither of you ever said—"

"She thinks I'll go back. She thinks thirty years of marriage makes it inevitable."

Alice looked at her pretty fireplace which she had filled with flowers and leaves.

"You've been an awful husband."

"I haven't been a *faithful* husband."

"That's awful. I couldn't stand it."

Sam finished the wine.

"I wasn't unfaithful in order to hurt your mother."

"I know that. It's just that she has nothing else."

"It was that I nearly died of."

Alice looked at him. She felt both a faint disgust and a mild affection for him, but mostly she felt that none of it had much to do with her.

"What will happen to Mum?"

"I don't know. Of course, I'll give her half of everything. But at the moment she won't discuss anything because she thinks I *must* return. So—" He looked across at Alice.

"So you want me to go and tell her that you are not coming back and she must think what she wants to do."

"Yes."

"All right," Alice said.

Her father stood up.

"You don't sound much concerned. One way or the other."

Alice said, with sudden temper, "You always want such an *emotional* reaction. Well, I haven't one to give you. Or if I have, I mightn't want to show it. Maybe I think you are right to leave and maybe at the same time I think Mum's future looks terrible, but I'm not going to talk to you about it. I'm not going to *wallow*."

Sam came over to her and put his hands on her upper arms.

"One day," he said, "one day when you wake up to real feeling and real pain, one day when you can't have something you long for or you see too late that you have closed the door on something you need, *then* you will understand about communication and communicating is, after all, the only end of life that makes any sense."

Alice said indignantly, "What d'you mean, when I wake up to real feeling?"

Sam dropped his hands.

"Just that."

When he had gone. Alice went into her kitchen to wash up his wine glass and cried a bit, out of confusion. It seemed a long time until Martin might be home and was she tempted to telephone him but restrained herself, just, and so wasted an afternoon in profitless fidgets around the cottage. When he did arrive, she told him at once, in a clumsy rush, and he came over to her and put his arm round her and said, "Oh, Allie, I'm so sorry, how awful for you, but really it was inevitable wasn't it?" And she felt suddenly and wonderfully better. Of course it was inevitable! What else could anyone have expected of that hopelessly ill-assorted pair manacled to one another by law and a perfect graveyard of impossible expectation and broken promises? She leaned against Martin. He said into her hair, "You've got a new life now, anyway. I mean, they'll just have to get on with it, won't they. You see, you're mine now, aren't you."

And it seemed then, standing there together, that he was both the answer and the refuge, and so she clung to him and was full of grateful love.

She did, of course, go to see her mother. They sat either side of the kitchen table with their elbows on the worn formica, and Elizabeth said at once, "I know he won't come back. I have to face having dedicated myself to a man who is quite able simply to remove himself and leave me with the ashes of our life together. My life was his. Now I don't have one."

"Perhaps," Alice said, "he didn't *want* all that dedication."

She felt sorry for her mother. Her eyes were quite dead, like pebbles, and she was painfully thin.

"There was no way to please him. There was no way to hold him. It was all I wanted, ever, and it was the one thing

I couldn't have." She began to cry, silently. "I don't want to live any more."

Alice put her hand out and held her mother's wrist.

"Stop it."

Elizabeth said, "You haven't the first idea what I am talking about. You have never felt passionately about anyone in your life. You are so immature."

Alice took her hand back again. With an immense effort she said, "I'd like to help. If you'll tell me how."

"You can't," her mother said. "It's nice of you to want to, but you can't. Nobody can except one person and he has finally refused."

Alice got up and leaned her hands on the table so that she could thrust her face at her mother.

"All right, then. Drown in self-pity if you want to. Refuse help. Keep your stupid melodrama. But just don't forget I offered and you turned me down."

Elizabeth turned her face away.

"Why should you care?" she said, in the low, bitter voice she had used since Alice arrived. "There you are, safely married to money and status before you are twenty-one. You're spoiled. The Jordans have seduced you but you'll regret it because nobody, *nobody,* has life *that* easy."

Alice left the house then, and went for a long and angry walk around the streets where her brothers had done their long-ago paper rounds, and when she returned her mother had made tea and announced, with no preliminary, that she was going to Colchester anyway, to live with her sister.

"So all that scene just now," Alice said, incredulous and on the verge of tears, "was for nothing? You *knew* all along, you were going to live with Aunt Ann?"

"I have nowhere else to go," her mother said. "Who would want me?"

"Who indeed," Alice said to Martin later, dolloping sour

cream into baked potatoes for their supper. "I don't know what to make of her. She's certainly a sensational mother, *that's* for certain."

Martin made soothing noises. In his book, parents were not for objective criticism; they should be exempt, somehow, from personal discussion. He hardly knew his mother-in-law and the unmanageable neurotic bits of her he simply closed his mind to. She had been to university and read law, and that he could encompass quite comfortably, but the rest—best for everyone's sake not to dwell on it. And however much cause she had, he didn't like Allie sounding sarcastic about her. He cut into his potato and cold ham with energy and told Alice about a colleague of his who had a flat in Verbier which he let to friends at reduced rates, and which he had offered to them, in February.

Two weeks later, Elizabeth Meadows left for Colchester and the neat villa of her widowed sister. She took almost nothing with her but her clothes, and left her wedding and engagement rings in a saucer on the kitchen table. Lynford Road was sold, and Sam bought a flat near the university where he could live the kind of life that his greedy, kindly temperament was best suited to. He came to Apple Tree Cottage several times a year, where his benevolent bohemianism made him a great favourite among Alice's new friends who treated him with the same indulgence they might have shown an elderly and affectionate Labrador who had suddenly learned to speak. Elizabeth never came. Once a year Alice, with a sinking heart, went to Colchester for a night with the two sisters, and sat miserably in their precisely tidy sitting room while their joint grievance at losing their men occupied the fourth chintz armchair with the strength of a palpable being.

The next three years were—happy. Martin was entirely so, not just in the possession of Alice, but also because he knew— and the knowledge pleased him enormously—his life's major decisions were taken. He had not only taken them, he liked them. His job, which would finally make him a partner, was exactly what he had unambitiously expected, he had a pretty cottage and enough money, and he had Alice. The having of Alice was an incalculable asset, both for what she gave him and for the way in which people saw him, having her. She had taken to plaiting her long hair high on her head on honeymoon, to keep it from tangling like weed in the sea, and now she wore it like that all the time, and people looked at her a good deal. She wore boots and shawls and clothes from India and Peru, while the wives of Martin's colleagues wore navy blue loafers and striped shirts and pearl earrings. She painted borders round the rooms of the cottage, and pictures on the cupboard doors, and gradually people began to want her to paint their cupboards and walls and to do watercolours of corners of their houses that they felt best expressed their personalities, which they then gave to one another for Christmas and anniversaries.

She made curtains for the cottage, great dramatic billowing things that she hung from poles, while her friends turned their own cottages into sprigged milkmaid boxes, and felt, returning to them after supper with Alice and Martin, that they were altogether too timid. Alice learned to cook too, and to garden, and brought to both the eye and the confidence that it is no good wishing for if you are born without. Alice, it was generally agreed, in the rural circles around Salisbury, Alice Jordan had *style*.

And when having style exhausted her, Alice went off, of course, to Dummeridge. For those first three years of her marriage she went two or three times a month, driving down the comfortable southern roads through Cranborne and Wimborne and Wareham to spend a night with Cecily. They were usually alone, but if Richard happened to be there, he made little difference to their aloneness, and Anthony had taken his demanding and difficult personality off to Japan, with an investment company. Cecily was writing a new book on kitchen gardens, which was an attempt to revive the ancient potager. A prototype was being laid out at Dummeridge, as complex and orderly as a knot garden, and Alice drew the plan, painting in each red-leaved lettuce, each gooseberry bush trained to grow like a lollipop, each radiating brick path, with the charming stiff precision of a sampler. Cecily had shown her the foreword to the book.

This book owes so much to other people besides myself. Some of them are dead, like those vegetable heroes of the past, Richard Gardiner and William Lawson. Some are very much alive, and foremost among those is my daughter-in-law, Alice Jordan, whose exquisite plan for my own potager here at Dummeridge you will find as a frontispiece.

"I would take you to America with me, next time," Cecily said, "but I don't think it would be quite fair on Martin."

However, to both of them, a trip to Venice seemed perfectly fair. Martin did not, after all, want to go.

"Honestly," he said, "I'm not brilliant at endless churches and pictures of saints. You know me."

Alice was torn. She felt quite easy at going without him,

but at the same time a small disquiet that he didn't *want* to come. This was somehow compounded by the fact that he was so manifestly satisfied at the prospect of his wife and his mother going off to be cultural together. He said this so often and so complacently to people that in the end Alice lost her temper with him and dispensed with her compunction. They had been married almost two years.

Venice filled her with a quite violent excitement. Long after she and Cecily got back—and they were only there for five days—Alice fed herself voluptuous fantasies of living there. She saw herself in a rooftop flat watching the sun sail round behind the bell towers and the domes, a flat with a balcony filled with pots of basil and a warm parapet on which to lean and gaze down into the still, olive-oily green waters of a canal. She saw herself going shopping with a basket, buying aubergines and long, sweet tomatoes from the vegetable boat by the San Barnaba bridge, and fantastic alien fish from the market, and pasta and parmesan cheese from the tiny crammed shops in the lanes of San Polo. In the background of these dreams, she could not disguise from herself, lurked a man. He was shadowy, but extremely satisfactory, and he was not Martin.

Then she became pregnant. She liked it. She was full of energy and aroused everyone's admiration. In their large circle of young couples, some had babies—almost all had dogs—and their mutual stage of marriedness was this possession of a first baby. Alice made no fuss about anything and bore Natasha with ease. Both mother and baby seemed instinctively to know how to handle one another, and Martin, who was not required by Alice to help with nappy-changing or midnight feeds, was deeply envied by colleagues whose wives had pointed out to them that the baby, with all its attendant troublesomeness, was half theirs.

Of course, with Natasha, she could not go so freely and frequently to Dummeridge. So she telephoned, every few days, and once a month Cecily came up to Wilton with armfuls of bounty from the garden and stayed in the third tiny bedroom, and was pleased with everything and enchanted by her grand-daughter. She even sang to Natasha sometimes, and Alice and Martin exchanged slightly conspiratorial smiles of accomplishment and pleasure. Alice's friends adored her. They would all pour in for coffee or for lunch round the kitchen table, clutching their babies and their toddlers, if they knew Cecily was there. At Christmas, they gave their mothers copies of Cecily's book which they brought proudly for her to autograph.

It was then that Alice met Alex Murray-French. Alex's father John lived at The Grey House in Pitcombe, a much admired village where all Alice's friends aspired, without much hope, to live. Alex's parents had divorced when he was eight, but The Grey House had been his childhood home, and he chose to return to it a good deal rather than go out to Australia with his mother and stepfather. On one of his visits to his father, he saw a painting of Alice's, a painting she had done for a mutual friend, of a flight of stone steps leading up to an archway and a tangle of creeper. He thought he would like such a painting to send to his mother in Australia, and so he drove to Apple Tree Cottage one afternoon, on the off-chance, and found Alice on the doorstep stripping currants with her baby asleep in a basket beside her under a patchwork quilt.

Alex fell in love as suddenly as Martin had done four years before. Alice did not fall back, but she felt she would very much have liked to. He was eager and sympathetic and cultivated. He came constantly, all that autumn, on the pretext of his mother's painting, and Alice basked in his longing and admiration like a cat in the sun. She never flirted with him and he never even tried to kiss her. He told her most eloquently of his feelings, and although she liked to hear him he did not strike an answering chord in her. In the end Martin grew suspicious and angry and Alex took his picture and himself away and left Alice with a real emptiness, a bigger one than she felt was in the least fair.

Martin watched her for a long time after this.

"There was nothing *in* it," Alice would say. "He had a crush on me and I didn't have one back. I liked talking to him, that's all."

Martin knew that, but he still felt sulky about it. He believed her and yet he felt at the same time that that part of her, that differentness in her, that had made him want her so much, was becoming elusive, that he couldn't catch it any more. Instead of feeling that life with her was a lovely chase, he began to feel that she was keeping something back. But because he could not, by temperament, speak of it, he watched her instead, and this made her cross.

Her second pregnancy was quite unlike the first. She felt sick, she was sick, and many days she was so tired that from the moment she dragged herself out of bed in the morning, she was obsessed, all day, with the prospect of getting back into it. James was born with difficulty and didn't seem to like life outside Alice when confronted with it. Cecily dispatched a New Zealand girl, from a London agency, to help Alice, and Apple Tree Cottage strained at the seams under the impact of her capable outdoorsy personality. She certainly worked, and Alice could rest in the afternoons and send Natasha off to nursery school every morning in clean dungarees not laundered by herself, but the privacy of their lives was quite gone. Jennie was only with them for four months, but when she left, in a gale of good will, for a family in Pelham Crescent, she left behind her the constraint between Alice and Martin that they had adapted to encompass her in their lives. Friendly and good-mannered towards one another, they moved through the rituals of Martin's job and Natasha's school runs and James's demands, and supper parties (small), and children's tea parties (large), without somehow either coming together or moving forward.

Alice pretended not to notice that she didn't want to paint. Her friend Juliet Dunne, whose husband Henry was agent at Pitcombe Park and who was blessed with a sharp tongue and keen percipience, made no bones about pointing this out.

"It's no good *hiding*, Allie. This awful baby business doesn't last long, and if you aren't careful you'll end up like my mother saying why is it every day takes a week. It doesn't matter if you don't *want* to paint. You just have to."

"I do want to—"

"No you don't. You just want to want to. You won't get real wanting back unless you kick yourself into doing something. Look at our useless husbands. They'll never get anywhere much because they couldn't *make* themselves if you paid them."

"Why did you marry Henry?"

"Oh," Juliet said, scraping apricot pudding off her newest baby's chin, "he was so suitable and so keen and everyone else in my flat was getting married. I quite like him, though."

"You mean love him."

"Yuk," said Juliet.

Alice did try to paint after that, and it bored her so much she was quite alarmed. She took out some things she had done before James was born and they looked to her the desirable achievements of a total stranger, so she put them away again, hurriedly, before they should demoralize her. She had, she told herself, plenty to do in any case and she did it all—a touch of pride here—without any help at all. None of her friends managed their houses and families with no help at all. Cecily was always offering her some, but she said the cottage was too small, and in any case she liked her privacy.

Small things happened. Martin was made a junior partner, Natasha started at a little private school in Salisbury—the children wore checked smocks and had to shake hands, *smiling*, with their teacher each morning—they built on a playroom and another bedroom at the cottage. In the late winter, Alice and Martin went skiing (Alice discovered, rather to her satisfaction, that she liked frightening herself), and in the summer Cecily rented a cottage for them on the north Cornish coast where the children could play on the calm sands of the Camel estuary. Alice began to read, hungrily, novel after novel, carrying lists of them around in her bag along with the purse and cheque books and cash cards and paper handkerchiefs and tubes of Smarties and clean knickers and sticking plasters that formed her daily battle gear. Titles like *And Quiet Flows the Don* stuck in her mind like burrs. She chanted them to herself in the car, while in the back the members of the school run bullied the most tearful, sucked their thumbs and surreptitiously took their knickers off in order to amaze the others with their wicked daring.

When she discovered she was pregnant with Charlie, her first reaction was relief. She felt a great gratitude towards this unexpected baby for mapping out her life for her again and threatening her with its needs. Martin seemed extremely pleased except for taking out, with immense ostentation, an insurance policy against school fees which he appeared to regard, Alice felt, as something he was nobly doing for *her*.

"Ignore him," Juliet said, "just fade him out. It's the only way to survive living with a man."

"But the baby isn't just mine!"

"You try telling any father that. Henry will acknowledge William and Simon when they are captaining the first eleven, and *strictly* not before. If you wanted anything else, you shouldn't have married an Englishman."

"No one else offered."

"Allie," Juliet said, "just get on with this baby, would you? You'll make a much better job of it than Martin in any case. I despair of myself but I think I envy you."

Charlie was born, suddenly, a month early, and Alice went into a deep, deep decline. Sunk in the fogs of a profound depression, she was carried off to Dummeridge with the baby where she remained for a month, struggling inch by inch out of the depths into which she had tumbled. Pills, frequent small meals, sleep, confiding conversation and gentle exercise were prescribed as her regime. Martin, thankful to surrender this dismal conundrum to his mother, telephoned nightly for bulletins and was spoiled tenderly by Alice's friends who pitied his male dilemma in the kitchen.

She came home pale and thin and slightly sad, but she was better. Martin was very sweet to her but at the same time anxious she should know that he had suffered too, alone at night with the two elder children and responsible for the morning whirlwind of rejected eggs and lost gumboots. The week Alice returned, Cecily wrote privately to Martin, to the office in Salisbury, and said she thought Alice needed both a change and more support. She suggested a house move and offered to pay for help and for a holiday, a holiday without any of the children, the moment Charlie was weaned.

And then the gods produced The Grey House, out of casual conversation at a dinner party, and presented it to the Jordans on a plate. It was not just the house they offered, but village life, the chance and the need to be part of a proper community, where you couldn't even go to buy stamps, Alice thought excitedly, without meeting several people you knew. There would be a church fête, and a flower rota, and a list for driving old people into Salisbury, or to the hospital, and men from the Park would bring loads of logs in winter, and a Christmas tree, and in the summer she would pityingly watch the neat tourists emerge from the parked Toyotas and peer hopefully—but fruitlessly—down the pretty, sloping street for a tea shop. She would, she knew it, envy no one, long for nothing. In Pitcombe she would feel again what she had felt at Dummeridge ten years ago when she was twenty-one—she would feel she had come home.

FOUR

"Now the county travelling *library*," said Miss Pimm with the separating articulateness of Marghanita Laski, "is a *great* blessing."

"Tuesdays, did you say?" Alice said, obediently writing it down on her list.

"Tuesday afternoons. Three to three-*thirty*. The librarian is an excellent vegetable gardener and to be relied upon for *brassicas*."

"Brassicas," wrote Alice.

James, leaning against Alice, thought, with wonder, that they were discussing underclothes. He had his finger up his nose. He pulled it out and offered it to Miss Pimm.

"Gucky," he said.

She averted her gaze.

"Mrs. Leigh-Brent runs the church *cleaning* rota. And Miss Payne is in charge of the *flowers*. I know Mrs. Macaulay would *gratefully* welcome help on Mondays with the community *shop* and of course Mr. and Mrs. Fanshawe will be happy to register you with the local *Conservative* branch."

Alice wiped James's nose hard enough with a piece of paper kitchen towel to make him whimper.

"Don't be a disgusting little boy. I don't think I really am a Conservative, but my husband—"

"Not?" said Miss Pimm, swivelling her gaze back.

"No," Alice said staunchly, remembering Sir Ralph, "I believe the Park—"

"That," said Miss Pimm, "is *quite* different."

She looked round the kitchen. It looked rather *loud* to her, though considerably cleaner than in Major Murray-French's day. But she did not like being entertained in kitchens, even the kitchens of people newly moved in who might perhaps be forgiven for having nowhere else. When Miss Pimm had brought her mother to Sycamore Cottage fifteen years before, the *first* thing she had done was to make the sitting room respectable for callers. She remembered standing on a chair hammering in nails for the "Cries of London" above the fireplace, the position they had occupied in all the houses of her life.

Natasha came in through the door to the hall carrying a doll dressed like a teenage fairy, and wearing an expression of faint disgust.

"Charlie's crying and he's pooey," she said.

Alice stood up.

"Would you forgive me, Miss Pimm?" she said, "I must just see to the baby."

Miss Pimm sat on. There was much information yet to impart. She inclined her head.

"I am in no hurry."

Alice left the room. Natasha came up to the kitchen table and put her gauzy doll down. She looked at Miss Pimm who seemed to have nothing about her that Natasha could admire. The texture of her stockings reminded Natasha of drinking chocolate powder.

"Pretty doll," said Miss Pimm with extra elaborate articulation, as if speaking to a half-wit.

"She's called Princess Power," Natasha said. Her voice was proud. "She's got net petticoats, pink ones."

She turned the doll upside down to demonstrate and Miss Pimm looked hastily away.

"But," said James slowly and earnestly, from across the table, "she hasn't got a willy."

Panic blotched Miss Pimm's neck with purple patches.

"Have you?" said James.

Natasha hissed at him.

"Shut up."

"Charlie's," said James with real sympathy, "is only little. But it'll probably grow."

"I'm afraid," said Natasha to Miss Pimm, "that in James's class at school they talk about willies *all* the time. But you must just ignore him. Like Mummy does."

"School!" cried Miss Pimm on a high note of relief. "And do you like your school?"

"No," said James. "I hate everything except being at home."

"He cries every morning," Natasha said. "It's so embarrassing. My best friend is called Sophie and she has Princess Power too only *her* petticoats are yellow. I like pink best."

"Yes!" cried Miss Pimm. "Yes! Pink!"

Alice came back into the room holding a large baby. Miss Pimm was afraid of babies. Alice sat down and picked up her pencil again, wedging Charlie into the space between her and the table.

"So sorry about that," Alice said. "Now, what else was there?"

Miss Pimm wanted to say that a cup of tea was one of the things. It was five past four. She would have liked a cup of tea and a Marie biscuit. She cleared her throat with meaningful thirstiness and said, "Well, there is our little *Sunday* group."

Charlie seized Alice's pencil and drew a thick, wild line across her list. Instinctively Miss Pimm's hand shot out to prevent the desecration of neatness, but Alice didn't seem to notice.

"Group of what?"

"Why, *children*." She looked at Natasha and stretched her mouth into an attempted smile. "We meet in the church room for songs and stories about *Jesus*."

"I know about *him*," Natasha said. "He gave some people a horrible picnic with bare bread and fish that wasn't *cooked*. And then he walked about all over a lake and made a girl who was dead be alive again. If you ask *me*," Natasha said darkly, "I don't believe that bit."

"Tashie—"

"We have eleven little *members*," Miss Pimm said hastily. "And I—" She paused and then said with quiet pride, "I play the ukelele."

They stared at her. To her misery Alice found she didn't even want to laugh. Miss Pimm took their silence as an awestruck tribute to her skills and opened her black notebook in a businesslike way to show she was quite used to such admiration.

"Now, may I tell Miss Payne you would be happy to join the *flower* rota? I believe Mrs. *Kendall* lacks a partner. And what about Mondays? The community *shop* is such a boon to our *old* people—"

Go, Alice said to herself in sudden frenzy. Go, go, *go*. I hate you here, you mimsy old spinster, I hate you in my kitchen. *Go*.

"We have unfortunately to share our vicar with King's *Harcourt* and *Barleston* which means mattins only once a month, but he is a *wonderful* man, and we must just be *thankful*—"

"C'n I have some crisps?" James said.

"No. Don't interrupt. I am sorry, Miss Pimm, but usually around now I give them—"

Miss Pimm slapped her notebook shut and stood up.

"Naturally. I am sorry to interrupt family *routine*."

"Oh no," Alice said, struggling to her feet clutching Charlie, and in a confusion of apology, "I didn't mean that at all, I only meant—"

"I *came*," Miss Pimm said, implying by her tone that at least some people were still in command of their manners, "just to *welcome* you to Pitcombe. I make a *point* of it, with newcomers."

"Yes," Alice said faintly. "It's very kind of you and I'm sure when I've sorted myself out a bit—"

"You should *see* upstairs," Natasha said. "It's the most utterest chaos."

Miss Pimm walked to the stable door and lifted the latch. She turned stiffly and gave a little downward jerk of her head.

"Sycamore Cottage. Telephone 204."

"Thank you—"

"Good afternoon."

"Goodbye," Alice said. "Goodbye—"

The door clicked shut, one half after the other. Alice subsided into her chair.

"Don't cry," James said anxiously.

"I'm not," Alice said through a river of tears.

"You are, you *are*—"

Natasha picked up Princess Power.

"I expect you're tired."

"Yes," Alice said. "Yes, I expect I am, I'm sure that's it—"

Charlie's face puckered. James came to lean on her again, his eyes filling with tears.

"Don't do it," he said. His voice was pleading. "Don't *do* it."

But she couldn't stop.

The community shop, Alice discovered, was a large and battered van, owned and driven by Mr. Finch, one-time boardinghouse keeper and failed poet, who ran Pitcombe Post Office and Village Stores. Twice a week, the shop van trundled out of Pitcombe with its cargo of old age pensions, tins of marrowfat peas and packets of bourbon biscuits, to serve outlying cottages and the smaller satellite villages of Barleston and King's Harcourt. It made thirteen stops in three hours, either outside the cottages of the most infirm, or by the clumps of people standing with clutched purses and plastic carrier bags at designated places along the route.

Mr. Finch was very excited to have Alice on board on Monday afternoons. Mrs. Macaulay, who was the long-standing other helper on Mondays, despised his artistic sensibilities, believing, as she did, only in good . sense and wire-haired dachshunds, which she bred with dedication. "My girls," she called her bitches. Within the first half-hour of her first Monday, Alice discovered that Mr. Finch was misunderstood by his wife who yearned still for their boardinghouse in Kidderminster which had catered for actors at the Theatre Royal, and that Mr. Macaulay had been called to the great dog basket in the sky ten years previously, much lamented by his widow and her girls.

"He was a wonderful man," Mrs. Macaulay said to Alice, as they jolted out of the village, the tins jiggling on their barricaded shelves. "He could do anything he liked with animals. He inspired perfect trust."

At the frequent stops, Mr. Finch came out of the driver's cab and sat in the doorway of the van at the seat of change. Every time he appeared holding not only his cash box and ledger but also a battered notebook bound in imitation leather which he left nonchalantly on the edge of his little counter, with many a casually pregnant glance thrown in Alice's direction.

"Take no notice," Mrs. Macaulay hissed at Alice, passing her a stack of All-Bran boxes. "Those are his terrible jingles. Don't give him the chance to mention them."

At every stop, the van filled rapidly with people, heaving each other up the steps into the interior like an eager crowd of hedgehogs. Alice was stared at.

"Who's 'er?" somebody said from close to the floor.

"Sh, you, Granny. That's the new lady—"

"Who's 'er?"

"Mrs. Jordan," Mrs. Macaulay said with great clarity. "She has just moved into the Major's house at Pitcombe."

There was a sucking of teeth.

"She won't like that. Miserable 'ouse, that is."

"But I *do* like it—"

"It's very good of Mrs. Jordan to help us," Mrs. Macaulay said, "because she has three little ones on her hands."

"Where's me spaghetti hoops, then?"

"Hang on, Gran, they're coming," and then, turning confidentially to Alice, "she loves them. She don't need her teeth in to eat them, see."

At the end of the third stop, Mr. Finch laid his hand slowly on his book of poems and looked roguishly at Alice.

"Care for something to read before Barleston, Mrs. Jordan?"

Mrs. Macaulay was ready for him.

"Sorry, Mr. Finch, I've got the cereal section to explain to Mrs. Jordan before we get there."

Mr. Finch placed the book flat against his chest, holding it in both hands.

"Are you a reader, Mrs. Jordan? I fancy you are."

"Novels," Alice said hastily. "As much fiction as I can get. But you know, with the children—"

Mrs. Macaulay tapped her watch.

"Time, Mr. Finch, time."

By the end of the second hour, Alice could gladly have lain down on the linoleum floor of the van and wept with fatigue. Spring it might be, but the day felt raw and cold, and the depressing contents of the shelves, the tins of butter beans and the packet puddings, only compounded the bleakness. Alice had asked Mr. Finch, in his shop the previous week, for an avocado pear, and Mr. Finch had made it elaborately plain to her that left to himself his shop would be a profusion of avocado pears, but that the brutish character of his non-poetry reading clientele demanded nothing more *outré* than cabbages.

"I should be only too happy," Mr. Finch said egregiously, hunting in his memory for scraps of Tennyson with which to flatter and impress this delightful newcomer, "to bring you anything you require on my visits to the wholesaler in Salisbury."

"Thank you," Alice said, "but I'm in Salisbury most days on the school run. It's just that I'd rather use your shop, I mean, I feel I ought—" She stopped. She had no wish to sound patronizing. But Mr. Finch had hardly heard her.

" 'Why should we only toil,' " cried Mr. Finch suddenly. " 'The roof and crown of things?' "

Alice looked startled. He leaned over the counter, laying his hand reverently upon a display box of foil-wrapped chocolate biscuits.

" 'The Lotus Eaters.' "

"Yes," Alice said.

" 'We only toil,' " intoned Mr. Finch, " 'who are the first of things, And make perpetual moan, Still from one sorrow to another thrown—' "

The shop door had opened then and in had come Miss

Pimm, in quest of a small loaf and a tin of sardines. Alice had seized her chance to flee, and had bought her avocado in Salisbury, later in the day, while picking Natasha up from school.

Now, sitting precariously on her little stool as the van rumbled onwards, she thought again of the avocado.

"If we put—slightly more interesting things on the shelves, do you think we could persuade anyone to buy them?"

"Not a hope," Mrs. Macaulay said. "Absolutely set in their ways. Same stuff every week, same quantities. See that jar of Mint Imperials? We get through one a fortnight, regular as clockwork. Same with cream crackers." She glanced at Alice. "You look tired, dear. I expect it's the move. It really is good of you to join in so quickly."

Alice said, "But I always meant to," and tried not to think of Miss Pimm's visit.

"I mentioned it to her ladyship," Mrs. Macaulay said. "I said now there's a young woman prepared to pull her weight. Has she called yet?"

"No," Alice said in some panic, thinking of the disordered rooms she somehow seemed unable to find the energy to disentangle. "No, she hasn't. Frankly, the house looks so awful—"

"She won't mind that," Mrs. Macaulay said approvingly. "She isn't one to stand on ceremony. My girls always know when it's her ladyship's car. They give her such a welcome."

When Alice got home, Gwen, who had consented to look after the children on Monday afternoons until Alice returned, was making them the kind of tea she thought they should have. James was gazing in misery at the thick slice of bread and jam on his plate. The jam was red and he was alarmed by red food. Charlie, on the other hand, was cramming sticky squares of bread into his already packed mouth with the flat of his hand. Natasha, who had decided she would simply wait until Alice's return, had declined to eat anything at all. She sat at the table, neat in her school uniform, and told Gwen about her dancing class where she had been praised for being the flutteriest butterfly.

Alice dropped into a chair.

"It's a killer, that shop," Gwen said, with satisfaction, putting a mug of thick brown tea in front of Alice.

"Peanut butter," James pleaded in a hoarse whisper.

"In a minute," Alice said. "Just give me a minute. Tashie, why aren't you eating?"

"I was slightly hoping," Natasha said, with theatrical quietness, "for Marmite toast."

"I brought them the jam," Gwen said proudly. "My kids used to go mad for strawberry jam."

"How sweet of you—"

"And look how old gorgeous loves it!"

Charlie's face resembled that of a character in the final scene of a Jacobean revenge tragedy. Sensing them all looking at him, he plunged his gory hands rapturously into his hair. Gwen said fondly, "Isn't he a card?"

"Gwen," Alice said, suddenly remembering, "Mrs. Macaulay said today that Lady Unwin might call. And there isn't a civilized corner, except in here, to take her—"

Gwen pursed her lips to indicate that even such a thought had already occurred to *some* people.

"She will, Mrs. Jordan. No doubt about it."

Alice looked up at her.

"Would you help me have a real blitz on the drawing room?"

She looked really, helplessly tired. Even Gwen, who didn't go in for pity, felt sorry for her. She looked what Gwen called pulled down.

" 'Course I'll help, dear. It'd be a sight easier to clean with all those boxes shifted, in any case. She's a shocker for just popping in, is her ladyship—"

"Peanut butter," James begged.

"All right," Alice said standing up and moving slowly to the relevant cupboard.

"Of course," Gwen said, "it's all excitement up at the Park with Miss Clodagh coming back."

Alice began to spread James's bread with peanut butter.

"Thinner, *thinner*."

"Shut up. Miss Clodagh?"

"The youngest. She's been in America for three years. She always was her parents' favourite. She was a monkey of a child, I can tell you. How can you," she said to James, "eat that nasty stuff?"

James gazed at her, chewing, but said nothing.

"I'm being very *patient*," Natasha pointed out.

"Heavens," Alice said, "I might get a whole deputation from the Park—"

The telephone rang. Going to the hall to answer it, Alice said, "Gwen, could you possibly make some toast for Natasha? I don't like her to touch the grill—"

The telephone was Cecily. She had resolved only to telephone once a week, and then only in the early evening when the children were in bed, because she felt that Alice's state of mind was very fragile just now, and that even if they were all worried sick, they must not let Alice know it. But today Alice had been on her mind so constantly for some reason that she could not restrain herself from ringing up.

"Hello," Alice said tiredly.

"Darling," Cecily said, "you sound absolutely whacked."

Alice's voice grew warmer, but no more energetic.

"It's the village community shop. I got involved somehow and I've spent three hours in a very cold van selling jars of beetroot to people who told me that I'd hate living here."

Cecily laughed.

"How funny."

"It wasn't really," Alice said. "It ought to have been. But it wasn't."

"Then I'm very glad I've rung. Darling, I'm going to be very firm. I *insist* you have some more help, a mother's help, even an au pair girl. You're worn out to start with, and here you are taking on extra things like the shop."

"I've got help," Alice said. "It's sweet of you, but there's Gwen. I've never had so much help—"

She stopped. This was quite true. She had never had so much help and nor had she ever lived in such a muddle. A lump rose in her throat. Sometimes she felt quite paralysed in her inability to sort herself out. She had felt desperate after Martin and Cecily had persuaded her to go to the doctor recently and she had spent two days in the gynae bit of Salisbury hospital while they did tests, and then there had been absolutely nothing wrong with her. Martin had been so pleased. She had felt frantic. If there wasn't something wrong with her, then why did she feel like this?

"You need someone living in," Cecily said. "You need a younger Dorothy. I intend to find you one."

"Please," Alice said, pleading, "please, no—"

"But, darling, why on earth not?"

"Because there is nothing the matter with me. You know that. Mr. Hobbs said so. I've just got to pull myself together."

"But why can't you be *helped* to do that?"

"Because," Alice said on the verge of tears, "I don't *want* to be. It's so nice of you, but I must get on myself. I'm fine, really I am. Gwen's going to help me with the drawing room and when that's straight I'll feel quite different. I know it."

There was a pause, at the end of which Cecily sighed.

"Would you consider a compromise?"

Alice sounded wary.

"What—"

"You struggle on for one more month, and if you don't feel any better, will you then let me re-open the subject?"

"All right," Alice said unwillingly.

"Look, my love, there is no shame in not being able to manage. You have *so* much on your plate—"

"*I* might feel shame," Alice said.

"Your standards are too high. Is Martin being a help?"

"He's fine. He's awfully busy but he helps a lot at week-ends."

"He's so proud of you."

Alice squirmed, involuntarily.

"He's doing really well—"

"How are the children?"

"Jammy at present. But fine."

"I shall have them here in the holidays. I want you and Martin to go away together. I said so two months ago. Shall I ring Verity about your honeymoon house in Patmos?"

"No," Alice said with too much emphasis.

"Darling—"

"One shouldn't ever try and repeat things—"

"Darling Alice," Cecily said sadly from Dummeridge, "how I long to help you and how difficult you make it."

"Sorry," Alice said in a whisper. "Sorry."

The drawing room was cleared, carpeted, but uncurtained when her ladyship's Volvo, with a brace of handsome springer spaniels penned in the back, drew up outside The Grey House. From her bedroom window, Alice watched Lady Unwin get out, smooth down her pleated skirt, stoop inside the car to bring out a huge hydrangea in a pot and then advance, looking

about her, towards the front door. Gwen, who had been washing the stone-flagged hall floor, let her in with alacrity.

"Ah, Gwen. How nice to see you. What a lovely day. Is
Mrs. Jordan in?"

Gwen showed Lady Unwin into the drawing room.

"Hm," Lady Unwin said interestedly, putting down the pot,
and moving towards the mantelpiece along which Alice's collection of old jugs marched in stout procession. "Charming."
She turned to smile at Gwen. "Do tell her I'm here."

Gwen was sorry that Alice was wearing jeans and an old
shirt of Martin's because she was unpacking tea chests, and
sorrier still that Alice didn't intend, apparently, to make any
changes at all to her appearance. She simply pulled her pigtail
over her shoulder and ran downstairs. Lady Unwin, immacu-
late in a pale grey skirt and soft jersey with handsome pearls,
was examining a drawing hung beside the fireplace. She turned
and held both hands out to Alice.

"My dear Mrs. Jordan. I'm a monster not to come before.
Will you forgive me?"

"Oh, of course. I'm afraid we're still in a terrible muddle—"

"Don't speak to me of muddles. My youngest is just back
from New York with enough luggage to fill a liner and I am
not exaggerating when I tell you that she has spread it over
the *entire* house."

Alice said, "Would you like a cup of coffee?"

"Thank you so much, but no. I am flying in, literally, on
my way to a meeting in Shaftesbury. Look, I've brought this.
I've always loved them. It's a lacecap."

"Oh," Alice said, "how kind of you—"

"I suppose," Lady Unwin said, "you are no relation to
Cecily Jordan?"

Alice said, smiling, "She is my mother-in-law."

Lady Unwin grasped Alice's hand with warm enthusiasm.

"My dear! What luck. Now *look*—" She dropped Alice's hand and opened a large, professional handbag from which she took a slim diary. "Now then. When can you dine with us? Let me see. Saturday fortnight? The eleventh?"

"Lovely," Alice said faintly. "Thank you, how kind—"

"And if you are speaking to your mother-in-law, tell her I am a devoted fan. I wonder if she'd *stoop* to talk to our little flower people here? Or perhaps a gardeners' brains trust for the hospice? I must think. Goodbye, my dear—" She waved a ring-glittering hand around the room. "*Too* pretty."

People like that, Alice thought, watching her enviously as she climbed swiftly into her car and turned it competently in the drive, people like that don't feel pain. People like Lady Unwin don't get into muddles and feel that their lives are without point and that they don't see the way forward.

"I've got a crush on Lady Unwin," she said to Juliet Dunne, later, on the telephone. "I want to be like her when I grow up."

"Margot?" Juliet said. "Don't be an ass. Of course you don't. It's an awful life. Luckily she's an old bossy boots so she rather likes it."

"But she looks as if she's beyond things being able to hurt her. She looks—"

"Allie," Juliet said firmly, "if you don't book a holiday for yourself and Martin sharpish, I shall come and do it for you. Oh Lordy, here's Henry, *early*, if you please—Don't," she said, away from the telephone, "those are for the children's tea. Allie, dins at the big house will be quite sparky, I promise, and you'll love Clodagh. She's been a frightful headache all her life and has been living with some lawyer in New York for years whom she utterly refused to let Margot and Ralph—What? Oh, Henry says he is a millionaire, the lawyer. Anyway, millionaire or not, she's left him and come home so Margot has gone into her *ultra*-clucking routine. But Clodagh's lovely fun. Allie, I've got to stop and beat Henry up. He's eating all the children's egg sandwiches. Honestly, Allie, Henry is my *cross*.''

⁓

"Am I your cross?" Alice said to Martin at supper.

He leaned across the table and patted her but he wasn't giving her his full attention.

"Of course not.''

"If I'm such a burden to myself, I must be a burden to you—''

"You're tired—''

"But that's the effect, not the cause.''

He had his mouth full. Through his fish pie he said, "Don't agree.'' He finished his mouthful and went on. "You've taken on so much. The village thinks you're great. Has the rector been?''

"No—''

"He will, then. I saw him in the shop. Seemed nice.''

"He'll only want me to do things.''

"Then say no.''

"But you see,'' she said, leaning forward to give him the second helping he always had, "one of the reasons for living here is to be involved.''

"Not in everything. Not so that you are so tired you can't see straight.''

She said, looking at him hard, "But I don't think it's that.''

Visibly he flinched. She saw his mind tiptoe away from the turn the conversation was taking, a turn he could not bear. He waved his fork at her.

"Frightfully good, this,'' he said.

⁓

72

Two days later, Alice was pushing Charlie in his buggy along the river path. It was a pretty, bright, chill day and there were catkins on the willows and clumps of primroses on the banks. She picked one and gave it to Charlie. He held it respectfully at stiff arm's length and she thought how he was learning because even a few weeks ago he would have tried to eat it.

A man came along the path towards them, a big man in a loose tweed overcoat whom she took to be John Murray-French, and was just raising her arm to wave when she saw he had on a dog collar. When he came nearer, he called, "Lovely morning!"

"Yes!" she called back.

He said, when he was near enough merely to speak, "I'm Peter Morris. And you are Mrs. Jordan. And I owe you what is known as a pastoral call."

He was about sixty, vigorous and upright with thick hair and a good colour. He stooped to Charlie who offered him the primrose.

"Thank you, old chap."

"I know you are awfully busy," Alice said.

He straightened.

"It's a shocking time of year for dying. They totter on all winter and then, just as it begins to get warmer and lighter, they give up the ghost. It's been one funeral after another. That's why I came out today, to see something *starting* for once." He looked down at Charlie. "You're starting, luckily. Is that your only one?"

"He's my third."

"You don't look old enough. I was going to come and tell you not to let the old biddies bully the life out of you. They will if they can. They do a wonderful job in the village but they know no mercy. Hope you'll be happy here."

"Oh, we *will*—"

"It's a nice place. And you've a lovely house. I used to go

up and play poker with John Murray-French in your house. I expect we'll start again in his cottage when he's settled. Two old bachelors together.'' He looked down at Charlie again. ''Never had any children. My wife died before we got round to it.''

''I'm so sorry—''

''So was I. I was a sailor. That is, before the old Admiral up there''—he looked up at the blue sky—''summoned me aboard. You'll find I speak my mind. If I can't abide something, I say so. And that applies to a large number of bishops. Woolly lot. Why don't they just see what the *Bible* says about things? You know where you are, with the Bible.''

Alice turned the buggy back towards the village.

''I've never really read it. Not since school.''

''Not surprised. People don't. But sixty-five million copies are sold every year, so *someone* reads it. You ought to try.''

''I wouldn't know where to begin.''

''No excuse,'' Peter Morris said heartily. He took the handles of the buggy from her and began to push.

''I hear they've got you on the community shop.''

''And the flower rota. But I've jibbed at the Sunday Group.''

''Good for you.''

''But the belonging, I mean, doing things, is part of living here—''

''So is getting on with everyone. I always say to newcomers, don't think living in a village is easy. In a town you can pick and choose your friends but a village is like a ship—you have to get on with everyone. Not easy, but not impossible. Hold on old fellow, here come some bumps.''

They emerged on to the broader path below the pub, the Pitcombe Inn. Late daffodils were drooping in the window-boxes and through the partly opened ground-floor windows seeped a stale breath of beer and frying. Peter Morris went on pushing Charlie, past the pub and round the corner up the village street where people hailed him. Alice felt comforted, walking beside him while he pushed and replied briefly to those who greeted him. He stopped at the corner of the lane to The Grey House.

"I'll return the chariot to you."

"Thank you," she said. She rather wanted to ask him to come with her.

He said, "I've a bereavement, a broken leg and a bad case of self-pity to see to before lunch, Mrs. Jordan. It was nice to meet you."

He held out his hand and grasped hers.

"Keep smiling," he said, and put a finger on the end of Charlie's little nose. "You too, old fellow."

FIVE

Alice dressed three times for dinner at Pitcombe Park, and when she finished she was more than half-inclined to throw off her final choice and go back to the first one. But there wasn't time, and in any case, Martin was getting impatient. She came downstairs holding the ends of a heavy Turkish necklace of silver and turquoise behind her neck with both hands and asked him to hook it up for her. He was wearing a dinner jacket and looked very sleek and remote. He turned her back to the light in the hall so that he could see, and muttered over the necklace. She stood with her head bent, holding her pigtail away from her neck to help him, looking down at the deep folds of her red skirt and the toes of her embroidered slippers which said "Made in Jaipur" on ribbons sewn to the insoles.

"There," he said triumphantly, and gave her shoulder a finishing pat. She let her pigtail fall again, down her back. She had woven it with ribbons for the dinner party and Natasha, who had sat admiringly on the end of her bed watching while she did this, was now sitting on the last step of the stairs trying to achieve the same effect on Princess Power. James sat on the top step crying quietly with his thumb in. He didn't want Alice to go out and he didn't want to be left with Gwen. He said now, removing his thumb just long enough, "What if there's a baddie?"

Natasha sighed.

"Quite honestly," she said, plaiting away, "you watch too much television."

James loved television. He watched it, clutching a cushion in his arms so that he could bury his head in it if anything on the screen looked as if it might become frightening. But when the television was turned off, the baddies on it seemed to lurk about his imagination much more powerfully than the goodies. He knew Gwen wouldn't be any good at dealing with his fears because she somehow had something to do with the baddies. Only Alice staying at home would be any good.

He stood up.

"Don't go!"

Martin climbed past Natasha up the stairs and knelt below James.

"Now, come on, old boy. We are only going out for a few hours and we are only going to the Park—"

"Don't go! Don't go!" screamed James, staring at his mother past Martin's face.

Gwen came out on to the landing holding Charlie in her arms. He was wearing a yellow sleeping suit and looked like a drowsy duckling. He saw Alice in the hall and yearned out of Gwen's arms down towards her.

"I'll be back so soon," Alice cried up to her two boys, "so soon. I'll come in and see you the minute I'm back, I promise—"

"I should just go," Natasha said, not looking up from her task.

"Oh, Tashie—"

James's crying rose to a howl. Martin gave him a despairing

look and scrambled back down the staircase to the hall.

"Dear me," Gwen said, "*what* a silly fuss. Now you've set Charlie off—"

Martin hurried Alice towards the front door, wrapping her coat round her.

"Come on, come on—"

"I *hate* this," she said unhappily, "I hate going out when he's so miserable—"

"He only puts it on for you. To try and make you do what he wants."

"Even so, he is frightened—"

Martin said irritably, "He is frightened of everything."

He got into the driving seat of the car and leaned across to open the passenger door for Alice.

"He'll be five soon," Martin said. "Three years until prep school. He'll have to pull himself together."

Alice said nothing. There were at least three things she wanted to say, chief amongst them being that she did not think James ought to be sent away to school at eight, but they only had five minutes' time for talk in the car, and they were bound to disagree and then they would arrive at the Park all jangled up and . . .

"Are you sulking?"

"No," Alice said in as ordinary a voice as she could manage.

"I wish James had a quarter of Tashie's spirit."

"I expect he wishes it too."

The Park gates, with their boastful stone triumphs, reared up briefly in the headlights' beam, and vanished past them.

"I say," Martin said, "this is rather something."

"D'you think it will be a huge party?"

"Dunno," Martin said. He peered ahead. Lights were shining through the dark trees.

"It's *huge*—"

"It sure is."

Alice thought of the black lace dress discarded on her bed.

"I've got the wrong clothes on—"

"No you haven't. Anyway, it's too late to think that."

The drive swung round and opened into a floodlit sweep in front of the house; nine bays, ashlar quoins, roof pediment, long sashed windows and, above the front door, the arms of the family, added by a mid-Victorian Unwin who wished the world, or at least that part of it that came to Pitcombe Park, to be in no doubt as to the antiquity of his lineage. Alice leaned forward.

"This is such a *weird* thing to be doing! It's like visits to Rosings in *Pride and Prejudice*. You know, best clothes, best behaviour, kindly patronage—"

"Nonsense," Martin said tensely.

"But—"

He stopped the car at a respectful distance from the steps to the front door.

"It's a perfectly normal thing to do. And very nice of the Unwins."

Alice said in a rude voice, "Well, it isn't normal for *me*."

Martin said nothing. He got out of the car, shut the door without slamming it and came round to open Alice's door.

"Allie—" he said, and his voice besought her to be amenable, "don't let James get to you. He'll be fine, once we've gone."

"It's nothing to *do* with James—"

The double front doors were opened above them and an oblong of yellow light fell down the steps. They were instantly silent, like children caught red-handed. Martin put his hand under Alice's elbow, and guided her up the steps. At the top, a small man like an ex-jockey was waiting to open the inner glass doors to the hall. He said, "Mr. and Mrs. Jordan," without a questioning inflexion, and Martin said, "Evening, Shad-well."

"How do you *know*?" Alice mouthed at Martin.

He ignored her. Shadwell slipped Alice's coat from her shoulders, murmured, "*This* way, Mrs. Jordan," and went across the hall—it was round, Alice noticed, so did that mean all the doors had to be curved, like bananas?—and opened another double pair, and there was the drawing room and Lady Unwin, swimming forward in a tide of green silk ruffles and ropes of pearls, to envelop them in welcome.

The room was large and grand and there were about a dozen people in it, grouped among the damasked chairs and the tables bearing books and framed photographs and extravagant plants in Chinese bowls. There was also someone particular by the fireplace. Everyone else was dressed as Alice would have expected—indeed, as Lady Unwin would require—in dinner jackets and the kind of silk frock that saleswomen are apt to describe as an investment, but this person looked like the cover drawing for *Struwwelpeter*, which Alice had had to hide from James's fascinated but appalled gaze. All Alice could see, because the person was half-turned away from her, was a wild head of corn-coloured hair and a bizarre costume of black tunic and tights. Whoever it was, Lady Unwin was leaving it until last.

"Alice, dear—may I?—Alice, this is Mrs. Fanshawe who lives at Oakridge Farm, simply brilliant with flowers, can't think how she does it, and Major Murray-French you know of course, and the Alleynes from Harcourt House—little ones just the age of yours I think, such fun—and Elizabeth Pitt, Mrs. Pitt who is my right *arm* on all these committees, truly I cannot think what I should do without her, and Susie Somerville who is—what are you, Susie? Calling you a travel courier seems so rude when all the tours you take are so *grand,* I simply shouldn't dare to aspire to one, I promise you—and

Simon Harleyford who is here for the weekend, so nice to have you, dear—and *Mr.* Fanshawe without whom we just wouldn't have our famous summer fêtes, and Clodagh. Clodagh, come over here and say hello to Mrs. Jordan.''

The black tunic and tights turned briefly from the small bright pink man she was talking to, said "Hi" and turned back again.

"I told her," Lady Unwin said in a stage whisper to Alice, "I told her to be especially nice to Nigel Pitt because I really *need* him for the hospice. Our present treasurer is threatening to retire, so tiresome but I suppose as he's nearly eighty I shouldn't bully. Come and talk to Susie. She knows everything there is to know about Indian palaces."

"I don't, actually," Susie Somerville said, when they were left alone. She was small and leathery and in her forties, dressed in an evening suit of plum-coloured velvet. "I only know how to get a porter wherever I am and how to change a colostomy bag. Being a courier is murder, sheer murder. Our outfit is so expensive that only the ancient can afford it so I haul these disintegrating old trouts round Baalbek and Leningrad and Udaipur and spend every evening mixing whisky and sodas and Complan. It's a nightmare."

"Why do you *do* it?" Alice said, laughing.

"Money. They give me vast tips, especially the Yanks who love it that I'm titled. I'd miles rather be married, but I only ever want to marry people who don't want to marry me. So I've got horses as substitute children and a lot of friends and this ghoulish job. D'you ride?"

"No," Alice said.

"You've got a man," Susie Somerville said, draining her glass, "you don't need to."

Ralph Unwin, in a deep blue smoking jacket and smelling of something masculine and Edwardian, came up to take Alice in to dinner.

"Is Susie trying to shock you?"

"I can't shock anybody any more," Susie said. She jerked her head towards the fireplace. "How's Clo, now she's back?" Ralph Unwin spoke quietly.

"We think she's fine. She won't speak of why she left, so we are simply biding our time." He glanced at Alice. "Our daughter, Clodagh. It looked as if she might be going to marry a chap in New York, but she's suddenly come home." He smiled very faintly. "Young hearts do mend."

Susie Somerville and Alice both looked across at the *Struwwelpeter* shock of curls. Alice said suddenly, surprising herself, "Of course it hurts, but it's better to feel something so strongly that it half-kills when it's over than—"

She stopped.

"Hear, hear," Susie Somerville said. "Story of my life. Come on, Ralph. Margot's gesturing like a windmill. Nosebag time."

In the doorway to the hall, there was polite congestion. Alice found herself next to Clodagh, whose face was difficult to see on account of her hair. Alice could not, out of delicacy, mention New York but she felt she ought to say something.

"We've just moved in to John Murray-French's house."

"I know," Clodagh said and moved on to catch up with her mother.

At dinner, Clodagh was next to Martin. When she turned towards him, Alice could see her face, which was neither pretty nor in the least like either of her solidly handsome parents. It was the face of a fox, wide-cheeked and narrow-chinned, except that her mouth was wide too. Because Alice was new to the village she had been put next to her host, and in order that she should not be alarmed by too much social novelty, John Murray-French was on her other side. In front of her was a bone china soup plate edged with gold containing an elegant amount of pale green soup sprinkled with chives.

"Watercress," John said. "They grow it further down the Pitt river. Are you liking my house?"

"Enormously."

"You're too thin."

"I don't think," Alice said, leaning so that Shadwell could pour white burgundy over her shoulder into one of the forest of glasses in front of her, "you know me well enough to say that."

"It doesn't need intimacy. It needs an aesthetic eye. I don't just know about ducks."

"Ducks," Ralph Unwin said. "Perfect bind. I gather they are coming off the river up the village street again."

"Does that matter?"

"Only in that someone, sooner or later, slips on what they have left behind, and as they are reckoned to be my ducks, I end up visiting the victim in Salisbury hospital. My dear girl, you haven't any butter."

Down the table Martin and Clodagh were laughing. She was doing the talking, very animatedly, and Alice could see her excellent, very white teeth. On Martin's other side, Susie Somerville and Mr. Fanshawe were having a boastfully comparative conversation about international airports, and opposite Alice a gaunt woman in a grey silk blouse pinned at the neck with a cameo was drinking her soup with admirable neatness.

"You know Elizabeth Pitt, of course," Ralph Unwin said.

Mrs. Pitt leaned forward.

"I know *you*. Two dear little boys and a girl. They look exactly the age of Camilla's three. And you've taken on the dreaded shop."

Ralph Unwin gave a mock shudder.

"The shop!"

"It's jolly good," John Murray-French said. "Has just the kind of food I like. Left to myself I'd live on beans and biscuits and whisky.'' He indicated his soup. ''Can't really see the point of vegetables.''

''Are you,'' Sir Ralph said to Alice, ''going to start a vegetable garden?''

Alice smiled at him.

''I'm hoping my mother-in-law will do that.''

''Not *Cecily* Jordan!''

''The same—''

''My *dear*,'' said Elizabeth Pitt.

''Does Margot know? You won't get a minute's peace—''

''Yes, she does.''

''I *told* you Martin was Cecily's son, you know,'' John said. ''It's odd how nobody listens to a word you say unless you are offering them a drink, when they can hear you clear as a bell three fields off.''

Sir Ralph bent his blue gaze directly upon Alice.

''What wonderful luck. Has Martin inherited her talent?''

She looked down the table. Martin was describing something to Clodagh and using his hands to make a box shape in the air. She looked utterly absorbed.

''Not really. I mean, he's very good at keeping a garden tidy, but he hasn't really got her eye.''

''This child's a painter,'' John said across her, ''but she won't paint.''

''Won't?''

''I can't, just now,'' Alice said unhappily.

Sir Ralph put a hand on hers.

''Sort of painter's block?''

''I suppose so—''

''I know!'' Elizabeth Pitt said triumphantly. ''Juliet Dunne has a charming one, in her sitting room. Now Juliet,'' she said, turning to Sir Ralph, ''has got a brilliant scheme for the hospice garden party—''

Sir Ralph bent towards her. John Murray-French turned

away to say to the woman on his far side, "I gather your trout have got some nasty ailment—"

Alice looked back down the table at Clodagh. She could watch her for a bit now, without distraction. It looked as if she hadn't touched her soup, and she had broken her roll into a hundred pieces and scattered it messily round her place, just like a child. She had very good hands. As far as Alice could see, they were without rings, but her nails were painted scarlet. Her eyes were set slightly on a slant, and even though her hair was light, her brows and lashes were dark. She didn't seem to have on any jewellery except an immense Maltese cross suspended round her neck on a black ribbon, invisible against her black tunic. She was saying something to Martin, looking down, and then she suddenly looked up and caught Alice gazing at her but her expression remained quite unchanged. Alice felt snubbed. She looked towards Sir Ralph and Mrs. Pitt, but they were deep in county politics, so she looked instead at all the Unwins on the walls in their gilded plaster frames, regarding the dinner party from beneath their unsuitable, practical twentieth-century picture lights.

When the salmon came, John Murray-French turned back and told her that his son Alex was married, to a French girl whom he had met in Athens. Alice said she was so glad. They ate their salmon talking companionably and Alice tried to be interested in Alex's new job as an investment analyst and at the same time tried to remember the flavour of Alex's brief, ardent interest in her. During pudding—a chocolate roulade or apricot tart—and cheese—Stilton and Blue Vinney—Sir Ralph devoted himself to Alice. He was very charming. He told her of his childhood at Pitcombe, and how two spinster great-aunts had lived in The Grey House then. He told her how his three children had exactly the same nursery rooms as he and his sister had had, which gave Alice the chance to ask a question to which she perfectly well knew the answer.

"And is Clodagh your youngest?"

He immediately looked fond.

"She is. Twenty-six. Of course, she could have been married a dozen times over, but she has impossibly high standards. She's much the brightest of our three. She worked in publishing in New York. Somebody and Row. I'm afraid I'm putty in her hands."

Alice rather wanted to say that it looked as if Martin was, too. But instead, she said, "Perhaps she could get a job in English publishing, now she's back."

"You must forgive a fond old father, but I rather want her here for a bit. Perhaps you could help me devise a scheme to keep her. I know she'd love to see your paintings."

"Oh no!" Alice said, genuinely alarmed.

"All you creative people, so modest. Now tell me, when are we going to be allowed to meet your mother-in-law?"

When the cheese had been borne away, Lady Unwin rose and swept the women out of the room before her.

"*Strictly* twenty minutes," she said to Sir Ralph, and then to her charges, "Clodagh thinks we are absolutely barbaric. Don't you, darling? I suppose Americans wouldn't dream of such a thing."

Clodagh said, "The Americans I knew ate in restaurants all the time," and then she went up to Susie Somerville and said, "Come on, Sooze. I want a horror story from your latest trip."

"Braced for it?" Susie Somerville said delightedly, going up the great staircase beside Clodagh. "Well, you simply won't believe it, but I had an eighty-five-year-old junkie who chose *Samarkand* as the spot to trip out—"

Margot Unwin took Alice's arm.

"My dear, I do hope they looked after you at your end of the table."

"Beautifully, thank you—"

"Let's find you a loo, my dear, the geography of this house is a nightmare for strangers."

They went up the stairs together behind Susie and Clodagh, Margot talking all the time, and across an immense landing peopled with giant Chinese jars to one of several panelled doors. Margot thrust it open with her free hand and pushed Alice into the pink warmth beyond.

"Take your time, my dear."

Alice was suddenly desperately tired. Shut into this baronial bathroom done up in a style Cecily would describe as Pont Street 1955, she could at last look at her watch. It was only ten past ten. There would have to be half an hour without the men, and then half an hour with them, before she could even begin to signal home to Martin across the room. She looked in the mirror. To herself she looked badly put together and amateurish. Perhaps it was time to cut off her pigtail.

Outside the bathroom, Sarah Alleyne was waiting for her. Sarah was fair and expensive looking, and Juliet Dunne had said that she was brilliant on both horses and skis.

"I wondered," she said now, languidly, to Alice, "I wondered if we could talk about sharing a school run. My wretched nanny's pregnant and I'm quite stuck, just for now—"

In the drawing room the ladies were gathered, holding cups of black coffee and feigning indifference to a silver dish of chocolates. Neither Clodagh nor Susie Somerville was there. Lady Unwin sat Alice beside her on a little French sofa, and talked about the village. She went through a kind of vivacious inventory of inhabitants, from old Fred Mott who was nearly a hundred through Miss Pimm and Miss Payne to some old thing called Lettice Deverel who played the harp. After twenty minutes, Alice realized that she had not been asked a single question. After twenty-five minutes, the men came in, and after thirty, Susie and Clodagh returned still absorbed in some conversation. Martin was holding both brandy and a cigar, neither of which he normally touched, and he sat down beside the gaunt Mrs. Pitt with every show of enthusiasm. Alice realized, with amazement, that he was really enjoying himself.

She could not drag him away until almost midnight, and only then because other people were beginning to look round for Shadwell and their coats and to say, "Come on, old thing, eight o'clock church tomorrow, don't forget." Both Unwins kissed Alice goodnight but Clodagh, talking to the Harleyford man whom Alice wondered if Lady Unwin intended to be the next boyfriend, just waved from across the room and called "Look at the beams!" to Martin.

"What did she mean?" Alice said in the car.

"She and her brother carved swear words into the beams in the room above our garage, for a dare, when they were little. She couldn't remember what the words were, though."

He began to laugh.

"Was she nice?" Alice said.

"Good fun," he said, still laughing. "Good fun."

At home they found James asleep in their bed, clutching Alice's nightie. Gwen said she was sorry about it, but he'd been a proper handful. Martin carried him to his own bed, and then drove Gwen home while Alice sat on the floor of James's room and waited for him to sink down into deep oblivion again. She sat with her arms round her knees and her head bent and thought, without enthusiasm, of the dinner party. When Martin came back, she crept out of James's room and went to their bedroom where Martin was chucking his clothes over the back of a chair.

"Did you enjoy it? Did you like tonight?"

He was down to his socks and boxer shorts. He pulled one sock off and dropped it.

"It was terrific," he said. He pulled off the other sock. "Wasn't it?"

She went past him to the cupboard where she kept her clothes.

"I think you did rather better than me at dinner."

"Oh-ho," he said sounding pleased. He seldom flirted, but he liked to be flirted with. "D'you think so?"

"I thought she was jolly rude," Alice said, from half inside the cupboard.

He began to hum. Clodagh had been far from rude to him.

"Give her time—"

"If I can be bothered—"

"Allie," he said, suddenly serious, "we can't fall out with the Unwins."

"Can't?"

"No. You just can't be bolshy."

He went off to brush his teeth. When he came back, Alice was in her yellow dressing gown, fiercely brushing her hair. When they were first married, he used to love watching her do it; now he got into bed, hardly looking, and punched the pillows into the shape he liked.

"You looked great tonight," he said absently.

"I felt a mess—"

"Rubbish." His voice was thickly sleepy.

She went over to the window and parted the curtains to look out. There was a bright hard white moon, and the shadow of the fence lay in a black grid on the silver grass. I would so like to be free, Alice thought involuntarily. I am so tired of myself and the muddle of everything. I wish . . . She stopped.

"Come to bed," Martin said.

She dropped the curtain and crossed the room to climb in beside him. He turned to roll himself behind her, cupping her breast in his hand. She stiffened, very slightly.

"OK, OK," he said. He rolled away. "Night."

She reached to turn out her bedside lamp. A silver slice fell through a gap in the curtains.

"Martin. Sorry—"

He grunted.

She turned on her side and lay there, staring into the dim room. Outside an owl called, from across the valley, and after a while another owl answered it from the beeches high above the Park. Then, from down the corridor, but coming nearer at every step, came the sound of James, crying.

"What do you want to go to church for?" Martin said.

They were both slightly hung-over, Martin because he had had quite a lot of brandy, and Alice because she couldn't drink much of anything, anyway.

"I feel I'd like to. That's all. It's only an hour and Charlie will be resting. If you could just put the lamb in at half past eleven—"

"I wanted to be in the garden."

"Then be in it. The children can come outside with you."

"But the lamb—"

"You come *inside* to do that. It will take you all of two minutes."

"I don't see why you want to go. You never go to ordinary church."

"But *I* see," Alice said, suddenly cross, "why you *don't* want me to go. It won't do you any harm to have the children for an hour. I want to be somewhere quiet. I want to think."

"Suppose I want to think?"

"Then you can go to evensong."

He went out into the garden then, banging both halves of the stable door which failed to latch and bounced open again. Alice had a bad quarter of an hour putting Charlie down for his rest and finding a roasting tin for the lamb and Natasha's other gumboot and persuading James out of his pyjamas and into clothes, so that she had to run to church, which was uphill, and arrived very much out of breath and ill-prepared for calm.

The church was simple and strong and medieval. It had only a nave and a chancel and there was no stained glass in the windows, so that whatever natural light there was came in, uninterrupted. At the west end was a famous Norman font, carved with scenes from the life of John the Baptist ending with his lolling head on a charger, a scene that Miss Payne, who was in charge of the church flowers, liked to screen with a brass jug of golden rod or Michaelmas daisies or delphiniums. Mr. Finch, of the shop, was sidesman in charge of books. He pressed *Hymns A & M* into Alice's hands most meaningfully.

She chose a pew at the back. The hassocks had been embroidered by the villagers to celebrate the Queen's Jubilee, each one representing animal or plant or bird life along the Pitt river. Alice knelt carefully on a bunch of kingcups. Ahead of her was a dozen or so backs, of which she recognized a few, and beyond them, Peter Morris in cassock and surplice. Idly she wondered who laundered its snowy folds. The organ began, a little breathlessly, played by Miss Pimm in her Windsmoor Sunday suit. The congregation rose stiffly to its feet.

Holding her prayerbook, Alice thought how much her father admired Cranmer's English. She remembered him giving a sudden impromptu lecture at supper one night on the iniquity of the banal and bloodless language of the modern service book. Pitcombe clearly had turned its thumbs down to the alternative services—what she held, she discovered, was in the still sonorous English of 1928. In the front of her prayerbook was stamped "The Church of St. Peter, Pitcombe" and underneath, in neat elderly script, "Given in memory of Hilda

Bryce, by her loving family.'' Did anyone, she wondered, commemorate people that way any more?

She did not really notice what they said or sang, nor did she hear properly what Peter Morris said comfortably for ten minutes, from his pulpit, about St. Paul's exhortations to the Romans, on being delivered from the bondage of corruption into the glorious liberty of the children of God. She had said she wanted to think, but she didn't think. She simply sat, and looked at the whitewashed walls and the little monuments in stone and brass lamenting matchless husbands and beloved mothers and sons and observed how the pale sunlight came in and lit up the brass ends of the churchwardens' staffs like tiny flames. And then she knelt with everyone else and read aloud with them the prayer of St. Chrysostom.

''Fulfill now, O Lord, the desires and petitions of thy servants, as may be most expedient for them.''

What, she wondered, *were* her desires and petitions, except that she wished to be rid of this preoccupation with the fluctuating graph of her unhappiness? She got up and followed everyone out, and Mrs. Macaulay said how nice it was to see her in church, and Mr. Finch smirked as he took her books, and Peter Morris clasped her hand warmly and told her to remember him to Charlie.

When she got home, they were all sitting round the kitchen table with mugs and the biscuit tin, and Clodagh Unwin was there too. She looked pale, and nothing like as self-possessed as the night before, and she was wearing butter yellow tights, and an enormous grey jersey that came half-way down her thighs, and grey suede boots. The moment Alice came in, Clodagh got up and went across to her, put her hands on Alice's arms and said, "I came to say sorry. Because I was so horrible last night."

Alice, startled, said, "Oh, you weren't—"

"I was," Clodagh said. "I was awful. Ma said would I be particularly nice to you, but I was in a temper with her for something that's too boring to mention so I was particularly horrible instead."

Alice moved away slightly.

"It doesn't matter," she said. "You were very nice to Martin."

He gave a pleased guffaw from the table.

"Oh, *please,*" Clodagh said. Alice gave her a quick glance and saw her eyes were full of tears.

"Don't make so much of it. It doesn't matter. I didn't notice."

"I don't know," Clodagh said, with the beginning of a smile, "if that doesn't make me feel *worse.*"

"Come on, Allie," Martin said. "Come on. Have some coffee."

Alice threw her coat over the chair back and reached for an apron on the hook behind the door to the hall.

"I've got to do the potatoes for lunch—"

"I'll do them," Clodagh said, taking the apron. "I'm a whizz at potatoes."

James, who had decided Clodagh was delicious, pulled a chair up to the sink, giggling, so that he could splash about while she peeled. Natasha, who felt a keen desire for Clodagh's boots, stayed by the table to devise a scheme by which she might try them on even if they were going to be too big, which they were, she knew, but all the same . . . Alice, not won over, went to fetch the potatoes from the larder and the peeler from a drawer and a saucepan. She dumped the potatoes in the sink and Clodagh seized her wrist.

"*Please* forgive me," she said. Her voice was an urgent

hiss and her curious grey-gold eyes were bright with intensity.

"You made me feel a fool last night," Alice said, "and you're doing it again now. I don't like it. That's all."

Clodagh dropped her wrist. In a voice so low only Alice could hear it, she said, "You were the only person last night who *didn't* look a fool."

Alice went away to find carrots and a bag of frozen peas. When she came back, Martin had gone out again, James and Clodagh were singing and splashing at the sink and Natasha, without being asked, was laying the table, back to front.

"Clodagh's staying," Natasha said. "Daddy asked her."

Clodagh turned round.

"But I won't if you don't want me to."

"Of course stay. It's very ordinary lunch—"

"You're really kind."

Natasha stretched up to her mother's ear.

"Oh I so *want* her boots—"

"Aren't they smart."

Without turning round, Clodagh kicked her boots off backwards.

"Try them."

Natasha gave a little squeal. James put his arms around Clodagh's waist in case the boots should create a bond between her and Natasha. She dropped a kiss on his head and he looked up at her with passion.

"You've no idea," Clodagh said, "how unutterable American children are. We had one that used to come to the apartment loaded with toys and if you admired the smallest thing, he'd say. 'Don't touch. OK?' at the top of his voice."

James thought this was brilliantly funny.

"Don't touch, OK, don't touch, OK, don't touch, OK—"

"Look—" Natasha breathed, bending over to admire her feet.

"You look like Puss in Boots."

"I love them." She looked up at Clodagh. "Are they American?"

"Sure thing, baby," Clodagh said with an American accent, "Henri Bendel, no less."

Martin came back with a bottle of wine. He was humming. He kissed Alice's cheek on his way to fetch a corkscrew and then again on his way to fetch the glasses. At the second kiss, she laughed.

"Feeling better?"

"Yes," she said, surprised.

"I expect church made you feel better," Natasha said, stroking the boots, "I think it's supposed to."

When everyone laughed she looked tremendously pleased and said, in Gwen's phrase, "Well, this really *is* my day and no mistake."

Martin poured wine for himself and Clodagh and Alice. Clodagh finished the potatoes and put them on to boil and scooped the peelings out of the sink into the rubbish bin. Alice stared at her.

"Isn't that right?" Clodagh said. She had pushed up the sleeves of her jersey and stood there, shoeless, like a grey and yellow bird.

"It's absolutely right. I just don't associate New York flat dwellers with—"

"Oh," Clodagh said quickly, smiling at her, "I always did things like that. I used to scrub floors and stuff as therapy when the whole scene got a bit heavy."

She came round the table to where Alice was peeling carrots and looked at her intently.

"Hello," she said.

Alice took a quick swallow of her wine.

"Is this another kind of game? Like last night?"

"No," Clodagh said. "I could kill myself for last night."

Alice's hands were shaking. She put down her wineglass not at all steadily.

"You haven't met my baby."

"He's so sweet," Natasha said, still mooning over her feet. "He's the nicest baby in my class."

Clodagh dropped her gaze and let Alice go.

"Can we go and find him?"

The children rushed to seize her hands, Natasha shuffling but determined in her boots. They went out of the room and Alice could hear them beginning to clatter, chattering up the uncarpeted stairs. Singing softly, without meaning to, Alice fetched a pan and put her carrots in it, beside the pan of Clodagh's potatoes.

SIX

It was not in the least lost upon Peter Morris that Alice hadn't attended to a word of his sermon; indeed, that she had hardly come to church for any orthodox spiritual purpose at all. This was hardly uncommon. The reasons that brought his congregations to church seemed to him quite as various and tenuous and peculiar as those that kept them away. Folding his stole carefully after the service, Peter decided that Alice had probably come because an hour in church meant you could step off life for a space, stop time. That at least was how she had looked. And no doubt while she sat there, drifting, that decent young husband of hers—good midshipman material—was gardening and minding the children. Peter sighed. The Jordans seemed to him a thoroughly late twentieth-century combination of emotion and imagination on the one hand and Anglo-Saxon aversion to intensity on the other. A polite and lonely alliance.

The village, needless to say, had minutely observed the outward things. Even old Fred Mott, day in day out at his cottage window next door to the post office, had sufficient sight left to say approvingly on Peter Morris's weekly visits, "That's a fancy piece. *That'll* make 'em all sit up."

"Who?" Peter said. "Who'll sit up—"

"All of them old dumps round 'ere. All them old bags."

His little wet mouth widened into a grin.

"You're an old scoundrel, Fred."

"Not 'alf what I was when I was young. Not *'alf.*"

It was all very well, of course, to observe that something was troubling Alice, but how to help was inevitably much trickier. When he asked people around the village, the general view was that she was extravagantly blessed among mortals— lovely house, nice husband, dear little children, more than enough money—so that even if she was being helpful in the matter of the shop and the flower rota, that really was no more than her duty, living where she did and having what she had. Rosie Barton, who ran a very successful little computer business in Salisbury with her husband, Gerry, and who had very decided views on the sort of village Pitcombe should be, said, with the seeming deep sympathy that was her stock in trade, that Alice simply had to learn about a village community. Peter had pointed out that Wilton had hardly been an inner city situation to come from, and Rosie said indeed no, but the measure of *involvement* in the village was unique. Peter had said no more. The Barton child, an anxious four-year-old in the care of a succession of au pair girls, seemed never to require from his parents the involvement their business or village life did. And they came to church.

Alice, Peter Morris knew, would have been amazed to find how much she was watched and how much the village knew about her. It had amazed Peter himself, at his first country living in Suffolk, to realize that not a line of washing could go up nor an order of groceries be placed without every item being noticed, and conclusions drawn. When he heard someone in the Pitcombe shop say, "She keeps the children nice," he knew that meant that the frequency of lines of socks and knickers blowing in The Grey House orchard had not gone unremarked.

Even with the great Admiral aloft to talk and pray to, Peter Morris was very conscious of his solitariness. He had not really meant to remain a widower so long—his marriage had only managed two years before his wife's cancer had killed her, in four months, start to finish—but he had never found another woman to whom he could talk as comfortably as he had to Mary. He had come very close to it in Suffolk, with a woman who, in the end, decided she could not be a parson's wife, and then, oddly enough, he had found quite recently an excellent friend in Lettice Deverel of Pitcombe. She was over seventy, scholarly, sharp and a Shavian socialist. She kept a harp in her muddled sitting room, and a green Amazon parrot in the kitchen and she had not a minute in the world for airs and graces. In the last three years, Peter Morris had taken to going up the lane from his sturdy early Victorian rectory to her Regency villa at the top of the village when he had a human knot to untie. Even if she said, as she often did, that she knew nothing about backward babies or neurotic spinsters or the male menopause or whatever the current problem was, she was a good sounding board, and simply went on making bread or potting up pelargoniums while he talked himself to some kind of conclusion.

Rose Villa contained an accumulation of a lifetime's energetic curiosity and culture. As a young woman Lettice Deverel had taught in an international school in Switzerland and had learned to ski in brown leather boots—there was a matching brown photograph to prove it. She had then come home to teach with the Workers' Education Authority, and gone on to be librarian of a famous collection on the history of women in England. All her life she had painted, cooked, gardened, written, read, travelled and kept animals and a diary. She played both the piano and the harp. She had always lived alone and had collected a wide and enthusiastic circle of friends. When Peter Morris added himself to the circle, she told him that she was agnostic and that she had never known a priest well before. He said in that case, she was about to learn. She said, meaning it, "But I won't stand for God being dragged in all the time," and he had replied, "Well, He won't mind that as there's nothing He dislikes so much as no reaction at all."

It had been a good start. Three years later, among a welter of weekly minutiae, they had together been through Clodagh Unwin's defection to America, the death of Miss Pimm's tyrannical but worshipped old mother, a crippling motorbike accident to the brightest boy in the village, cot deaths, Down's Syndrome babies, broken marriages, drunkenness, unemployment, fire, flood and pestilence. Alice Jordan seemed to Lettice Deverel a very minor problem indeed. She went on thumping her dough while she said, "Of course, you wouldn't trouble yourself about her if she wasn't good-looking."

"Good morning," the parrot said from his cage. "And who's a pretty parrot then?"

"I might," said Peter Morris, who never minded being found out, "not trouble myself quite so *much*—"

"She may be a very spoiled young woman, for all we know. And of course spoiled people inevitably become discontented in time."

"I don't think she's spoiled. I think she may be unhappy, but I don't think it's discontent. It might be disappointment, of course. In her marriage, maybe."

Lettice Deverel had encountered Martin several times in the village; once, outside the shop, she had dropped a bag of flour and he had helped her, most assiduously, to scoop it into the gutter. She gave a faint snort.

"The English public school system—"

"Well?"

"—renders most men incapable of recognizing or acknowledging their own states of mind. Makes them emotionally inarticulate." She poked a floury finger at Peter. "Makes most of them afraid of women. Drives any of them who go to Winchester quite round the bend."

"I think Martin Jordan went to Rugby."

"Stands out a mile off."

She dumped fat sausages of dough into loaf tins and set them at the back of her ancient Rayburn to rise.

"If you're trying to make me say I think you should go and talk to her, you're out of luck. You leave well alone."

"Laugh like parrots at a bagpiper," said the parrot. "Good morning. Merchant of Venice. Pretty parrot."

"She's rather a good painter, you see," Peter said, "and she won't paint. Or can't paint."

"Creativity isn't like carpentry."

Peter Morris stood up.

"Why have you taken against Alice Jordan?"

"I've done no such thing. I've admired her about the village and I've noticed what you have noticed. But I haven't woven sentimental fantasies about her. You leave her be. She's got pride. Now come outside and have a look at the camellia I thought the frost had done for. You never saw such leaders—"

The last week of the spring school holidays was soft and warm, with the sun shining bright and hard through the still bare branches of trees. Pitcombe began to break the winter seal on its doors and windows and pot plants were put out on doorsteps, like invalids, to take a little reviving air. Lettice Deverel washed the blankets on her bed as a gesture to spring cleaning, and started to go for walks again, declining to do so in winter because she said there was no point in walking when you had to keep your eyes on your feet rather than the view. In rubber-soled brogues and grasping a thumb stick, she set off most afternoons at a determined pace and the village, noticing her departures, said to one another, grinning, that spring *must* have come if Miss D. was off again. Fred Mott's grandson, Stuart, who was unemployed and a competition gardener, took advantage of these walks to take a wheelbarrow up to Rose Villa by the field path where he would be less observed, and to help himself to some excellent and well-rotted compost.

Sometimes Lettice went up the hill and round the edge of the Park. Sometimes she went either way along the river path, or across fields by bridleways to King's Harcourt and Barleston. Her favourite walk, however, was to skirt the higher boundary of The Grey House garden and strike east along the hillside, with the river below her and a widening valley view opening out ahead. She noticed, with approval, that the window frames of The Grey House were being painted and that someone had begun to thin out the depressing hedge of mahonias that John Murray-French had simply ignored. There was a new sandpit on the lawn outside the kitchen door, and a tricycle and a pleasingly full washing line. Lettice had never wanted to marry but she was a staunch supporter of family life.

Two fields beyond The Grey House, she could hear children. She dropped down the slope a little so that she could see the river, and there some way below her in the grass sat Alice Jordan and Clodagh Unwin with a basket and a baby, while a girl and a boy were jumping about over the trunk of a fallen willow near-by. It was a very pretty scene. It might have been, Lettice thought, the subject of one of those Victorian narrative paintings on which her artistic teeth had been cut. Alice wore blue and Clodagh was wrapped in a strange cloak of yellow and black. Lettice, who had known Clodagh from a child and believed her to be thoroughly spoiled and the only original child of the Unwin family, considered going down the slope to join them, and to meet Alice Jordan properly. But they looked so complete in themselves that she decided against it, and tramped on above them with her stick in her right hand and her face set determinedly to the eastward view.

⁓

"Don't you have any curiosity about me?" Clodagh was saying.

She had been wearing a long string of yellow amber beads under her cloak, and she had taken them off and given them to Charlie who was collapsing them, up and down, up and down, on his knees.

"I'm dying of it," Alice said, "but I thought it was generally accepted that no one must ask."

"Ask *what*—"

"About New York."

"Jesus," Clodagh said, "what *about* New York?"

Alice leaned on one elbow, turning herself towards Charlie and Clodagh.

"Well. I may have got it all wrong, but I understood that a love affair that might have ended in marriage went wrong and you have come home with a broken heart."

"Broken heart?" Clodagh said. "Hah! Marriage. *Honestly.*"

Alice waited. Charlie swung the beads from side to side and talked excitedly to them.

"I see," Clodagh said. "I'm the poor little jilted fiancée, am I?"

"*I* don't know," Alice said, "I don't know anything. And if you want to be mysterious, I never shall."

There was a pause. Then Clodagh said, "I don't want to be mysterious. Not to you."

Alice lay down in the grass and waited. It was ten days since the dinner party at Pitcombe Park, and she had seen Clodagh on eight of them. Clodagh had come down to The Grey House constantly on some pretext or other, bringing with her a tabby kitten and a significant change of atmosphere. It was she who suggested this picnic, just as she had suggested a number of other things—getting the drawing room curtains up, learning songs to her guitar, making fudge, choosing old roses to climb through apple trees—that had made them all feel that life was markedly improved.

"There was a love affair," Clodagh said, "and it did end. But I ended it."

Alice turned her head sideways. She could see the backs of Charlie's and Clodagh's heads against the sky.

"Then even if you're sad, you aren't as sad as you would have been if you had been thrown over."

Clodagh didn't turn around.

"I'm not sad at all. I'm thankful to be out of it. I was nearly stifled with possessiveness. Couldn't go out without saying where, couldn't telephone without saying who, couldn't buy so much as new socks without being asked who they were meant to impress. And as I was being virtually kept, after I gave up my job, I wasn't in much of a position to object."

"So he wanted to marry you?"

Clodagh turned round suddenly and lay on her front so that her face was close to Alice's.

"There wasn't any question of marriage."

"Oh Lord," Alice said. "Was he married already?"

Clodagh raised her eyes so that she was looking straight at Alice, only a foot away.

"Alice," she said, "he was a woman. That's why."

Alice thought she had stopped breathing.

"My lover was a woman," Clodagh said.

Alice sat up.

"So all this millionaire lawyer stuff was just a smoke-screen—"

"She was a millionaire. Is, I mean. And she is a lawyer. And she'd have married me like a shot. As it was, she did everything but eat me. So I had to leave."

"Clodagh—"

Clodagh sat up and put an arm across Alice's shoulders, above Charlie's head.

"Have I shocked you?"

"No," Alice said. "Yes. I don't know—" She turned to look at Clodagh. "Do you hate men?"

Clodagh began to laugh.

"Oh, Alice—"

"Shut up," Alice said angrily, twitching her shoulders free.

"Listen," Clodagh said, "I like men a lot. I don't sleep with women because I *have* to. I do it because I *choose* to. We all have a choice, you, me, everyone—"

Charlie tipped himself sideways and began to crawl ener-getically down the grassy slope towards his brother and sister. Alice made as if to follow, but Clodagh held her.

"He's fine. We'll go after him if we need to. We haven't finished."

"I don't know what to think—"

"Don't try then."

"Tell me—"

"What?"

"Oh, Clodagh, I don't know, I don't—just, tell me—tell me what happened, what's happened to you—"

"Nothing's *happened*. Before I was twenty I slept with boys and girls—girls first of course because of boarding school—

and I liked girls better. Nothing happened to me unless you can call the discovery of preferring girls a happening. I've had two proper affairs, one with a writer in London and then this one, with an American lawyer whom I met through my first lover and some libel action over a book of hers. The first affair was really better because we were more equal and I don't like being dominated. If I did, I'd probably like sex with men more. I got stuck in the New York business. I was very bowled over by all the glamour and Concorde and skiing in Aspen and stuff, and by the time that had worn off I was up to my neck, New York job, amazing apartment and this besotted woman. All her friends said she'd kill herself if I left, so I stayed. And then I realized that if I didn't leave, I'd kill *myself*, so I went. And she did try to kill herself but they got her to hospital in time and pumped her stomach and the lover who'd preceded me in her life and always wanted her back anyway has taken her to Florida.''

Natasha came stumbling up the field to say that James had got river *in*side his wellingtons.

''Tell him to take them off and play in bare feet.'' Alice was astonished her voice should sound so ordinary.

''And Charlie's eating all kinds of things. We thought we saw him eat a ladybird—''

Clodagh laughed.

''Did he spit it out?''

''No. He sort of crunched it—''

Alice began to get up.

''Perhaps we should go back—''

''No,'' Natasha pleaded. ''Please not yet. We're on a voyage. *Please.*''

She went dancing back to the fallen tree. Alice followed her with her eyes, devouringly.

''Did you love her?''

''Of course,'' Clodagh said. ''At the beginning. Or at least,

I was in love." She looked at Alice, smiling. "Are you suggesting I'm only in it for the sex?"

"Of *course* not—"

"Alice," Clodagh said, and her voice was warmly affectionate, "you don't know a thing about a thing, do you?"

Alice said nothing.

"A husband, three children but you aren't even awake. You haven't one clue about how wonderful you are, nor how to live—"

Alice's voice was choked with angry tears.

"Don't be *cheap*. Living isn't your jet-setting, sexually indulgent merry-go-round. Living is getting on with things, bearing things, making things work—"

"Oh my God," Clodagh said. She put her hands over her face. After a while she took them away again and said, in the gentlest voice, "My poor little Alice."

"I'm not poor. And don't patronize me."

"Believe me," Clodagh said, "that's the last thing I want to do."

Alice began to rip up single grasses, like tearing hairs out of a head.

"It's you who don't know what life is for. You don't live, you just pass the time. You only want to enjoy yourself—"

"Ah," said Clodagh, quite unperturbed, "the puritan ethic yet again, I see." She stretched across and very gently but firmly took hold of Alice's agitated hand. "Alice. If I'm so wrong and you are so right, why are you so cross and unhappy?"

"I'm not—"

"*Alice*."

Alice took her hand away and wound her arms round her knees and put her head down on them. She said, muffled, "I've tried so hard—"

"Too hard, perhaps."

"You couldn't call my children not living properly—"

"I don't. But you won't have them for ever and you'll *always* have you."

"Sounds to me like the usual live-for-yourself pseudo-psychological American claptrap—"

Clodagh let a little pause fall and then she stood up so that her voice should come down to Alice from a distance.

"If you aren't happy with yourself, you aren't any use to anyone else. And I should think that should satisfy even your masochistic puritanism."

And then she went down the slope to the children, who were delighted to see her and let her come on board their ship and sail over the grassy sea. Above them, in a perfect turmoil of fury and relief and misery and excitement, Alice sat where Clodagh had left her and cried copiously into her folded arms.

When they returned to the house at teatime, Clodagh carrying Charlie and Alice the picnic basket, they found Cecily in the drive, in her car, reading a magazine. Natasha and James were entranced at this and rushed forward with pleased screams but Alice felt, for the disconcerting first time, less pleased than she expected to. She said, "My mother-in-law," to Clodagh and went forward behind the children.

Cecily got out of the car all smiles and hugs. She took no notice of Alice's wariness and hugged her too, with her usual warmth, and kissed Charlie and said hello to Clodagh. She had never done this before, never arrived on impulse without warning—it was one of her rules—but then she had never felt so out of touch, so—so *excluded* from Alice's life as she had recently. Even given Alice's precarious state of mind, the telephone had been abnormally silent and when she had, after intense self-examination, tried to ring, there was either no one there or only Gwen who answered the telephone with an affectation that set Cecily's teeth on edge—"Mrs. Jordan's residence"—and was then elaborately, unnecessarily, discreet about Alice's whereabouts.

"Darling, I should have rung—"

"Not at all," Alice said politely.

Clodagh said, "I'll go in and put the kettle on," and went into the house with Charlie on her hip and the others dancing behind her. Cecily watched her go.

"Is she an Unwin from the Park?"

"Yes. The youngest."

Cecily wanted to say that Clodagh seemed very much at home but stopped herself. She put an arm round Alice.

"It is lovely to see you. I've been longing to see how you were getting on with the house. And I thought, heavens, the holidays are nearly over—"

"We've been so busy," Alice said. "I don't know why moving should take up all one's life, but it seems to."

"And what about some help?"

"I'm fine," Alice said.

"And a holiday?"

"Honestly," Alice said, and there was an edge of impatience to her voice, "we don't need one just now."

"There's Martin," Cecily said, dropping her arm and catching Alice's tone, "as well as you."

Alice began to move towards the house.

"Come in and have tea."

The kitchen looked undeniably a happy place. There was a blue jug of yellow tulips on the dresser, and on the table James and Natasha were putting out plates and mugs haphazardly on a yellow flowered cloth. Charlie was already in his high chair gnawing on a carrot, and by the window, still in her wizard's cloak, Clodagh was slicing and buttering currant bread. There was a kettle on the Aga and the top half of the stable door was open. In a Windsor armchair by the fire a tabby kitten lay asleep on a blue and white cushion. It was all entirely as it should be and the sight of it caused Cecily's heart to sink like lead.

She had paused, on her way to The Grey House, at the Pitcombe shop and post office. She was not quite sure why she had done this, nor why she had said vivaciously to Mr. Finch, "I am on my way to The Grey House! I am Mr. Jordan's mother, you see."

Mrs. Macaulay had been in the shop at the time and so had Stuart Mott's wife, Sally. Mrs. Macaulay had beadily taken in Cecily's clothes—very good but my, wouldn't it be a treat to have that much to spend—and Sally Mott, who was tired of having Stuart out of work and under her feet all the time, came boldly forward and said she wondered if Mr. Jordan could do with some gardening help because Stuart could probably spare him a bit of time if . . .

Cecily was delighted. The suggestion suited her every wish to help and it gave her a purpose in arriving at The Grey House unannounced and clearly not just passing. She took Sally's telephone number, bought two tins of dog meat—not the brand, Mrs. Macaulay noticed, that her girls favoured—and a box of chocolate buttons, and went out of the shop leaving a breath of "Arpège" behind to daze Mr. Finch. He took the washing powder and the packet of aspirin that Mrs. Macaulay held out to him and heard his mouth say, "Will that be all?" While his heart sang Swinburne:

> *Strong blossoms with perfume of*
> *manhood, shot out from my spirit as rays.*

Now, Cecily put the chocolate buttons down on the table beside the milk jug. James's eyes bulged with immediate desire and Charlie, using his carrot as a baton, pointed at them with it and mewed urgently. Clodagh stopped buttering and with a winglike swoop of her cloaked arm vanished the box into her pocket.

"After tea."

"Now, now, *now*," said James.

"After tea."

"*Now—*"

"*James*," Alice said, "you know the rules perfectly well."

"So sorry," Cecily said stiffly. She looked round the room. "You've made this so pretty. And how lovely to have a kitten."

Natasha slid into a chair next to her grandmother.

"He's called Balloon because of his tummy. Clodagh says he's a lousy kisser."

The other side of the table, James began to giggle.

"Personally," Natasha said, "I don't kiss him a lot because his breath is fishy."

"I'm glad to hear it," Cecily said.

"There's hens," James said.

"Hens, darling?"

Alice said, "We've got a dozen pullets. White Leghorn crossed with Light Sussex. Clodagh knows about hens and we are learning."

"They can't do eggs yet," James said, "but they can when they're bigger."

Cecily eyed Clodagh.

"What a knowledgeable young woman—"

Clodagh put the plate of buttered bread on the table and then went over to the Aga and said something quietly to Alice who was making the tea. Alice laughed and said something inaudible back. They came back to the table together and began in a practised mutual way to give the children their tea, cutting up Charlie's bread into little squares, putting honey on

James's, pouring milk into mugs. Alice gave Cecily a cup of tea and sat down beside her.

"Darling," Cecily said, "I think I've found you a gardener this afternoon. Someone called Stuart Mott—"

"He's a rogue," Clodagh said.

"All gardeners are rogues," Cecily said, "more or less."

"This one's more."

"But does he know about gardening?"

"I think he must. He's mad about prizes, marrows like hippos, yard-long runner beans. If you lick off all the butter, Charlie Jordan, you will simply have to eat your bread bare."

Smiling angelically, Charlie laid the bread on his high-chair tray and began, with tiny, neat fingers, to pick out the currants. Alice, Cecily noticed, had hardly spoken.

"Darling. Mightn't he be worth a try?"

Alice said slowly, "I'll suggest it to Martin—"

"I *long* for you to come down to Dummeridge. The potager is having its first real spring and as you were in at its conception—"

"Alice," Clodagh said, "are you a *gardener*?"

"You know I'm not—"

"Alice painted the most lovely frontispiece for my book. She was a kind of inspiration—"

"You must beware of my mother," Clodagh said, stretching over to rescue a sticky knife that had fallen from Natasha's plate. "She thinks you are a gardening genius but she's quite unscrupulous in bending people to her will. You'll find yourself talking to the Evergreen Club, none of whom can hear a word you say."

Cecily turned to Alice who was cradling her cup in both hands and drinking dreamily out of it.

"When can you come? Come for the night. Bring everyone, before the end of the holidays."

"It would be lovely," Alice said remotely.

"I've started the recorder," Natasha said to her grandmother. "I can play 'London's Burning' after only two lessons. Will you come and hear me?"

"Yes," Cecily said unhappily, "I should love to."

She got up. Alice said, "Five minutes only, Tashie."

Natasha took Cecily's hand and led her out of the room. When the door had closed behind them Cecily had a sudden angry, irrational feeling that everyone in the kitchen was bursting with suppressed laughter the other side of it.

"Do you," she said to Natasha, despising herself for doing it, "do you like Clodagh?"

"We adore her," Natasha said, "*and* I can play the first two lines of 'Frère Jacques' too—"

"And does she come here a lot?"

"Oh, every day. And when Mummy was doing the shop she took us on a walk and got us some frog spawn. It is *disgusting*. Of course, a lot of interesting things *are* disgusting. Aren't they?"

"Yes, darling," Cecily said sadly. "Yes, I'm afraid that they are."

When Cecily returned to Dummeridge that night, Richard was at home. She had known he would be and although the knowledge hadn't in any way affected her impulsive drive to Pitcombe, she discovered that she was surprisingly pleased to find him when she got back. He was sitting in the drawing room with an open briefcase and a whisky and soda, and when she stooped to kiss him he said, "What's the matter?"

"Tired, I think. I've just come back from Pitcombe."

He went on flipping through papers because it was what she expected of him.

"All well there?"

"Oh yes—"

"Drink?"

"Please—"

He put his briefcase down and went to the drinks tray on the sofa table. He poured a gin and tonic and took it back to her.

"Alice any better?"

"Alice," Cecily said with some edge, "was looking fine." She paused, took a swallow of her drink and then said carelessly, "There was really no chance to talk to her."

"No chance?"

"She has a new friend. The youngest child of Pitcombe Park. Seemed very much at home—"

Richard, perceiving at once what was the matter, picked up his papers again and said, "You should be pleased she has found a friend locally. I thought you were worried she was lonely—"

Cecily got up, rattling the ice in her glass.

"Of course I'm glad."

Richard said quietly, without looking up, "Alice had to leave home some day."

Cecily said angrily, "Richard, she isn't *well*."

He said nothing.

"I can't talk to you about it," Cecily said. "You can't relate to humankind at all, only to business. I don't suppose you give Alice any thought at all. I don't suppose you ever have."

He said, in a perfectly ordinary voice, "How do you know what I think?"

"The evidence of my eyes and ears."

"I'm a patient man," Richard said, "but sometimes you try me to the limit. You don't know what I think because in forty years you have never once asked me."

Cecily was close to tears. She still stood by her armchair holding her drink because she had meant to walk out on some Parthian shot and go off to the kitchen to grill trout for their dinner.

"Then I'll ask you. I am asking you—"

"What I think about Alice?"

She subsided on to the arm of the chair.

"Yes."

"My feelings for her are considerable. I am fond of her and I admire her. But I think she has taken a long time to grow up. If she is being awkward now—"

"I didn't say she was being awkward."

"—if she is disappointing you—"

"I didn't say—"

"Shut up," Richard said, suddenly angry.

Cecily got up.

"I don't want to hear any more. You haven't a clue. But then you have no idea what women are like or what they need. You never have."

"Is that so?"

She almost ran to the door.

"I'm going to get supper." She waved an angry hand at his papers. "You go back where you belong."

When the door had shut, Richard sat for a moment and looked ahead of him without seeing anything. Plainly, Alice had in some way defied Cecily, and although he was sorry for Cecily, he was also glad. He sighed and went back to his papers. The considerableness of his feelings for Alice were a self-forbidden luxury.

"Juliet?" Cecily said into the telephone.

It was a quarter to eight. Juliet Dunne had just read the last word of the last bedtime story and had come down to find that the dog had eaten most of the shepherd's pie she had left by the cooker for supper, and then the telephone had rung. So she had answered it with a snarl.

"Oh, Cecily," Juliet said, "so sorry to be cross but *really*.

Sometimes I hate domestic life so much I am not responsible for my actions. The fucking dog. And, frankly, fucking Henry for needing supper at all. I'd give anything to be a kept woman at this minute.''

Cecily made soothing noises.

"I really rang to talk to you about Alice—''

"Allie? Why, is something—''

"Well, I'm not *sure*—''

"I thought she was looking miles better," Juliet said. "I saw her on Tuesday. We had a tots tea party.''

"Do you know Clodagh Unwin?''

"Clo? All my life, practically.''

"She seems," Cecily said, "almost to be living there.''

"Whoopee," Juliet said. "Best thing in the world. She's the most lovely fun. She'll cheer them all up. Oh Lord, Cecily, here comes Henry. He'll have to have dog food, there isn't anything else. If you'd had daughters, Cecily, would you have encouraged them to get married?''

"Probably not—" Cecily said, thinking of the briefcase in the drawing room.

"Of course, with sons, I can't wait to be shot of them. But I'm stuck with Henry. Look, I think it's brilliant about Clodagh and Alice and I should think the Unwins are thrilled. They always want Clo to settle down, so a nice dose of happy family life—''

"Is—is she *safe*?''

"Safe?" Juliet said. "Safe? Clo? Heavens, no. What do you want a safe friend for Alice for? Henry's safe and he bores me to tears, don't you, darling? Cecily, I must go and open his tin of Chum.''

Cecily put the telephone down. Then she went over to the refrigerator and took out the trout that Dorothy had left, ready gutted, on a plate. She looked at their foolish dead fish faces. Tomorrow, she resolved, she would telephone Martin. He was, after all, her son.

SEVEN

Martin Jordan and Henry Dunne met for lunch in the White Hart in Salisbury. Henry had telephoned Martin at his office and said, rather mysteriously, that he had something to discuss and could they meet somewhere that their crowd didn't frequent. Martin said what about the White Hart as it was so large, and so they met there in the foyer, conspicuous in their moleskin trousers and tweed jackets among two busloads of spring tourists, one checking in and one out, in a welter of nylon suitcases and quilted coats in pastel colours.

Henry found them a table in the corner of the bar and went away for two pints of beer and several rounds of prawn sandwiches. When he came back he said, "I sneaked a look at The Grey House the other day. I must say, you're doing a great job. John's a wonderful fellow, but of course he never much minds how things look."

Martin was extremely pleased. He had worked tirelessly at weekends in the garden, and was allotting himself four hours' outside painting a week. Alice said "Oh well done" rather absently to him, quite often, but he didn't feel she quite took in the scale of his achievements, and anyway, he liked other people to appreciate the improvements he was making. He shrugged his shoulders self-deprecatingly.

"Those mahonias had really had it—"

"Awful things. Only worth it for the scent of the flowers in March—"

"Absolutely."

Henry took a large bite of sandwich, chewed, swallowed, took a pull at his beer and said, in a much more solemn voice, "Martin, nice as it is to see you, this isn't just a social lunch."

"I rather gathered that—"

"Fact is, I'm here as Sir Ralph's emissary. To test the water. To put something to you." He took another bite. "A proposition."

Martin immediately and wildly thought that Sir Ralph might want to buy back The Grey House. For all the difficulties involved in getting there, now he *was* there he felt extremely possessive about it as well as being conscious that living there added several social cubits to his stature. He put on a soberly considering expression.

"I won't beat about the bush," Henry said. "Thing is, Sir Ralph needs a new solicitor. He's decided he must have local advice, particularly for the estate and—this is strictly in confidence—I think he's fallen out with the London lot, naming no names. He wants to change a lot of things—I'll tell you about that later—and he asked me who I would recommend. I suggested your outfit. He thought for a bit and said why not you."

Martin was scarlet.

"I-I'm not a senior partner—"

"I said that. He said he didn't mind about that, and that one day you would be. Fact is, I think it's your living in The Grey House that's done it. He feels it would be keeping everything in the family, so to speak."

"I haven't any experience in estate work—"

"I have."

"I *say,*" Martin said, and beamed.

"Like it?"

"I'll say. That is—if I can do it—"

"Nice piece of business to brandish at your senior partners. I wouldn't like to promise, but it's my guess that estate business will lead to all personal business too in the end, Lady Unwin and all. Pitcombe Park's pet lawyer. Thing is," he looked at Martin over the rim of his beer glass, "it'd help me a lot, having you on my side. He can be the devil to handle, used to having his own way. Clodagh takes after him."

Martin was full of excited generosity.

"She's amazing. She's cheered us all up like anything. Allie's quite different and the children think she's wonderful."

"That's another thing. You see, the Unwins are pleased as Punch she's taken to you all. Any friend of Clodagh's is likely to be beamed on by them but your family is exactly what they want for her. They were in a frightful state when she got back from the States, made worse, of course, by the fact she wouldn't tell them anything. Margot was all for rushing her off to some frightfully expensive trick cyclist in London to have her head seen to. But life at The Grey House seems to have done the trick for nothing. Sir Ralph said this morning he hadn't seen Clodagh in such good form for years."

Martin, whose private thoughts about Clodagh were of a guiltily excited kind, said, well, she was the greatest fun . . .

"Oh, she is. But she's a bad girl too. Has those poor old parents running round in circles." He looked at his watch. "Can I take it that your answer is at least a preliminary yes?"

Martin said, with enormous self-control, "You may."

Henry got up.

"I think the next step is—I mean, before you breathe a

word at your office—to see Sir Ralph together. All right by you?''

''Absolutely.''

''Saturday morning? Sorry to cut into gardening time, but it wouldn't interfere with a working week and it's the one morning I have the remotest chance of his undivided attention for three minutes at least—''

Martin rose too.

''Suits me fine.''

They went out into the foyer which was now entirely empty except for an enormously fat woman wedged in an armchair and grasping a Curry's carrier bag on what remained of her knees beyond her stomach. Outside in St. John's Street they turned instinctively to one another and shook hands.

''Henry,'' Martin said, ''I'm really awfully grateful.''

''Fingers crossed. If it comes off, I'll be the grateful one. See you Saturday.''

And then they separated, two pairs of well-polished brown brogues going purposefully off down the Salisbury pavements among the dawdling shoppers and the pushchairs.

Dutifully, Alice took the children down to Dummeridge for the day. Clodagh had wanted to come, but Alice had said no.

''*Please*. Why not? It's another pair of hands to help with Charlie—''

''I can't explain why not, I just know I couldn't handle it. Clodagh, it's *duty* I'm going for, not particular pleasure.''

''What am I going to do all Thursday?''

''Make us an amazing supper to come home to,'' Alice said jokingly, but knowing Clodagh would take her seriously.

''OK then. But I'll have my pound of flesh some other way.''

Alice said happily, ''I know you will.''

At least the children had been pleased about going. Natasha had dressed herself with immense care in fancy white socks and a pink plastic jewellery set, including earrings, which Gwen had given her and which Alice knew would cause Cecily real grief. James had submitted to Alice's desire to compensate for the pink earrings by substituting brown lace-ups for his prized trainers with silver flashes on the heels, and Charlie, promoted from his carrycot to an egg-shaped safety seat in the back of the car, dah-dah'd contentedly to himself while taking off his first shoes and socks and throwing them on the floor.

It was a long drive, but all three were remarkably good. Alice talked to them a lot over her shoulder, because she felt nervous, and because the first thing she was going to have to say was that they couldn't, after all, stay the night. She should have said that at the outset, but she hadn't, and now Cecily would have made up beds and told Dorothy to set up the cot and altogether it was an awful prospect and all her own fault. And then, driving through Wareham, she had thought, with sudden indignation, that she had no idea why she should feel guilty about *Martin's* mother. Martin never seemed to.

Once this had occurred to her, her indignation grew. *She* was the one who made all the running with Dummmeridge, and it was a running she had now made for over a decade. Just because she had been so conscientious, they all of course expected her to go on being conscientious, so that Martin would have been amazed to be told to remember Cecily's birthday himself, or to bring the children down to see her at Dummeridge. The last mile to the house, the leafy, sun-flecked familiar mile that Alice used to drive with such a joyfully lifting heart, seemed to have lost its charm entirely. She rounded the last curve of the road, went over the little stone bridge that spanned the remains of an ancient moat and pulled up in front of the studded front door with a kind of dread.

The children squealed for release like piglets and went racing into the house shouting for Cecily. Alice followed slowly with Charlie under one arm and his discarded shoes and socks in her free hand. Natasha and James and Cecily had collided on the stairs and were hugging and chattering, and, watching them, Alice felt small and cold. Charlie stretched out of her arm towards his grandmother, so Alice put him down on the flagged floor and let him stagger across on his soft bare feet, bleating for attention.

"Darling," Cecily said at last, reaching Alice, "this is a highlight. I've been looking forward to it so much you can't think. Richard's coming home tonight specially, so you really are honoured. I saw him lurking about with champagne bottles and I've got a salmon trout—"

"Where'm I sleeping?" James said.

"Jimmy James. Where d'you think? In your always bed—"

James, recalled to his own babyhood language, dissolved with pleasure.

"And I," said Natasha, turning her pink bracelet admiringly on her wrist, "am in the blue room. Where Mummy used to sleep. In the *golden* bed."

It was too late. Alice made a feeble last try.

"D'you know, I've done such a dotty thing, I've forgotten all our night things—"

Cecily, jiggling Charlie in her arms, began to laugh.

"Oh darling, how funny! But it couldn't matter less. We'll just have to put Charlie in a hot-water-bottle cover for the night. Won't we."

The children were visibly happy. Cecily had packed their lunch up in little baskets so that they could elude the tedium of a table and also so that she could have Alice to herself while Dorothy dotingly spooned mashed carrot and liver into Charlie in the kitchen. There were two places laid for lunch in the dining room, either side of a shallow copper bowl con-

taining a brilliant cushion of yellow-green moss studded with
scyllas. Cecily helped Alice to a fragrant stew of chicken and
cashew nuts, poured her a slender glass of Chablis and said,
in the businesslike tone she had promised herself she would
use all day, "Now then. I want to know when you are going
to start painting again. No excuses now. Your house is almost
straight, the children are settled, the village clearly thinks you
are wonderful, so what are you waiting for?"

"Nothing," Alice said coolly. "I've started."

Cecily stared.

"Darling!"

"Two days ago."

Cecily raised her glass.

"It's wonderful! Here's to you. Tell me all about it, exactly
what happened."

Alice was in no hurry to finish her mouthful. She said deliberately, "Clodagh locked me into the studio. It was as simple as that. She got the children to help her and they all said
I couldn't come out until teatime. At five o'clock, they un-
locked the door and stood there with a chocolate cake."

Her face was faintly glowing. It had all been so extraordinary, she had been taken completely by surprise. It had begun
with Gwen coming in during the morning with a painting of
a straw hat on a chair by an open French window and saying,
"I hope I'm not speaking out of turn, but this was just lying
about in the spare bathroom and I picked it up and thought it
was ever so pretty and then I looked and saw—"

Alice was sitting on the edge of the kitchen table sewing
name-tapes on James's summer school uniform.

"Yes. I did it."

"Mrs. *Jordan*—"

Clodagh came over from the sink.

"Let me see."

She turned the painting towards her and examined it.

"Hell's teeth, Alice—"

"I can't do it any more," Alice said. "I don't know why, I just can't. I tried and it was hopeless."

"It's ever so clever," Gwen said. "Now my cousin—"

"What d'you mean, hopeless?"

"I mean that I couldn't draw or paint and so I felt rather desperate."

"When was that?"

"About four years ago—"

"Four years? Now that's odd, because my cousin—"

"Shut up, Gwen," Clodagh said. She peered at Alice.

"Four years is an age ago. Why don't you try again?"

"I'm afraid to."

"Just what my cousin—"

"Afraid?" Clodagh said. "You afraid? This is seriously good, you know, *seriously*."

And then she had given the painting back to Gwen and gone back to the sink, and when she spoke again it was about a Canadian novelist called Robertson Davies that she said Alice must read.

It was after lunch that it happened. Clodagh and Natasha and James had been giggling away about something and they lured Alice up to the room above the garage on the pretence of needing to find the croquet set, and simply locked her in.

"You can come out," James had shouted, highly delighted with the whole game, "when you've painted a picture!"

At first she thought frenziedly that she couldn't, she hadn't any water, or paint rugs, but Clodagh had thought of all that. So in a curious state of being at once both exhilarated and quite calm, she had set up her easel and painted a corner of the dusty window, on whose sill John had left a half-carved duck. A couple of fronds of ivy had pushed their way in and a spider had woven a truly copybook web between the duck's head and the window frame. She painted very fast and quite absorbedly. When they let her out she was so pleased with herself she was almost sorry they had come. She said now, with a small swagger, "I always said I'd be able to paint at The Grey House."

"*Did* you?"

"Oh yes."

Cecily watched her. She was pleased for Alice but wished very much that it had not been Clodagh who waved the magic wand.

"It all sounds a bit melodramatic to me."

"It was. But it worked."

Cecily pulled herself together.

"I'm more pleased than I can say. Not least because it will get all those people off my back who think I can get them an Alice Jordan just by whistling."

Alice took a swallow of her wine.

"I don't think I want any commissions just yet—"

"Darling, why on earth not? I thought that was the point—"

"I don't want," Alice said, spacing the words out in a soft, even voice, "to be beholden to anybody about anything just now. I want to be free to do what I need to do."

"I don't think I quite understand."

"No."

"Could you explain?"

"No," Alice said. "No. I don't think I could. I just feel it very strongly."

"Forgive me, darling," Cecily said sharply, getting up to put a dish of big gleaming South African grapes on the table, "but you sound like a spoiled adolescent to me."

"I expect," Alice said politely, "that that is because I am not behaving exactly as you would like me to."

Cecily sat down and pushed the grapes towards Alice.

"I have never tried to influence you in any way."

Alice said nothing.

"If I have ever given you any kind of guidance—reluctantly, mind you—it is because you asked me for it. When you came here, a gauche girl—'' She stopped.

"Are you going," Alice said serenely, "to tell me how much I owe you? It reminds me of conversations long ago with my mother."

Cecily held her hands together tightly to prevent herself from reaching over and slapping Alice. She closed her eyes for a second and said, "Don't let's quarrel."

"I don't want to."

"No." She opened them again and gave a small smile. "Neither of us do."

Alice rose.

"May I use the telephone? There's something I forgot to tell Clodagh about Martin's supper."

"What has Clodagh to do with Martin's supper?"

"She offered to get supper for him," said Alice as if it were the most natural thing in the world, "because I am here."

She went away to the kitchen telephone and rang The Grey House. There was no reply. She dialled the Park and Lady Unwin answered and was excessively friendly and said she would fetch Clodagh at once.

"I've lost," Alice said. "I've got to stay. Out-manoeuvred."

"*Alice*," Clodagh said. "You're pathetic. How old are you? And I was going to do my Upper East Side Swank Foodie's Fish Curry."

"Could you do it for Martin?"

"OK."

"Clodagh. I'm really sorry."

"Me too."

"I'd better go. I'm so grateful."

"What for? For feeding the family lawyer?"

"*What?*"

"Tee hee," Clodagh said. "Serve you right for staying away. See you tomorrow—"

"*What* about the family lawyer?"

"I couldn't *possibly*," Clodagh said, "tell you a state secret over the telephone," and she put the receiver down.

Alice went out into the garden where Cecily and the children were feeding the goldfish with special grains out of a little plastic cylinder.

"I hate him," James was saying, peering into the water, "his face is all gobbly—"

"Just like yours, my dear," Natasha said, tossing her head to feel her earrings swing.

"All well?" Cecily said to Alice.

"Perfectly. She's going to make him a fish curry."

"I'll make you into a curry!" James shouted excitedly at the pool. "That's what I'll do! I'll make you into a curry!"

Natasha put her hand in her grandmother's.

"Sometimes, I'm afraid, Charlie eats beetles."

"Does he, darling?"

Natasha sighed.

"Oh yes. He's a great responsibility. Can we go to the sea?"

It was a long, long afternoon. Alice could not believe the strength of her wishing to be at home. She looked at familiar, beloved Dummeridge in the glory of its spring garden, as if through the wrong end of a telescope, tiny, remote and impersonal. When Richard returned, she kissed him with unusual warmth and Cecily, noticing this, said before she could stop herself, "And what has he done to deserve all this?"

"She thinks I'm going to open some champagne for her," Richard said. "And she's right."

Dinner was better because Richard was determined, it seemed, to keep things impersonal. He talked about the Middle East, made Cecily talk about her last trip to America—"Potagers are now sweeping Georgetown like *measles*"—and when the talk inevitably drifted round to the state of things at Pitcombe, he said, "Guess who rang today."

Cecily, fetching a wedge of perfect Brie from the sideboard, said, "Who?" without interest.

"Anthony."

"Anthony!"

"Coming home," Richard said. "Changing continents, changing jobs—"

"Why didn't he ring here? Why didn't he ring me?"

"I expect he will—"

"How odd," Alice said. "I haven't seen Anthony for almost ten years. Ten years in the Far East. Before the children—"

"He sent you his love," Richard said to Alice.

"Me?"

"Dangerous stuff, Anthony's love—"

Cecily said, "When is all this happening?"

"Soon. A few weeks."

"I see. My eldest son chooses to come home after a decade at a fortnight's notice and does not seem to think it necessary to inform *me*."

"He rang me with the facts," Richard said, pouring more wine. "I expect he will ring you for analysis and interpretation."

Cecily drew in her breath, but she said nothing more except, after a pause, "Darling Alice, tell Richard what's happening to Martin tonight. Too amusing—"

Richard looked at Alice. She took a leisurely swallow of wine, returned his look and said, without any emphasis, "He's being fed fish curry by the youngest child of Pitcombe Park."

Richard's mouth twitched.

"Is he now."

Alice nodded.

"I promise you."

"Isn't that," Richard said measuredly, "something."

But Alice couldn't reply because she was suddenly seized with a helpless fit of giggles.

On his way home from the office, Martin stopped at Pitcombe shop to buy seeds and brown garden twine. He was slightly irritated that Cecily had landed him with Stuart Mott who was the kind of gardener whose surface friendliness concealed a sneering contempt for any employer's opinion. If it wasn't for Stuart, Martin would not now be buying carrot and cabbage seed, both of which he considered wasteful to grow and dull to eat. He had meant to start Stuart's employment with the friendly firmness he had heard his father use to junior colleagues on the telephone, but Stuart's faintly curled lip had thrown him off key from the outset. When Cecily had telephoned him the other night with some idiotic objection to Clodagh as a friend of the family, Martin had been so aggrieved with her over her interference about Stuart that he had been quite short with her and the call had ended very coolly on both sides. Of course, being Martin, he had repented of this and had rung back to say sorry and his mother had said she quite understood, they were all clearly rather on edge just now, and no wonder. When she said that, Martin's regret quite evaporated and he wished he hadn't bothered to apologize. Standing in the shop now, spinning a rickety wire rack of seed packets, he felt indignation bubbling comfortably up in him all over again. This was aggravated further by Mr. Finch coming stealthily up to him—he knew Martin was no candidate for bursts of lyric poetry—and saying, "You've an exotic supper to look forward to tonight, Mr. Jordan."

Martin said, without looking up from the printed merits of Nantes Express carrots, "Have I?"

Lettice Deverel, who disapproved exceedingly of Mr. Finch's separate and obnoxious manner to his upper- and working-class customers, and who was half-obscured by a plywood unit of paper plates and doilies, said firmly, "Mr. Jordan's supper is no concern of yours, Mr. Finch."

Mr. Finch tiptoed back to his counter and began to make an unnecessary pyramid of nougat bars.

"Miss Clodagh was in this afternoon," he said in self-justifying tones, "buying nutmeg and cinnamon. She told me they were to put in Mr. Jordan's supper because Mrs. Jordan is away taking the children to their grandmother."

Lettice Deverel emerged and put a packet of sunflower seeds for the parrot down in front of Mr. Finch.

"Two wrongs don't make a right, Mr. Finch."

"Seems to me," Martin said in a jocular voice, coming forward with his seeds, "that everyone round here knows all about my supper but me."

"Village life, Mr. Jordan," Lettice Deverel said.

Martin offered Mr. Finch a five-pound note.

"Is Miss Clodagh getting supper for me, then?"

"I couldn't," said Mr. Finch in offended tones, taking the note between finger and thumb, "possibly say."

Lettice and Martin emerged into the street together.

"He's a dreadful fellow," Lettice said, jerking her head backwards, "but then, running a village shop is enough to addle the sanest wits."

Martin laughed.

"He's not so bad. Made me rather look forward to my evening." He bent to open his car door. "Can I give you a lift?"

Lettice shook her head.

"Thanks, but no. My conscience is burdened by the fruit cake I ate for tea and will only be quieted by a little vigorous exercise.'' She looked at Martin with sudden keenness. "The whole village will know you and Clodagh had dinner together by tomorrow. Take no notice. Tell Clodagh from me that it's time she went off and got herself a proper job. A job where she is *stretched.*''

Martin got into the car and started it and went slowly up the hill. As he passed Lettice, she brandished her thumb stick at him, and a bit further on he passed Stuart Mott talking to Sir Ralph's tractor driver, both of whom gave a brief, unsmiling nod. When he turned into his own drive, the kitten raced across his path in its usual ritual kamikaze greeting, and there—his insides gave a brief and pleasurable lurch—was Clodagh, taking washing off the line in the orchard beyond. She was wearing jeans and a black jacket embroidered with big, rough, silver stars.

He got out of the car and went to lean on the orchard fence. It was a soft pale early evening and some of the fat buds on the apple trees were beginning to split over the bursting pinkness within. The air, having smelled of cold or mud for months, smelled of damp earth. The hens were muttering about in the grass around Clodagh's feet. Last weekend, she had shown Martin how to measure their progress in coming into their first lay by the number of fingers you could place between the pelvic bone and the breast bone. "Not yet," she had said, "it ought to be four fingers. But coming on." He bent over the fence to make clucking noises at the hens, of which they sensibly took no notice, and then he said to Clodagh's galaxied back, "What's going on?"

"Don't sound so thrilled," Clodagh said, dropping the last garments into the basket at her feet. "Alice meant to get home but your mother had killed the fatted calf so she couldn't. And you aren't deemed capable of scrambling your own eggs."

"Wouldn't dream of it," Martin said, opening the gate for her, "if you're the alternative."

"You have very bizarre fish instead."

"Wonderful."

He followed her into the house and the kitten joined them, mewing faintly in anticipation of supper. Clodagh stopped and scooped it up and dumped it on the laundry.

"You pig, cat. You've known there was fish in the house, all day, haven't you."

"The whole village is talking about us. Apparently, you told Mr. Finch you were getting supper for me."

"Yippee," Clodagh said. "At least it'll take their minds off Pa's rent rises—"

"Rent rises?"

"I do believe he's putting up cottage rents a whole three pounds a week." She put the basket down on the kitchen table and picked out the kitten, who began at once to purr like a generator. "Anyway, you'll know all about that soon, won't you. As our new family lawyer?"

Martin frowned. Spontaneity was one thing, indiscretion quite another. He hadn't even been up to the Park to see Sir Ralph.

"What do you know about that—"

"Quite a bit."

"I suppose your father talks to you?"

"Yes, he does. But this is different. This was my idea."

"Your idea? But Henry—"

"Henry suggested your firm. I suggested you. Simple as that."

Martin was not at all sure if he was pleased about this. Being beholden to Sir Ralph for a benevolent idea was one thing, but to feel you were simply the result of a chance and frivolous notion of Clodagh's was another.

"You're frowning," Clodagh said.

"You make the whole thing sound so—so off the cuff—"

"It was, rather."

Martin said stiffly, "I don't like that."

Clodagh watched him.

"If it had been a man, my father or my brother, you wouldn't mind. It's only because a woman suggested it, you feel insulted."

"No."

Clodagh went off to the larder and came back carrying a covered plate and an onion. Martin was still standing rather woodenly by the kitchen table. She put down the plate and the onion and came up to him.

"Just because I thought of you," she said, "doesn't mean it's a silly suggestion. Pa wouldn't have taken it up if it were silly, even for me. He was really thrilled. I promise you. You'll see, when you go and talk to him."

Martin looked at her warily. His gaze was defensive.

"I don't like favours."

"Martin—"

"I like to earn my way—"

"But you are! Why should anyone offer you this if they didn't think you'd be good at it? And good for us?"

And then Martin, in some confusion of feeling and propelled by an urgency he was suddenly quite unable to control, leaned forward and kissed her. He then put his arms round her and held her very hard against him and bent his head to kiss her again. She said, very quietly, "No."

He smiled at her. He thought he was in charge.

"Why no? I want to, you want—"

"Because," Clodagh said, bending her head away, "I love Alice. You see."

He dropped his arms at once and turned away. He could feel his face grow fiery with shame and humiliation. He had broken his own rules.

He mumbled, "So do I."

"I know you do."

"Sorry," he said. "Sorry. I don't know what came—"

"Shh," she said. She came over and took his hand. "Forget it."

He thrust his chin out and removed his hand from hers.

"I think I will scramble my own eggs."

Clodagh sighed.

"As you wish."

She picked up the plate and the onion and took them back to the larder and returned with a wicker basket of eggs.

"I'll just feed Balloon."

"It's all right," Martin said, desperate both for her to go and for a drink.

"Martin," Clodagh said, and her voice was kind, "no big deal. It simply didn't happen," and then she went out through the stable door and after a while he heard her car start up and drive away and then Balloon came and pleaded penetratingly for food.

Later, when he had poured himself a drink and fed the kitten, he went into his study and sat in the spring dusk and was very miserable. He was bitterly ashamed of himself, both for abusing Alice's absence and for choosing someone who, by her own admission, was capable of better loyalty to Alice than her own husband was. He tried to comfort himself by remembering how unresponsive Alice had been recently—it was literally weeks since they had made love—but it was thin comfort and he had no faith in it. He wondered if he was going to be able to face Sir Ralph on Saturday because he felt his folly might be written on his brow for all to see. Not only had he behaved badly, but he had been rebuffed and rebuked. Martin was not a flirtatious man because he didn't have the confidence to be one. He knew he feared rejection and that that fear made him unadventurous, and because he disliked very much being both unconfident and unenterprising and saw no way to remedy either, he sat in the deepening gloom and let his shame stagnate into bitterness. He had far too much whisky while this happened, and then grew maudlin, and wandered about the empty house and forgot his eggs altogether. He went over and over the little incident, foolishly and pointlessly, and finally went to bed in a very bad way indeed, forgetting to lock up downstairs so that Balloon, finding the larder door unsecured, levered his way in and achieved his ambition of three-quarters of a pound of monkfish.

EIGHT

Morning sunshine, coming in through the tall east windows of Pitcombe Park, fell upon the breakfast table, upon a jar of marmalade made by Mrs. Shadwell the previous January, upon folded copies of *The Times* and the *Daily Mail* and upon a large biscuit tin bearing a Dymo-stamped label reading "Her Ladyship's Ryvita." Her Ladyship was not eating Ryvita. She was drinking a cup of coffee very slowly and trying very hard to concentrate on doing that, rather than on quarrelling with her husband.

The subject was Clodagh. The subject between them in the last six weeks had almost exclusively been Clodagh. At first they had been united in loving anxiety and relief at having her home, and then in approving pleasure over her friendship with The Grey House, but then Sir Ralph had begun to devise schemes to make it possible for Clodagh to remain at home, financial schemes, and what had been a mere crevice of difference between them had widened into a rift.

Margot Unwin loved her youngest daughter with quite as much energy as her husband did, but with more levelness of head. Clodagh's adolescence, a roller-coaster ride of scrapes and truancies and broken-hearted friends who always seemed more loving than loved, had made her mother aware that she needed, in riding parlance, a short rein. Clodagh's elder brother and sister had both been quite safe on longer reins, being more orthodox, less volatile and much duller, and Sir Ralph had always persisted in believing that Clodagh, left to herself, would emerge as tractable and conventional as young Ralph and Georgina had done. Attempt to coerce Clodagh into anything, he had always maintained, and it's like throwing a lighted match into a barrel of gunpowder; give her all the space she needs and she will come, in her own time, as good as anyone could wish.

"Don't," Margot Unwin said, "say gunpowder to me again."

"Sorry," Sir Ralph said, faintly huffy. He had grown fond of the image, over the years. "I am only trying to illustrate what I believe."

"I know what you believe."

Sir Ralph began to butter toast vigorously.

"And I'm right. Her coming home from America proves I'm right. She couldn't, she found, be as bohemian as she thought she could, so she came home, very sensibly."

"I don't think," Margot said, putting down her coffee cup, "you could call being half-engaged to an immensely successful American lawyer very bohemian. I suppose you mean it was bohemian of them to live together. And it wasn't sense that brought Clodagh home, it was the need of refuge—"

There was a knock and the door opened. Shadwell and two liver and white springer spaniels looked in.

"Mr. Dunne's here, sir. And Mr. Jordan. I've put them in the library. Mr. Dunne said not to hurry as he knows he's early."

"Thank you, Shadwell."

The door closed. Sir Ralph rose and shook out his huge napkin like a sail cracking in the wind.

"We'll talk about this later, Margot."

She did not move, but she said in her most commanding-committee voice, "You must know, Ralph, that I absolutely disapprove of what you are about to suggest to Henry. It is quite wrong. It is unfair to young Ralph and to Georgina and it will be disastrous for Clodagh. I may not be physically present at the meeting, but my astral self will be." She paused, and then added, "Very forcibly."

And then she picked up the *Daily Mail*, shook it flat and, with the skill of long practice, opened it at Nigel Dempster.

"Who are all those?"

Henry Dunne squinted up at the marble busts along the top of the library bookshelves.

"Roman emperors, I think."

"Heavens," Martin said. "*Real?*"

"Oh yes, Grand Tour stuff. This room was done about seventeen-eighty."

"It's amazing—"

"It's lovely," Henry said, with the carelessness of one quite familiar with amazingness, "isn't it?"

It was a long room, with three floor-length windows at one end, lined entirely with books. Over the books at one end was pinned a huge map of the estate. By the windows a vast partner's desk was heaped with papers, and parallel to the fireplace an amiable elderly red leather sofa faced a handsome portrait of the Unwin who had made the room and furnished its corners with a marble goddess, a Roman senator and a bronze, after Flaxman, of St. Michael slaying Satan. The rest of the room was comfortingly filled with map cases and loaded tables and dog baskets. Here and there enormous hippeastrums reared out of Oriental urns, and turned their majestic striped trumpets to the light. The air of the room smelt of man and dog and polished leather and history. Martin sniffed. This, he thought in the phrase he had once used to himself about Alice, this is *something*.

Sir Ralph and two spaniels came in on a benevolent tide of greeting. He was carrying a file of papers and was followed by Shadwell with a tray of coffee. They sat down round the fire after shaking hands, and the third baronet looked down on them from his place on the over-mantel panelling as he had looked down for two hundred years already. Sir Ralph waved an introductory hand towards him.

"Sir John. His elder brother, Ralph, died when only a child. He's the only John Unwin in an unbroken line of Ralphs, back to James I. So you see," handing Martin a cup, "you'll be taking on, if you agree, over three hundred of us."

"Henry did say—"

"Did he? Good. Excellent. I wanted to see you at once but Henry is frightfully cautious. Aren't you, Henry? Insisted on seeing you first. What do you say?"

Martin was afraid that his eagerness was written on his face.

"Well, of course, Sir Ralph, if the idea meets with the approval of my senior partners, I'd be more than happy—"

"I'll make sure they're happy. My dear fellow, of course they'll jump at it. Can't tell you what a difference it will make, having you a stone's throw away."

Henry, recollecting how he and Juliet were constantly at the mercy of midnight telephone calls about estate business, busied himself with his coffee cup. Martin could discover the job's little hazards for himself.

"The first thing I want to discuss, you see—and this is urgent—is my provision for Clodagh. I know," Sir Ralph said, waving a dismissive hand at Martin's rising objection of professional inability even to hear the legal problem of someone who was not yet his client, "you can't tell me anything yet. But I want to tell you. Because it's the first thing I'll want you to deal with."

He got up and went off for the coffeepot. Behind his back, Henry signalled Martin to smiling acquiescence about anything Sir Ralph might say, however bizarre. He came back and refilled their cups with alarming swoops of his tweed-clad arm.

"Of course, this house and estate go to young Ralph. Goes without saying and I'm only thankful he wants it and doesn't feel he ought to be running a soup kitchen in Stepney or some pop group thing. As to the girls, I've got a couple of farms in trust for them, Georgina's in Wales, Clodagh's not far from here, near Wimborne. They aren't supposed to have them until my death but I want Clodagh to have hers now. I think she needs the income. What do you think? Am I going to have a problem unscrambling the trust? To be honest, Martin, I don't like problems."

Martin swallowed.

"It's a bit difficult, not knowing anything about—"

"But you must," Sir Ralph said with energetic friendliness, "know about trusts. You are a *lawyer*."

"There are a lot of complications," Henry said, coming to the rescue. "And until Martin has seen all the documents—"

"It's an express trust," Sir Ralph said to Martin.

Martin shifted and put down his coffee cup.

"Usually, if all the beneficiaries of a trust are of age and in agreement, they can put an end to a trust—"

"Excellent!"

"But of course, that may not apply in this case because of other factors I don't know about."

"What I want, you see," Sir Ralph said, turning the full charm of his smile upon Martin, "is to be able to provide Clodagh with enough to live on, without her feeling under pressure to take the wrong kind of job. You have seen enough of Clodagh to agree with me that that must not happen.''

Henry, seeing on Martin's face the as yet unspoken question of what was the right kind of job for Clodagh, cleared his throat loudly and frowned.

''Yes,'' Martin said lamely, to Sir Ralph.

Sir Ralph went over to the windows.

''Come here and have a look.''

Martin followed.

''See all the new planting? Every tree indigenous. I hate to tell you how many elms we lost and now Henry tells me there's honey rot in the beech hanger. Well, what'd you say?''

He turned and faced Martin.

''My trees, my tenants, my daughter. You and Henry between you, hm? Keep us all in order. Ring Henry later in the week when you have told your partners, and he'll put you in the picture.'' He held out his hand and shook Martin's warmly. ''I'm so pleased, so very pleased. Give my love to your pretty wife.''

On the days when Clodagh did the school run, for Alice, Alice painted. She began to paint much bigger, more abstract things, and to think, much more than she ever had before, about colour and light, as well as shapes. When she wasn't painting, or doing things for the children or the house, Clodagh took her round the village, to introduce her to all the cottagers. Clodagh knew everyone. As a child she had made a point of it, partly out of social curiosity and partly out of an appetite for oddness. The village had grown perfectly used to her, so used that she got slapped and shouted at along with their own children. In the village she learned obscene words for parts of the body which she took back to the Park to alarm Georgina with, and scrumped for apples (this was pure affectation for the Park glasshouses yielded white peaches and Black Hamburg grapes) and joined the Bonfire Night gangs that put jumping jacks in village dustbins. Watching the dustbins dance, clattering their lids, had been, she told Alice, one of the purest joys of her life.

In return, the village preferred her to any other Unwin, even though, inconsistently, they would have been shocked to see Sir Ralph or Lady Unwin being as impudently approachable as Clodagh. She had entrée everywhere. Alice, a little self-conscious and anxious not to intrude or patronize, went in her wake in and out of a series of sitting rooms, where the television blethered on unwatched in corners and where old beams and fireplaces had been boxed in with plywood to modernize their old-fashioned shortcomings. She drank a good deal of dark tea, listened to endless monologues about health, and helped to wash up in kitchens where potato chips and motorbike parts bubbled companionably away side by side in their pans of oil. In the newer cottages picture windows let in blank blocks of light and fireplace surrounds rose in pyramidal steps dotted with brass animals and ornamental china thimbles. There weren't enough children, Alice noticed, not enough prams in back gardens and tricycles blocking hallways.

"Can't afford it," Sally Mott told her. "No one can afford to live here *except* in a tied cottage. Our Trevor's had to go to Salisbury when he married, same as our Diana did. Pitcombe's going to fill up with outsiders now, once the old ones have gone. Dad's cottage now—"

"I expect we'll sell it to weekenders," Clodagh said, "from London. Don't you think?"

"You can laugh—"

"I'm not laughing, Sally. I'm teasing. Lots of employment for all of you, looking after weekenders, so why should you complain?"

Sally Mott had learned a great deal about complaining from Rosie Barton. Rosie's life ran the way Rosie wanted it to and she had been anxious to put some of the village women on their guard about being exploited. Sally was ripe for such views, ripe for grievance. She gave up her job cleaning at the Park soon after Rosie Barton came to the village, and she wasn't going to start again, scrubbing for weekenders, not for anyone, thank you.

Lettice Deverel, too, had her views on weekenders. Clodagh took Alice to meet her as well as to drink Nescafé and eat shortbread in the comfortable rectory kitchen. Lettice Deverel said that mud always got the better of phoney weekenders in the end and Peter Morris said they were good for the collection but not really much good for the congregation. When Clodagh and Alice had gone, Peter went up to see Lettice and ask her if she thought Alice wasn't looking very much happier and very much better. Lettice agreed, but she did not sound particularly pleased.

"Sometimes, you give a very good imitation of being a crabbed old spinster—"

"Clodagh Unwin," Lettice said, "needs a good *hard* job. She's simply avoiding the issue, queening it over that poor girl."

"Poor Polly," said the parrot suddenly. "Pretty Polly. *Poor* Polly is a sad slut."

"Why poor?"

Lettice Deverel turned on her kitchen tap and ran water vigorously into a stout black kettle.

"Because two reasons. One, Clodagh is indulging herself. Two, because Alice Jordan is ripe for the picking."

Peter Morris began to laugh. After a while, having pondered the joke to itself, the parrot joined him.

"So you disapprove of an excellent friendship?"

"I disapprove of people being made fools of."

"Fool!" the parrot cried with energy. "Fool! Good morning. Who is a pretty bagpiper, may I ask?"

⁓

"Oh dear," Clodagh said, pushing Charlie up the village street beside Alice, "Lettice is disapproving of me again. She does it about every three years and she will never tell me why."

"Perhaps," Alice said, "she pays you the compliment of thinking you ought to know why."

"This time I do know. And what's more, she's ahead of me—"

"What do you mean?"

A car drew up beside them and a woman's voice said clearly, "Mrs. Jordan?"

They stopped. The face looking out of the driver's window was brightly made up under careful hair, and surmounted a blue blouse tied at the neck with a bow. Clodagh, behind Alice, hissed faintly.

"Cathy Fanshawe, Mrs. Jordan. I've been meaning to come for weeks, but what with one thing and another, I've been so rushed I haven't known whether I'm coming or going. It's the Conservatives—"

Alice stooped to the car window.

"Conservatives?"

"My husband is the local chairman. We're so thrilled you've moved in. Geoffrey said—"

Clodagh gave Alice a sharp dig from behind.

"Mrs. Fanshawe, I'm afraid that I'm not really a Conservative—"

"Surely," Mrs. Fanshawe said, thinking of The Grey House and Martin's appearance and the school run to Salisbury in unmistakable uniform, "you can't think the Liberals are any kind of alternative just now?"

"No," Alice said, "I don't. I—"

Clodagh came to stoop beside her.

"She's a babe in arms about politics, I'm afraid. And about most things. Too sad."

Mrs. Fanshawe looked nervous. A well cared-for hand crept up to adjust the bow on her blouse.

"Perhaps your husband—"

"He," said Clodagh firmly, "is worse. Much worse. Practically a Communist."

Alice began to shake.

"So sorry—"

"Perhaps I might just call one evening? With the forms." She looked directly at Alice. "We could have a proper chat about it."

Helplessly, Alice subsided in silent laughter on the pavement. Charlie watched her gravely from his pushchair.

"You see?" Clodagh said to Mrs. Fanshawe. "So sad. Not fit to make an adult decision really. I don't think the Conservatives *could* want her. Do you?"

Pink with indignation, Mrs. Fanshawe put her car into gear.

"It's really," Clodagh said gloomily, "a hopeless case."

Alice gave a little yelp. Mrs. Fanshawe wound her window up with great speed and let the clutch out too suddenly in her agitation so that the car leaped forward like a kangaroo. Across the street, old Fred Mott watched them from behind his cactus collection; the jerking car, Alice still sitting giggling and helpless on the ground, Clodagh standing above her in an attitude of the profoundest regret. He began to giggle faintly himself.

"What's up with you," his granddaughter-in-law Sally said, bringing in a bowl of pot noodles from the kitchen.

"Them girls," Fred said, wheezing. "Them girls there. Them bad girls."

Sally looked.

"You don't want to take no notice of them. That's just Miss Clodagh, bullyragging again. That's all."

Clodagh put her hand under Alice's arm.

"Get up, do. *Honestly*. What will people think? First you upset nice Mrs. Fanshawe who utterly worships my mother and then you sit on the ground and giggle like a glue-sniffing schoolkid. Charlie's quite shocked."

"Bah," Charlie said.

Alice struggled up, wiping her eyes.

"Clodagh, you are absolutely *shameless*—"

"On the contrary. I'm trying to get you off the street and into the privacy of your own home before the whole village thinks you are on the bottle." She waved across at Fred Mott, chumbling through his pot noodles, and he grinned back and shook his spoon. "If Sally Mott has seen us, we might as well be tomorrow's headline in the *Sun*." She began to push Charlie briskly uphill, talking as she went. Weak with spent laughter, Alice followed.

"Stupid," Sally Mott said, resolving to tell Gwen. "Too old to behave like kids."

"I like a bit of fun," Fred said, letting the noodles dribble down his chin. He glared at Sally. "I like a gay girl, I do."

After lunch, Clodagh took Charlie upstairs and put him in his cot and pulled the cord of his musical box so that it began to play "Edelweiss," over and over, luring him into sleep. Charlie liked his cot. He put his first finger into his mouth, turned on his side and gave himself over to the tinny little tune. Clodagh dropped a kiss on his warm round head, drew the curtains and went down to the kitchen where Alice was putting plates into the dishwasher before she went up to the studio to paint until Natasha and James came home. The room was full of contented post-lunch quiet. Alice shut the dishwasher door and straightened up.

"Don't go," Clodagh said.

She was standing just inside the doorway to the hall, still holding the doorknob in her hand.

"What, not paint? But I thought—"

"I want," Clodagh said, "to talk to you."

Alice found she was holding her breath. She stayed where she was, by the dishwasher, silhouetted against the window. Clodagh went round the table to the two wooden armchairs by the Aga, lifted Balloon off one, and sat down with him on her knee.

"Come here," Clodagh said. "Come here where I can see you."

Alice came, very slowly. She sat opposite Clodagh, upright and on the alert as if bracing herself for a row.

"What—"

"Wait," Clodagh said, stroking Balloon.

"What do you mean, wait—"

"Wait until you aren't exuding anxiety and apprehension like a blue flame." She looked at Alice. "What are you afraid of?"

"I'm not afraid."

"Sure?"

"Only—excited afraid—"

"That's all right then."

There was a pause. It was a silent pause except for Balloon's purring and, far away, a distant aeroplane. It's two o'clock, Alice thought, two o'clock on a Wednesday afternoon . . .

"It's time," Clodagh said. "Isn't it."

"Time? Time for what—"

Clodagh sighed gently.

"Time for me to tell you that I love you. Time for us to begin."

Alice said nothing. She sat absolutely still and stared at Clodagh. Clodagh picked Balloon off her knee, kissed his nose and put him on the floor. Then she looked back at Alice.

"You know what a spoiled brat I am," Clodagh said. "You know how I always want what I want right *now*. Well, by my standards, I've waited for you because I knew it was going to be worth it. I've waited since I saw your reflection in the mirror when you came into the drawing room at home and I felt my stomach turn over. Love at first sight. *Love* Alice."

She stood up and crossed the few feet between them and knelt in front of Alice.

"What about you?"

In a slightly strangled voice, Alice said, "Me?"

"Yes. You. What do you feel about me?"

Alice leaned forward and put her hands either side of Clodagh's face.

"I feel," Alice said, "that I hate it when you go out of the room."

"More," Clodagh said.

"Everything I do with you is more fun, better, than anything I do with anyone else or by myself. I like myself better. I feel more—more *able*. I'm so happy," Alice said, putting her arms round Clodagh's neck and burying her face in her hair. "I'm so happy I feel quite mad."

Clodagh undid Alice's arms so that she could push her away a little.

"Kiss me."

Alice bent again.

"No," Clodagh said, "on second thoughts, I'll kiss you. I think you need a bit of handling."

After a considerable time, watched detachedly by the kitten, Clodagh drew away and said, "Wrong again. You don't need any handling. You just need lots more of the same."

She stood up.

"Come on."

"What do you mean?"

"I mean bed."

Alice gave a tiny gasp.

"Bed!"

Clodagh knelt and undid Alice's shirt and put her hands inside and then, after a few seconds, her mouth. Alice sat with her eyes closed. Relief flooded slowly, heavily through her, relief and release and a sensation of glorious blossoming, like a Japanese paper flower dropped into water and swelling out to become a huge, rich, beautiful bloom. Clodagh turned her face sideways so that her cheek rested on Alice's skin.

"Look at you," she said, and her voice was as thick as honey, "look at you. You're like all bloody women. You thought, didn't you, that when two women fall in love, one at least has to have the same sex experience as a man. And that there has to be a woman one, one that behaves as a woman does, with a man. Are you beginning to see? Are you beginning to see that it's so great for us because we know what the other wants because we want it ourselves?" She took her face away and looked up. Alice was in a kind of trance. Clodagh stood up and then bent to take Alice's hands.

"Alice," she said, "Alice. Come with me."

NINE

In June, Anthony Jordan completed the sale of his luxurious, impersonal flat on Tregunter Path, Hong Kong, cleared his office desk, told the girl who had optimistically hoped for four years that he might marry her that he never would, and took a taxi out to Kai Tak airport with ten years' worth of Far Eastern living packed economically into only three suitcases. He told friends that he was exhausted by the climate and the claustrophobia of Hong Kong and that he wanted to try his hand at something other than corporate finance. He did not say that he would otherwise become lumbered with a largely unwanted wife but everyone knew that that was the case, and took sides in the affair, sides that were very largely weighted against Anthony. Enough people had endured his combination of exploitation and exhibitionism to feel nothing but gratitude towards Cathay Pacific for carrying him firmly homewards. When he had gone, Diana McPherson, who had loved him very much despite her better self, found herself asked out a good deal so that people could tell her that it was better to be an old maid for ever than to be married for five minutes to someone like Anthony Jordan.

His father met him at Heathrow. They had met on Richard's travels about once a year, and Anthony had come on infrequent leave, infrequent because he preferred to go to California than to come home. Anthony thought his father was looking well and fit and distinguished and Richard thought Anthony, despite his expensive clothes, was looking slightly dissolute. They took a taxi into Central London to Richard's tiny flat in Bryanston Street, and then went to the Savoy Grill for dinner. Anthony talked a great deal about why he had left Hong Kong and even more about the extraordinary number of alternatives he now had for a job in the City. He said he thought he would like to work for one of the big accepting houses. Richard listened, noticed that Anthony drank too much and ate not enough and then said, gently, that the City was of course a changed place. Anthony said rudely that his father didn't know a thing about the City and Richard sighed because, even if the City had changed, Anthony plainly hadn't.

Only when they were on the way back to Bryanston Street did Anthony ask about his family.

"You must go and see for yourself."

"Old Martin," Anthony said, staring out of the taxi window at the seedy muddle of Piccadilly Circus, "old Martin seems to have done all right."

"Certainly."

"More up your and Mother's street, really, what Martin has done—"

"I can only speak for myself and I wouldn't agree with you. As long as you both do what suits you best in life, insofar as that is ever possible, then that's what I want for you, and I should think what your mother wants, too."

"Very diplomatic."

Richard said nothing.

"Nice house," Anthony said and his voice was faintly sneering. "Lovely wife. Three children. Solid job. Getting on nicely. Pillar of the community. *Good* old Martin.''

''Yes,'' Richard said, ''all true.''

''And what you wish I'd done—''

''Not at all,'' Richard said in the level, patient voice he used a great deal of the time now, to Cecily, ''unless you wish it yourself.''

Anthony gave a little yelp.

''Bloody *hell*—''

The taxi crossed Oxford Circus and turned left.

''Go and see them,'' Richard said again. ''You will really like the children.''

Anthony turned in his seat.

''How would you know? Mother said you hardly ever see them.''

How many middle-class fathers, Richard wondered in a burst of fury, longed passionately sometimes to hit their sons, and envied working-class ones who sensibly just *did,* and thus avoided sleepless nights of emotional torment and pointless days of fruitless negotiations. He took a deep breath.

''I am lucky,'' he said, ''in that I have in my life a few people who recognize that I am a human being. I am unlucky in that my family are on the whole not in that number.''

Anthony burst into an exaggerated, cackling laugh.

''Oh it's good to be back! Oh it is! Some things don't change and paternal pomposity is one—''

The taxi stopped. Richard turned to look at Anthony.

''Are you thirty-six?''

''Yes—''

''Thirty-six.'' Richard opened the taxi door and climbed out. Anthony heard him sigh and then say to the cab driver, ''Give me forty pence change, would you?''

On the pavement together, when the cab had driven off, Anthony said, ''Why did you ask?''

''I am not,'' Richard said, ''going to give you the satisfaction of an honest answer. Nor of a row your first night home. Come on. Bed.''

In the lift, Anthony said, ''I could do with a nightcap—''

''Help yourself.''

''Join me?''

''No thank you. I have to be up at six.''

Grinning, Anthony began to hum, his eyes on his father, and Richard tried to smile back as if they were sharing a joke rather than a mutual animosity.

After a few days in London, Anthony went down to Dummeridge. It was a rare and perfect June afternoon, with a clear and brilliant light, and Anthony congratulated himself on leaving the breathless mists of Hong Kong for weather which behaved as weather was meant to. He had a lot of presents for Cecily, a length of silk, a magnum of pink champagne, an imitation Gucci handbag and a miniature nineteenth century Korean medicine chest. They had talked every day on the telephone since he had come home, long frivolous conversations that had done much to soothe the soreness in Anthony's heart, a soreness exacerbated by three days in his father's aloof company. *Why* Richard couldn't unbend was beyond Anthony. He was only an engineer after all, however successful. What gave him the right to *judge* all the time, as he undoubtedly did, and then make it very plain indeed if and when he found things wanting. The last three evenings in London, they had, by mutual agreement, gone their separate ways, and Anthony had no idea where his father had been. The flat was as tidy as a ship's cabin. Anthony had a good look round it, a good look, in all the cupboards and drawers, and was surprised to find a photograph of Natasha and James and Charlie on Richard's chest of drawers, and one of himself—quite a recent one, taken on a trip to Manila—and a paperback of Sylvia Plath's poetry beside his bed. Otherwise it was a man's functional flat: clothes, coffee, whisky and aspirin. Anthony could see why his mother never came near it. She called it Father's *other* filing cabinet. She was right.

The lane to Dummeridge was lined with May blossom, thickly pink and white. The grass, Anthony noticed, was not only bright green, but shiny, with the deep gloss of health. He drove the last half-mile slowly, looking at the wooded hills on either side, sniffing for a whiff of the sea and feeling an excited curiosity to discover how he would seem to things at home after all these years and, to a lesser extent, how they would seem to him. The hall door was open as he pulled up, and almost at once Dorothy came hurrying out in a flurry of fond pleasure at seeing him again, and told him that Cecily was out in the garden with Mrs. Dunne and the children.

He gave Dorothy a kiss and held her away from him so that he could look at her.

"Totally unchanged."

She gave a little squeal.

"Rubbish," she said. "Nonsense. Cheeky as ever. Go on through, quick. Your mother's panting for a sight of you—"

He went through the hall and caught the familiar scent of polish and flowers and age. The garden door was open and through it he could see a strip of bright green lawn on which a small boy was standing, bent double, and watching Anthony through his legs. Anthony did not much like children. They were, he found, too honest on the whole.

"He's here!" the little boy shrieked, his voice strangled by being upside down. "He's coming! He's coming!"

He stepped out into the sunlight. Cecily came almost running across the grass and flung herself into his arms. He thought she might be crying. She held him in a tremendous embrace, her face pressed fiercely to his.

"Darling. Darling Ant. Oh, how lovely. You can't think, you simply can't—"

A small, plump young woman with red curls held back by a band was watching them from a group of chairs under the willow tree. The little boy who had called out ran over to her and said with piercing distinctness, "But you said he was a *boy*. You said he was Mrs. Jordan's *boy*. And look, he's only a *man*."

"Just what I feel," Juliet Dunne said, laughing and getting up, "every time Daddy comes home." She came over to Anthony and Cecily, holding out her hand. "I'm Juliet. And you are awful Anthony who wouldn't come home and now you have. I've been sort of adopted here, for the summer. Such luck!"

Cecily put out one arm to encircle Juliet so that they were all three linked.

"Anthony, you must take no notice of her. She has a wicked tongue but I put up with her because she makes me laugh." There was a tiny pause. "She is a great friend of Alice's."

"Alice?"

Juliet sighed. She was extremely pretty, like a kitten, with little features grouped close together in a creamy freckled face.

"So boring. Allie's got a new friend and won't play with any of her old ones just now."

Cecily drew them away across the lawn to the willow.

"I'm not awful really," Anthony said, "I'm just lonely and misunderstood."

"I expect," Juliet said, looking straight at Cecily, "you had a simply horrible childhood."

Cecily nodded, laughing.

"Horrible."

"It *was*," Anthony insisted. "Martin was the goodie who could do no wrong. I was the baddie."

The small boy was trotting beside him. He looked up at disappointing Anthony.

"Mummy likes the baddies on television best."

"Mummy sounds very promising."

They sat down in the cane chairs in the speckled, drifting shade.

"Let me look at you," Cecily said to Anthony.

"I shouldn't. Father didn't like what he saw."

Juliet said, "You have bags under your eyes."

Anthony turned to his mother.

"Is she always like this?"

"I'm afraid so."

"I feel I've stumbled into a dormitory party—"

"Not quite," Juliet said. "It's more like a coven. We're plotting."

"What?"

"How to get Alice back."

Cecily said warningly, "Juliet—"

"Oops. Did I say something I shouldn't have?"

"You might be making too much of too little."

Anthony scented intrigue.

"What's going on? What is Alice up to?"

"She has thrown herself into village life," Cecily said. "That's all. So she hasn't much time for any of us, and we miss her."

"She used to ring *all* the time," Juliet said. "She was the one person I could have a really good complain about Henry to. Your mother's no good at all because she thinks Henry is a dear. I suppose he is really, in rather the same category as a dear old armchair. Or pair of bedsocks." She began to squeal with laughter. "You know what's *really* the matter. Allie thinks I'm so funny and I've got no audience just now. Cecily thinks I'm *quite* funny but not nearly as much as she ought to. Oh dear. I suppose I ought to be going." She looked about her. "Do you think my luck has turned and I've actually lost two children out of three for good and all?"

Her son, who was clearly used to this kind of thing, said his brothers were in the stable yard.

"Do go and get them, there's a little treasure. Isn't it sad," turning to Cecily, "how exactly like his father he looks?"

"She worships Henry," Cecily said to Anthony.

"I want to know more about Alice."

"Why do you?"

"I used to fancy Alice—"

Cecily gave a little sigh.

"I know. I used to worry that you were going to make trouble. To spite Martin."

"I did try—"

"What happened?"

"She froze me out."

"Oh dear. How tiresome virtue is. There it stands, blocking every path to pleasure. Here come my beastly little children." She stood up. "I shouldn't be cross about Allie. She looks as beautiful as the day, so clearly good works suit her."

Cecily went out to the car and saw Juliet and her boys drive away. When she came back, Anthony was lying in the long cane chair where Alice had lain her first afternoon at Dummeridge, with his eyes shut. He didn't open them when he heard his mother return, he simply said, "What a rattle."

"She's sweet."

"Really. Tell me more about Alice."

"Why are you so obsessive?"

"I'm not. I'm keenly interested in my brother's family in a most suitable way."

"You always have a *motive*."

"Not this time." He opened his eyes and turned his head towards his mother. "Tell."

"There's nothing to tell," Cecily said. "It is exactly as I

said to you just now. She had a bad post-natal breakdown after the last baby, and then a big house move, and now she has taken on a whole load of village responsibilities. She's extremely tired, so that she can't see reason and take a holiday.''

"And her new friend?"

"The youngest daughter of the big house in their village."

"Isn't that utterly suitable?"

Cecily said flatly, "Utterly." She took a breath. "I want to know about you."

Anthony shut his eyes again.

"Unemployed."

"Temporarily?"

"Oh yes. No problem. Quite rich."

"Also temporarily?"

"Probably. Is Martin rich?"

"No."

"Comfortable?"

"Yes," Cecily said doubtfully.

"Rich then. Isn't he too perfect."

Cecily let a little silence fall, then she said, "I did rather hope you would bring a wife home with you."

Anthony yawned.

"I was besieged. Literally. But I didn't seem able to fall in love back. I think I'm still carrying a torch for Alice."

"You haven't seen Alice for almost ten years. Very useful, supposing yourself to want someone you can't have, so that you need never commit yourself to anyone else."

"I *did* want her."

"Only in the same way that you wanted Martin's Meccano and Martin's friend Guy and Martin's diligence over examinations."

"That's not very flattering to Alice."

"It's meant," Cecily said, "to be not very flattering to you."

"Oh, me. I've a hide like a rhino."

"I know."

"First Father's unpleasant to me and now you are. I shall go to Pitcombe."

"No," Cecily said suddenly.

Anthony sat up slowly and put his feet on the grass.

"Why not?"

"Because you are a troublemaker."

"I don't want to make trouble. I just want someone to be nice to me. Alice will be nice."

"Alice," Cecily said, "has enough to cope with, without you," and then she gave the game away completely by beginning, with great dignity, to weep.

Anthony could not remember seeing his mother cry before. Indeed, her self-possession had been one of the chief things that had enraged him, as a teenager—*nothing,* it seemed, that you could do or say shook her composure. But she was shaken now. He knew she adored Alice. The main reasons for his own desire for Alice long ago were that his mother adored her, his father liked her a great deal and Martin wanted her. And then of course there were the additional, tantalizing reasons of Alice's personality and her fascinating dislike of him. Perhaps Cecily and Alice had quarrelled. Perhaps Cecily was an interfering grandmother. Perhaps Alice's youthful infatuation with Cecily had died and there had grown up instead, as there so often did in such cases, a robust dislike of the former idol. Anthony, turning these interesting speculations over in his mind, was rather inclined to the last view. He thought he would spend a few more days at Dummeridge, or as long as it took for the festal return of the Prodigal Son atmosphere to wear off, and he would make a few calls to contacts in the

City—he left a Morgan Grenfell telephone number lying about prominently—and then he would invite himself to Pitcombe. So he made himself very charming to Dorothy, and to the two young men in the garden whom his mother was training, and at meals he tried to elicit more information from Cecily about Pitcombe, information which, he was interested to notice, she seemed peculiarly reluctant to give.

"Anthony!" Alice said into the telephone. She was leaning against the kitchen wall, with Charlie, eating a biscuit, on her hip.

"I want you to ask me to stay."

"Of *course*. Where are you?"

"Dummeridge."

"Oh—"

"Exactly. What have you done to my mother?"

"Absolutely nothing."

"Sure?"

Alice smiled at Clodagh across the kitchen.

"Just a teeny bit of independence—"

Anthony laughed.

"I see. Look. When can I come? Nobody is being very kind to me, which is tough when I'm so vastly improved."

Alice said dreamily, her eyes on Clodagh, "I'll be kind. I'm kind to everyone just now."

"Why?"

"Because I'm happy."

"What, doing the church flowers?"

"Yes."

"Extraordinary. You do, however, *sound* happy."

Clodagh bent over James, who was painting a tiny, neurotic picture of a very neat house in one corner of a large piece of

paper. He leaned against her and Alice heard him say, "*You
do it.*" "No, Jamie, you." "Clo-clo do it," he said in a loving
baby voice, gazing at her.

"Are you listening?" Anthony demanded down the telephone.

"Sort of."

"If I come on Friday pour le weekend, how would that be?
If you're very kind to me, I might have to stay."

"Do," Alice said, rubbing her cheek on Charlie's head,
"whatever you like."

"Is your house lovely?"

"Oh yes," Alice said. "It's perfect here. It really is. You'll
see."

She put the telephone down.

"Martin's brother."

Natasha, who was importantly doing her homework—this
term's novelty—looked up from an extremely neat English
exercise book to say kindly to her brother, "Uncle Anthony.
Who you have never seen."

"Nor have you!"

"I *nearly* did. I was more nearly born in time. More nearly
than you."

"Was she?" James whispered up into Clodagh's hair.

" 'Fraid so—"

"Won't I *ever* be the bigger?"

Clodagh kissed him.

"In size, you will be."

Alice came to the table and sat down with Charlie. She
wanted to tell Clodagh about Anthony but Natasha's beady
presence made that impossible just now. So she smiled at Clodagh, and Clodagh came round the table and kissed her, and
then Charlie, and then Natasha said, "What about a kiss for
good little me doing my homework?"

Clodagh picked her off her chair.

"You're a little Tashie madam, you are—"

Natasha put her arms round her neck.

"I'm going to be like you when I grow up."

"No. You're going to be like your lovely mother."

"Can I too?" James said.

Clodagh put Natasha back on her chair.

"Look at you," she said to Alice.

"Why, what—"

"The cat that got the cream—"

"Oh but I am, I *am*—"

"You are so bloody *beautiful*."

"Dear me," Natasha said, "in front of James."

"Bloody," James said softly to his picture, "bloody, bloody, bloody beautiful."

Clodagh leaned towards Alice.

"Beautiful."

"You too."

"No. I'm a ratface." She put a finger on Charlie's cheek. "And Charlie's a moonface."

"And James," Natasha said with deadly quietness, "is a fishface."

James gave a yelp. Then a car came swooping past the house and there was a chorus of "Daddy! Daddy!" and Charlie, who had been dozing against Alice like a human teddy bear, became galvanized by the desire to join in.

It was exactly the homecoming Martin wanted. It was the best day he had had at work since the day he had been made a junior partner. He had been summoned in by Nigel Gathorne, the senior partner, to be congratulated, personally, on securing the Unwins as clients for the firm, and to be told, quite plainly, that this, particularly if he made a success of it, would contribute materially to Martin's upward rise. He then gave Martin a glass of fino sherry, a mark of approval all the junior partners recognized as being equivalent to a CBE. He was so genuinely pleased that Martin even managed to put aside all the complications and tribulations that seemed to have dogged his path since his lunch with Henry Dunne at the White Hart. If Nigel Gathorne could offer such warm and *professional* congratulations, then Martin's achievement must be real indeed. Coming out of Nigel's office, he felt he almost owed Clodagh an apology for his petulance over her part in it. Even thinking of her now was possible without an involuntary blush, but of course *she* had made that easy by being so ordinarily friendly to him and such a help with the children and such a good friend to Alice. He had, in his glow of gratitude and achievement, actually had a preliminary look at the Unwin trust papers at once, and really, it wasn't, at first glance, going to be too difficult to unscramble. He visualized a business conversation with Clodagh. It was a happy little fantasy in which he retrieved the self-esteem he had lost in that undignified little scene in the kitchen when Alice was away. At twenty past five, Martin left his office and went back to his car past the Victoria Wine Company so that he could buy a bottle of champagne, which luckily they had on a very reasonable offer indeed.

"You'll be able to handle Georgina," Clodagh said, admiring the light through her champagne glass. "Easy peasy."

They were sitting in the drawing room, to celebrate.

"Is she like you?"

Clodagh avoided looking at Alice.

"Georgina is absolutely straight in every way. She'll be just like Ma, in the end, only quieter. She buys day clothes from

Laura Ashley and evening ones from Caroline Charles and shoes from Bally and knickers from M & S. She's a dear."

Alice said, head back against a chair cushion, eyes half-closed, "Why don't you go and see her more?"

"Because, for some reason, I really like being at home just now."

"Never," Alice said, on the edge of laughter. She turned her head towards Martin. "Anthony's coming. On Friday."

Martin pulled a slight face.

"Oh well. It had to happen. How long for?"

"Don't you like him?" Clodagh said, interested. "Why don't you?"

Alice began. "He's—" and Martin, fearing family criticism, said quickly, "We fought a bit when we were growing up, that's all. He's been in Japan and Hong Kong for almost ten years. He's probably changed a lot."

"Didn't sound it," Alice said. "Sounded exactly the same."

Clodagh stood up.

"I'm going to read to Tashie. And then you can say what you really think about the Unwins in peace."

Martin tried not to look priggish.

"I wouldn't say anything behind your back that I wouldn't say to your face."

"I know," Clodagh said, and went out of the room, laying a hand lightly on his shoulder, and then on Alice's, as she went.

"I'm so pleased for you," Alice said to him.

He ducked his head. He looked suddenly as young and vulnerable as James. Alice felt so fond of him. It was only when he wanted to touch her that she . . .

"Allie—"

"Yes?"

"Allie, sorry to sort of mess up the mood, but there's something that's rather been on my mind—"

She took a slow swallow of champagne.

"Tell me."

"It's, well, it's about us. I mean, we seem to be fine and everything's going really well and—" He stopped. He loathed this kind of conversation, but a necessity was a necessity. "Look. It's—about bed. I mean, I may be no great shakes but you don't seem to want me anywhere near you at the moment. I can't remember the last time—weeks, months, I don't know." He looked at Alice pleadingly. "Is it me?"

She sat up and put her glass on the floor and folded her hands on her lap. She looked straight at him.

"No," she said. "It isn't your fault. That is, it isn't anything you do. Or don't do."

"Then—"

"It's me," Alice said. "I just don't want you to make love to me. I don't in the least want to hurt you but I must be truthful because it's kinder, really, in the end."

There was a silence and then he said, looking down at his crossed arms resting on his knees, "D'you think we should get some help? I mean, Marriage Guidance or something—"

Alice said gently, "I don't want to do that. I want to say sorry, but I won't because I don't want to patronize you. But I don't want to talk to anyone."

"But will you change?"

"I don't know. I can't tell."

"So you just want me to wait. Grin and bear it—"

"Yes please. Just for now. Yes—please."

He got up and walked about a bit and went over to a window and fingered the stiff gleaming billow of the curtains.

"Allie. I've got to ask you this."

He stopped.

"Ask me then—"

"Will you give me a truthful answer? However much you think it'll hurt me?"

Alice's voice had a little quaver.

"I promise."

Martin came back to his chair and put his hands on its back and looked at her.

"Is there another man?"

Alice raised her chin and looked at him squarely.

"No," she said. "There isn't another man."

And then Martin gave a long, escaping sigh, and grinned at her and said he thought they had better finish the champagne, didn't she?

TEN

In the Pitcombe Stores, Mr. Finch was patiently explaining to his new assistant, Gwen's daughter Michelle, about the arrangement of tinned vegetables on the shelves. It was not that Michelle was stupid, but rather that she wanted to work in Dorothy Perkins, in Salisbury, and they had said she couldn't until she was eighteen, so the village shop was to her no more than a tiresome stopgap at one pound eighty pence an hour. She was elaborately bored, all week, except on Mondays when, this being the show season for Mrs. Macaulay and her girls, Mr. Finch allowed her to help Mrs. Jordan in the travelling shop. Michelle didn't just admire Alice, she really liked her company. When she got home on Mondays, Gwen always wanted to know what Alice had said to Michelle, but Michelle went mulish and wouldn't tell. Her Mrs. Jordan, she felt, was different from the one her mother worked for. Her Mrs. Jordan talked to her like an equal and lent her books and once gave her a pair of silver earrings like shells so that Michelle had to lock herself in the bathroom and pierce new holes in her ears with a needle stuck into a cork and an ice cube to deaden the lobe.

She said, "Yeah, OK. Right. OK," to Mr. Finch but she wasn't really listening. Who cared whether carrots went next to butter beans or peas? She stood and bit her nails and thought about the black leather jacket she'd seen on Saturday that she'd set her heart on.

"There now," Mr. Finch said, "quite clear I think. Now you just load up from these boxes while I go and give Mrs. Finch a hand with the freezer delivery."

Michelle gave the faintest snigger. Everyone knew Mrs. Finch and the freezer delivery driver fancied one another, though why the sight of Mrs. Finch with her blue eyelids and purple hair didn't make the freezer man want to crack up Michelle couldn't imagine. He came twice a month, and Mr. Finch always shot out to the back to give a hand. Michelle imagined a really good punch-up going on among the fish fingers and ice lollies in the glacial van while Mrs. Finch sobbed theatrically into the little lace handkerchiefs she favoured.

When Mr. Finch had gone, Michelle began, laboriously, to take the tins out of their cartons and bang them on the shelves. After a few minutes, Miss Pimm came in and scuttled about in pursuit of a ball of string and a packet of custard powder. Long ago, Michelle had briefly been in her Sunday School, manifesting, Miss Pimm was mortified to remember, an unwholesome curiosity in Mary Magdalene and the woman taken in adultery.

"Michelle," Miss Pimm said, displaying her purchases with exaggerated honesty, "I believe I owe Mr. *Finch* exactly seventy seven *pence* for these two *items*."

"Right," Michelle said, getting up without a smile.

She took Miss Pimm's proffered eighty pence over to the till and was an age with the change.

"Three pence," said Miss Pimm.

"I know," said Michelle. "I'm not daft."

Miss Pimm, reddening in her characteristic blotches, opened her mouth to object to being spoken to in such a way and managed no more than a hoarse and humiliating caw. Michelle stared at her. Then the shop door twanged open and Michelle's gaze moved beyond Miss Pimm and lit up. A man's voice said, "I *am* in Pitcombe. Aren't I?"

Michelle was delighted. She dropped Miss Pimm's change very approximately into her outstretched hand, tossed the wing of hair she liked to let fall into her eyes and said, "Sorry. This is Las Vegas."

"Same thing," Anthony said, coming forward. He looked down at Miss Pimm. She reminded him of a moorhen. He said with great charm to her, "I'm sure you can help me. I am Martin Jordan's brother. I am looking for The Grey House."

Frenziedly, Miss Pimm fixed her eyes on his silk paisley tie.

"Yes!" she said. "Yes!"

Anthony waited. Michelle leaned on the counter and gazed frankly and greedily at him. Miss Pimm raised her troubled eyes to his striped shirt collar. She licked her lips and swallowed.

"Welcome," she said. "Welcome to *Pitcombe.*"

The propriety of her own behaviour encouraged her and her eyes moved to Anthony's chin.

"*Up* the village street until you pass, on the *right*, a cottage with an ornamental *well* in the garden. Turn right there, a very *narrow* lane, and The Grey House is *ahead* of you."

"How very kind," Anthony said gravely.

His voice was so pleasing, Miss Pimm dared one fleeting glance at his eyes. He was winking at Michelle. Seizing her custard powder and her string, and gobbling to herself faintly in her distress, she scuttled from the shop into the street. Fred Mott watched her unpityingly from his window and then observed that the tall bloke who had just gone in was now com-

ing out and was climbing back into the brand of car the telly
ads promised would always get you a sexy bit in a slit skirt.
Fred fingered his trousers. Sally had sewn up the slit in his
pyjama bottoms. He sniggered. She couldn't sew up the slits
in his *mind*.

Anthony drove up the street slowly, Miss Pimm and Michelle quite forgotten. It all looked very pretty and neat, grey
stone and bright gardens. Trust Martin not to dare to live anywhere more adventurous than this. By the ornamental well—
it was an immense affair with a fretted wooden roof like a
Swiss chalet and had a plaster cat creeping along the ridge—
he turned right, and beyond the cottages he saw the stone
gateposts and the clipped hornbeams and the grey-gold gravel
and he said to himself again, *trust* Martin.

He stopped the car outside the very pretty façade. The front
door was open. A kitten, past the sweet stage of babyhood and
fast approaching a gawky adolescence, was sitting just inside
in a patch of sunlight, washing nonchalantly. It took no notice
of him.

"Alice!" Anthony called.

There was no reply. He walked into the hall and across it
into the kitchen. There was no one there but several people
had recently had tea and there was a muddle of mugs and
crumby plates. Anthony called again.

In the open doorway to the garden, a small, neat girl appeared.

"Are you Anthony?"

"Yes," he said. "And you must be James."

She sighed. That was the sort of joke James liked. She said
severely, "I am Natasha."

"I am sorry. Where is your mother?"

"Doing the church flowers. Clodagh's out here. Come and
see Clodagh."

Anthony went out into the garden. There was a sandpit with

a very large baby or a very small child in it and a larger child
on a little bicycle and a girl in a sort of camouflage boiler suit
and a lot of brass jewellery shelling peas into a red enamel
pot. She looked up at the sound of footsteps and Anthony
thought he had seldom seen anyone look less welcoming.

Clodagh held out a hand.

"You must be Anthony."

He sat down on the grass beside her. The children all came
closer and regarded him. The baby one came very close and
poured a cupful of sand over his foot and into his shoe.

"*Charlie*," Natasha said. She stopped and brushed at the
shoe, making clucking noises.

"I gather," Anthony said, "that Alice is doing the church
flowers. And that you are Clodagh."

"That's right."

Anthony took off his shoe and poured the sand out into the
grass. Charlie watched interestedly and then took off his own
shoe and shook it hopefully.

"Which of you children is which?"

"I'm Natasha. I told you. And that's James and that's Charlie."

"And I am your uncle."

"It's so sad," Natasha said, "we have three of you and we
never see any of you. One is in America."

"You are seeing me now."

He looked at Clodagh. He wanted to provoke her.

"Are you the nanny?"

Clodagh wasn't even going to look at him. She went on
zipping her thumb along the pea pods so that the peas pattered
into the pot.

"No."

"She's the friend," James explained.

Clodagh shot him an affectionate look.

"Mummy's friend?"

"All our friend."

Anthony turned round.

"Bit of all right, here."

Natasha felt a social obligation. She said, "Shall I show you round?"

"I'd rather you showed me Mummy."

Clodagh said, "Take him to the church, Tashie, there's a love."

"Won't you?"

"No," Clodagh said. "I won't."

Anthony got to his feet.

"Lovely welcome—"

Clodagh said nothing. She was full of loathing.

"Don't I even get any tea?"

Natasha said comfortingly, "It'll be time for a drink soon. And we ate *all* the chocolate crunchy." She paused and then she said, "I could give you a banana, I should think."

"Certainly," Clodagh said. "As many as he can eat."

Natasha led the way back into the kitchen. She peered into the fruit bowl.

"They're all speckly. Do you mind? I only like them very smooth."

"I don't really want a banana."

Natasha looked puzzled. He was a most peculiar uncle. She thought uncles laughed a lot and gave you pound coins and took you for rides in sports cars with the top down. Anthony's car looked very boring. It was even black. She said, "Shall I take you to the church?"

He sighed and nodded. She led the way out of the house and up the garden to a field path. She told him about her school and about Sophie having to have glasses and about her intense longing to have some too. He nodded a bit but she didn't think he was conversationally very responsive. She asked him if he ever wore glasses and he said "No," rather crossly, and she began to be disappointed in the role of hostess.

"The church," she said in a last effort to entertain him, "smells exactly like my cloakroom at school."

But he only grunted. They skirted the churchyard wall and Natasha thought of several interesting remarks about the headstones but hadn't the heart to utter them. In silence, they walked up the path to the south porch, and went from the bright warmth outside to the damp cool dimness inside. There were several women dotted around the nave, and dustsheets and trugs of greenery and flowers and pairs of secateurs, and in the aisle a very beautiful woman was sweeping with an almost bald broom. The woman, Anthony recognized with a start, was Alice. Her hair fell in a river down her back from some high-crowned arrangement on her head, and she was wearing something swirling and green. Natasha ran forward and seized the broom, and said, "Here's Anthony!"

Alice stopped sweeping. She looked up and smiled at him angelically. Then she gave the broom to Natasha and came quickly to Anthony and put her arms round him.

"*Anthony*—"

He held her back. He felt, as he so seldom did, full of a large and happy warmth.

"You look *amazing*—"

She laughed. Then she looked closely at him and said, suddenly sober, "Oh, poor Ant. I wish you did."

"Everyone is so horrible to me. Your baby filled my shoe with sand."

"He didn't mean it!" Natasha cried indignantly, her eyes full of sudden tears. "He's only little!"

Alice took her arms away from Anthony.

"Don't be an ass, Ant."

"I *rely* on you to be kind."

"Are you whining?"

"No. Only pleading."

She gave him a sideways look.

"If you say so—"

A faint scream came from the west window. On a ladder insecurely poised against the high sill, Miss Payne, as small and round as a blue tit, was losing out to an immense and purposeful white stone vase that she was attempting to fill with cow parsley and iris. Anthony, who liked all diversions for their sakes, sped away from Alice and caught Miss Payne as she tottered, cradling her in his arms like a large pale blue knitted football. He then came back up the aisle with her, as if she were some kind of trophy. She was pink with distressed excitement. The other flower ladies left their assigned corners and crowded round with twitters of concern. Peter Morris, who had been in the vestry screwing up a modest little looking glass so that he could inspect himself before he emerged into the chancel every service, came down into the nave and for a fleeting moment thought Miss Payne was being abducted. Then Anthony set her gently on the floor and she began, quite helplessly, to giggle. Everybody watched her.

"Of course, nobody her age should even be *asked* to go up that ladder—"

"I've always said we could do with a nice cheerful arrangement of silk flowers up there, no trouble to anyone, only need an occasional shake—"

"You all right, dear?"

"Better sit down, Buntie dear, after a shock like that—"

"Perhaps *next* time, Mrs. Jordan, you being so much younger, you could volunteer for the west window?"

"Of course," Alice said, "but Buntie wanted to do it."

Miss Payne nodded violently. Anthony stooped over her.

"Shall I carry you out and lay you down on a nice tombstone to recover?"

She gave a little squeal of delight and horror. Peter Morris moved calmly through the little group and steered Miss Payne to a pew.

"I don't know, Buntie. Cradle-snatching I'd call it."

Miss Payne began to cry. Peter Morris pulled out what he always called his public handkerchief and handed it to her. Anthony looked at Alice.

"I'd *no* idea doing the church flowers could be such a lark."

Natasha said in distress, looking at Miss Payne, "But it's *sad*."

"Heavens," Anthony said, "*what* a sentimental little party." He turned to Alice. "Wouldn't you like to come home now and pour me a huge welcoming drink?"

"Not much," Alice said.

"Allie—"

Alice did stern battle with her temper.

"I must finish sweeping up. Tashie will help me. You go and sit in the churchyard and I'll be out in five minutes."

"All right," he said reluctantly.

He went down the aisle and Miss Pimm and Mrs. Macaulay and Mrs. Fanshawe watched him go as if to see him safely off the premises.

"Hold the dustpan steady," Alice said.

Natasha knelt down and leaned her weight on the dustpan.

"Is sentimental," she said, looking downwards, "nice or silly?"

At supper, which they ate in the kitchen with the upper half of the stable door open to the dim summer night, Anthony talked a great deal about the Far East, and, by inference, of the depth and breadth of his experience of life. Alice heard him with affectionate pity and Clodagh with contempt. Martin felt, as Anthony meant him to feel, faintly insecure. He tried, eating his chicken casserole, to tell himself that whereas Anthony had passed ten years, he, Martin, had lived them. Anthony had stories; he, Martin, had a wife and children, a house and friends and a solid career. Perhaps, Martin thought, getting up to go round the table with the second bottle of Californian Chardonnay, if Alice would let him make love to her, he would be able to hear anything, absolutely *anything*, Anthony chose to say, with equanimity. He believed Alice when she said she wasn't interested in anyone else. He believed that she loved him—heavens, she was more loving to him and appreciative than she'd been in ages, years even—but there was this bed thing. Suppose she never wanted sex with him again, what the hell would he *do*? It was bad enough now, he sometimes felt quite obsessed by it, thinking about it, wanting it. On top of the physical difficulties there was the siren call of self-pity. Martin knew Alice despised people who were sorry for themselves, but sometimes, after a messy little session alone with himself in the bathroom, he would look at himself in the shaving mirror and say piteously, "What about *me*?" He got angry with Alice then, and showered himself furiously, muttering abusive things about her into the rushing water. And after that, he felt as he supposed women did after they'd had a good cry, absolutely wrung out and forlorn. He hated the whole business and, try as he might, he couldn't escape the fact that he wasn't the one who had brought it about.

"Don't I get any?" Clodagh said.

Martin came slowly out of his trance.

"And after I've ironed seven shirts of yours today and put new slug pellets round the delphiniums and done the school run?"

He put his hand on her shoulder.

"Sorry. Miles away."

"Are you thinking about my farm?"

Martin was a poor liar. In a kind of shout, he said, "Yes, actually."

Clodagh looked briefly at Anthony.

"Martin is our family lawyer now."

"How *deeply* respectable."

Alice said mildly, "What an old bitch you are."

"I *needn't* be."

Clodagh gave a snort. She got up and cleared away the plates and put a blue china bowl of strawberries in the middle of the table. Anthony watched her. He thought that when he next telephoned his mother, he would tell her that he saw exactly why she had reservations about Clodagh as a friend for Alice. He turned to look at Alice. He held his wineglass up to her. She must be sorry for Clodagh.

"Here's to you."

"Thank you," she said. But she said it absently. Taking a bowl of strawberries from Clodagh, she said, "What is your farm like?"

"Lovely."

"What kind of lovely?"

"A square flint house with brick chimneys and a wonderful Victorian yard. Six hundred acres—"

"Six hundred and thirty," Martin said.

"It's grown!"

"No. It just wasn't measured properly. I've had it measured. For valuation."

"Martin," Clodagh said, putting an enormous strawberry on top of his helping as a reward, "you are wonderful."

Anthony said, "Why don't you live there?"

Alice held her breath.

"It hasn't been mine. When it is, I might."

"Do you," Anthony said, leaning forward, "live here?"

She looked straight at him.

"I live at home. I spend most days here."

"Why?" Anthony said.

Alice said, without looking up, "Because we like her to."

There was a tiny, highly charged pause.

"I see," Anthony said.

Clodagh said spitefully, "Do you know how to like people?"

"I know how *not* to like them."

Martin waved his spoon.

"Pax, you two."

"We might just, you see," Clodagh said, embarking on the high wire, "be about to have a most interesting conversation about love."

"*Love*?"

Alice looked up. Her eyes were enormous.

"It's the most important thing there is. I always knew it would be."

Martin, alarmed at this kind of remark being made in public, said quickly, "Are there any more strawberries?"

It was all the poetry Alice was reading, a sort of sequel to all those novels she used to devour. He shot a glance at her. She was looking at Clodagh but her mind was clearly miles away. Anthony picked up the strawberry bowl.

"There's about six. I'll share them with you."

He put two in Martin's bowl.

"You don't change, do you?"

"What I don't understand," Anthony said, "is why everyone expects me to."

After supper, Alice put a pot of coffee on the table, and then she and Clodagh moved about in the dimness outside the candlelit circle round the table, clearing up. They were talking together softly, and at the table Martin and Anthony were talking about Dummeridge. After a while, Alice and Clodagh said that they were going to tuck the children in and left the kitchen. When he could hear their feet safely on the stairs

Anthony said, "Come on. Tell me about Clodagh. Why is she here?"

Martin poured a spoonful of brown sugar into his coffee.

"We met her up at the Park. She's been an absolute godsend. A sort of unpaid nanny and companion. It's made all the difference in the world to Alice."

"Maybe," Anthony said. "But is she going to stay for ever?"

"Lord no. She had a bit of a crisis of some kind in the States, so she came home. She'll be off to do something else after the summer. She's that kind."

"Do you like her?"

Martin flinched a little.

"Of course—"

"When you were younger, you'd have been scared of a girl like that."

"Well," Martin said jauntily, "I'm older, aren't I?"

"Mother doesn't like her."

"Mother doesn't have to live with her."

"*Why* doesn't she like her?"

Martin shrugged.

"I don't know."

"You do."

"Shut up," Martin said loudly, suddenly angry. "Shut up, will you?"

"No good losing your temper."

"I haven't—"

Anthony got up and went over to the open door and lit a cigarette.

"This is quite a place."

"Yes."

"Three children. Steady progress up career ladder. Well done."

Martin said nothing. Anthony came back to the table and dropped into his chair again.

"To be quite honest, I envy you. My future is rather bleak."

"Surely—"

"Surely what?"

"Surely you can get another money job?"

"Oh sure. But it seems a bit pointless. What *for*? You know."

Alice and Clodagh were coming back down the stairs. They were laughing.

"I get lonely," Anthony said, thrusting his face at Martin.

"I'm sorry—"

The kitchen door opened and the women came in. Martin waved the coffeepot in relief.

"Coffee?"

"Lovely," Alice said, and then to Clodagh, "It was everything you see, comic *and* pathetic, I wish you'd—" She stopped. "Charlie has got out of his cot," she said to Martin, "and gone to sleep underneath it."

"Why didn't you put him back?"

The women looked at one another.

"It seemed pointless," Alice said. "And not very kind. We rather admired his enterprise."

"I won't admire it when he appears in our room at dawn."

Alice looked deflated.

"I'll put him back then. Later."

Clodagh picked up a bunch of keys from the dresser.

"I ought to go. The drawbridge goes up at eleven."

Alice moved across towards her. "I'll come and see you off."

Anthony was watching. Clodagh, observing this, said lightly, "No need."

"I'd like to. You've worked so hard today. Anyway, I must shut up the hens."

"No," Clodagh said, and shook her head. "I did the hens. Before supper."

She crossed to the stable door and unlatched it.

"Night everyone—"

Alice was gripping the chair back. She saw Clodagh go every night but tonight it was dreadful, heaven knew why. The door closed. She wanted to rush out through the front door and intercept Clodagh's car and get into it with her and just *not* be separated, not be made to be apart, again . . . Instead of doing that, however, she sat down slowly and poured herself some coffee and wished that Anthony wouldn't keep looking at her.

"Brandy?" she said to him.

"Love it—"

Martin got up.

"I'll get it."

He went out to the dining room.

"Pretty good," Anthony said. "For my little brother to find himself the Unwin's lawyer."

"It was Clodagh's idea."

"Was it now?"

"Her father is thrilled—"

Martin came back with a bottle.

"Only half an inch I'm afraid."

He poured brandy into Anthony's empty wineglass. For no reason at all, Alice remembered her father asking for brandy when he came to tell her that he had left her mother and that she hadn't had any then, indeed had never been even part owner of a bottle of spirits in her life. She hadn't been near her mother for a year but she would go now. She and Clodagh would take the children to Colchester to see Elizabeth and perhaps—Alice's heart gave a little lurch—stay in an hotel nearby. And they could go to Reading on the way back and see Sam. Sam would love Clodagh. Perhaps—perhaps they could stay away for a few days, free, just roaming with the car . . .

She said to Martin, "I can't think why brandy should make me think of my mother, but really I *must* go and see her."

"Of course," Martin said.

"Maybe Clodagh could come and help me with the children—"

"Good idea."

"Next month—"

Martin stood up, yawning.

"Whenever you like. I'm dropping." He gestured at Anthony. "Sleep well. No hurry in the morning."

"You must feel very proud of him," Anthony said, when Martin had gone.

"Of course I do."

"So glad."

"Anthony," Alice said, "enough games for one evening. Time for bed," and she leaned forward to blow out the candles, and as she did so Anthony found that his long scrutiny of her and of Clodagh had been rewarded and that he had made a most interesting discovery. And so, in order to consider it at leisure, he was quite happy to be shooed upstairs with the remainder of his brandy. The goodnight kiss he gave Alice on the landing was compounded both by admiration and appreciation of the probable complexity of the future.

ELEVEN

O n fine afternoons, Lettice Deverel carried the parrot in its cage outside and hung it in an apple tree. It liked this and made bubbling noises of deep appreciation. As long as she was in sight, bent over a nearby border in an ancient Italian straw hat, it continued to bubble contentedly, but if she moved too far away it grew agitated and screamed at her that she was a surly bagpiper. Sometimes she wished she had not confined its education solely to literary references to parrots because now it seemed resistant to learning anything new. Peter Morris had attempted to teach it prayers but it became overexcited and shrieked "Parrot, parrot, parrot" at him and then cackled with ribald laughter.

Margot Unwin, finding no one in Rose Villa, one warm, still, late afternoon, came round the house into the garden, calling for Lettice. Lettice was at that moment tipping a barrowload of weeds on to her compost heap, but the nearest apple tree remarked conversationally in Lettice's voice, "Well, Polly, as far as one woman can forgive another, I forgive thee."

Margot Unwin gave a faint squawk. Lettice appeared with

her barrow through a gap in her immense and burgeoning borders. Margot flapped a hand at her.

"I always forget about your wretched bird."

"Did he say anything improper?"

"Only that he forgave me."

"Oh," Lettice said looking pleased, "that's his bit out of
The Beggar's Opera. He hardly ever says it. You are much
favored."

Margot inserted her face sideways under the hat brim and
gave Lettice a kiss.

"I need to talk, Lettice."

"Clodagh?"

"Clodagh."

"Come and sit over here. No, not near the parrot. He always
wants to join in and I wouldn't put eavesdropping past him."

"Why *do* you have a parrot?"

"I like him," Lettice said, brushing garden bits off a
wooden seat. "He is contrary and amusing and independent.
Margot, you look tired."

"So annoying. But I'm worried."

Lettice sat on a second chair and removed her hat. Underneath it her grey hair was tied up in a red spotted snuff handkerchief. She wore a rust linen smock over wide blue trousers
and elderly espadrilles. Margot Unwin wore a sweeping print
frock.

"I shall get us some tea."

"No, dear. Don't trouble. It's the sympathy I've come for."

"I doubt there's anything I can *do*."

"You can listen."

Lettice had been listening to Margot for thirty years, from
the time she had bought Rose Villa and had only been able to
spend weekends and holidays there, travelling up and down in
the train from Waterloo with her pockets stuffed with sketches
of what she would do to the garden. Only young Ralph had

been born then and Margot was pregnant with Georgina and very handsome and spirited and impatient with being pregnant at all. There were endless parties up at the Park, weekend parties and shooting parties and tea parties for the children where the guests were accompanied by nannies in Norland uniforms. Margot started by inviting Lettice up as a curiosity, relying on the fact that she would wear breeches or a cloak or clogs and that she would express her decided opinions in a fresh and unconventional way. But then, at one lunch party, Lettice told the table at large that she was not a performing monkey, and went home. Margot followed her. She stood in Lettice's extraordinary and absorbing sitting room in her Belinda Belville dress and the Unwin pearls and said she was sorry. Very sorry. Then she burst into tears and Lettice, who recognized a true if incongruous friend, forgave her.

They had not quarrelled since but Lettice had always, tacitly and tactfully, retained the upper hand. As with Peter Morris, Lettice came to represent a confidante. When Margot Unwin supposed herself out of love with Ralph and very much in love with someone else, when Clodagh ran away from school, when a rampantly attractive and unprincipled Argentinian polo player besieged the defenceless Georgina for months on end, it was to Lettice that Margot came. Perhaps, Lettice sometimes thought, it was simply because their backgrounds were so different that their friendship was so real. Lettice, growing up in an austere academic household in Cambridge, might have come from another planet to that of Margot's adolescent society whirl. But after the apology, Lettice knew an excellent heart beat beneath the Hartnell suits and cashmere jerseys, and, as she grew older, she was inclined to think she valued excellence of heart above all things. She leaned across now and patted Margot's hand.

"I've had half a mind to speak to Clodagh myself. It's time she got on with her life."

"That's exactly it. And Ralph has made it infinitely worse and has insisted on breaking up the trust so that Georgina and Clodagh get their farms now. Poor George. She doesn't even *want* hers yet but of course she's much too obliging to object. And now Windover becomes Clodagh's and neither she nor her father, it seems to me, have any intention she should do anything other about it than treat it as a giant piggy bank. I'm quite appalled and Ralph is as stubborn as a mule. As for Clodagh—"

Lettice stood up.

"I *am* going to make some tea. Or would you rather have gin?"

"*Much* rather."

"I won't be a minute. You sit and admire my white delphiniums. All descendents from the ones you gave me."

"Lettice," Margot said, "you are a prop and stay."

She sat and looked obediently ahead of her and tried to be sensible and not seized with wild envy of Lettice's single blessedness. After a few minutes, Lettice returned with two magnificent gilded Venetian tumblers and a yoghurt pot of pine kernels for the parrot. As she crossed the grass having put these in its cage, it could be heard exulting over its luck.

"It's a nice parrot, really," Margot said.

"It's a dear parrot. There you are. Now then. It seems that all incentive for Clodagh to do anything enterprising ever again has been removed from her."

"Exactly."

"And she is still dancing attendance on those young Jordans?"

Margot took a swallow of her drink.

"Do you know, I was so pleased about that! They are charming, Alice particularly, and those dear little children, and I thought how lovely for Clodagh, how *normal*, how good for her. And now she never goes anywhere else, never wants to do anything else, never wants to see anyone else. I wish them no ill, Lettice, but I wish they had never come. I thought I might try another angle and wheedle Alice's mother-in-law here by getting her to talk to the county WI but she was most peculiar on the telephone. I was unnerved, to be honest. She said she had promised herself to keep quite clear of Alice's territory.''

"Perhaps," Lettice said, "you should simply throw Clodagh out."

"I thought of that. I even said it. She said of course she wouldn't stay for ever and the moment I wanted her to go she would go down to The Grey House or to a farm cottage at Windover. Then she told Ralph about this conversation and we had the most horrible evening. Thank goodness it was Shadwell's night off.''

Lettice pushed the lemon slice in her drink under the surface and watched the bubbles streaming upward.

"Then you must talk to Alice Jordan."

"Poor girl. She's done nothing wrong except befriend my bad daughter.''

Lettice was silent for a moment, considering how to economize with the truth.

"She is fond of Clodagh. Fond enough it seems only to wish all the best for her. If she sees that hanging about here for too long is bad for Clodagh, she may help to urge her to go. She ought to go——'' She stopped.

Margot looked at her.

"Go on."

"Young marriages like that," Lettice said, "don't need permanent extra adults hanging around them.''

Margot looked indignant.

"Clodagh would never do a thing like that! In any case, Martin Jordan isn't in the least her——''

"All the same——''

There was a pause. It would not be, Margot considered, the first time Clodagh had made mischief; made it not out of malice but purely because she had the power to do so. She stood up.

"I shall talk to Alice Jordan. After the fête."

"The fête—"

"Saturday, Lettice, and don't you dare to pretend you didn't know about it."

"Oh I do, I do. That plant stall—"

Margot smoothed down her skirt.

"If we don't make a thousand, I shall suggest we put our herculean efforts into something else. The work is quite appalling." She looked up at the sky. "Pray for a fine day."

"I have never," Lettice said staunchly, "prayed in my life." She stood up and drained her glass. "But if I *did*," she said reflectively, "I'd save it for Clodagh, not the weather."

"In the old days," Stuart Mott said, leaning against the shop counter and eyeing Michelle, "the shop'd always give something for the fête. Dad said."

Mr. Finch disliked Stuart Mott. He disliked all the Motts. He thought them shiftless and dishonest. They were also a plain family. At least the Crudwells, who proliferated in Pitcombe as the Motts did, had some Romany blood and were picturesque to look at, even if their girls were without morals and were constantly being caught up at the army camp at Larkhill. Mr. Finch had come to abhor human sexuality. He supposed that his abhorrence was the result of thirty-three years of Mrs. Finch. He leaned on the other side of the counter and said to Stuart, "The old days were different. The village shop got used properly then because nobody had cars to take them into Salisbury. I can't afford to give away so much as a packet of cabbage seeds.''

"Don't need cabbage seeds," Stuart said, still looking at Michelle. "Got more'n enough cabbage plants. We'd like a nice box of chocolates for the tombola, though.''

Michelle was friends with Stuart's daughter Carol and she thought Stuart was dirty to keep staring at her like that. She wasn't going to open her mouth and give him the chance to speak to her, though, so she turned round with her back to him and began to rearrange hairslides on a blue card hanging against the shelves where Mr. Finch kept what Mrs. Finch called toiletries. Along the shelf where the soap and talcum powder stood, Mrs. Finch had tacked a swathe of mauve net and an imitation orchid.

"I'll give you a box half-price," Mr. Finch said, "and bang goes my profit and then some.''

Michelle was going to help Alice and Clodagh on the white elephant stall. They'd asked her themselves. And Martin had made a sort of speed game with pegs on a wooden board which you had to cover with plastic cups, as many as you could in thirty seconds, because Lady Unwin had asked him to. Gwen was doing teas with Sally Mott and Miss Pimm was taking the money for them. Mrs. Fanshawe was in charge of the cake stall and at this moment, to judge by the smell, Mrs. Finch was in her kitchen in a ruffled nylon apron making her contribution of iced fancies. "My specials," she called them. Even Michelle, who could eat four Twix bars at a sitting, wanted to throw up at the sight of all that pink and yellow fondant icing. While she baked, Mrs. Finch was working her way through the score of *The Merry Widow*. She had reached the waltz. Stuart Mott pointed to the largest box of chocolates.

"I'll give you two quid for that one.''

Mr. Finch lifted down a small box of fudge which said it had been made of clotted cream in a cottage.

"This is my best offer. Sixty pence is all I'm asking."

With elaborate reluctance, Stuart Mott counted out sixty pence in very small change.

"You helping Mrs. Jordan, then," he said to Michelle's back.

She shrugged.

"Might be."

"She's taken a fancy to you, hasn't she. I know all about that. Nothing goes on up there that I don't see."

He picked up the box of fudge. Michelle hadn't turned round and Mr. Finch, priggishly mindful of Lettice Deverel's opinion of gossip, turned aside to wipe his bacon slicer.

"That brother's staying on," Stuart said. "He's a funny bloke. Nice car. You seeing our Carol later?"

"Dunno—"

Stuart walked over to the door.

"See you Saturday."

"Goodbye," Mr. Finch said, wiping vigorously.

Michelle said nothing. The one thing her eleven years of schooling had taught her was that you could be infinitely ruder if you kept your mouth shut.

"If I wasn't here," Anthony said to Martin, surveying Pitcombe Park just before the fête opened, "I wouldn't believe this sort of thing still went on."

Martin was trying to wedge a card table sufficiently steady to hold his game.

"It goes on all over England. Every summer. Thousands and thousands of village fêtes. Can you find me a flat stone?"

They had been allotted a corner of the great grass terrace below the house, under a laburnum tree. To their left Lettice Deverel, in a blue hessian apron with a sort of kangaroo pocket

in front for money, was pricing geranium cuttings and cour-
gette plants rooted in old cream cartons at ten pence each.
Miss Payne, her helpmeet at the plant stall, was surreptitiously
marking most of these down to five pence before arranging
them invitingly on a trestle table draped in green dustsheets
that had been dyed expressly for this purpose ten years before
and which spent three hundred and sixty-four days of the year
folded up in Miss Payne's box room.

Beyond the plant stall, an old kitchen table by a magnificent
yellow peony bore a depressed collection of second-hand
books, mostly paperbacks, the throwouts of the village's col-
lective holiday reading. Mrs. Macaulay, who never read anything except *Good Housekeeping* and dachshund breeding
handbooks, arranged her stall according to the width of books,
so that *War and Peace* and old medical dictionaries lay between hefty doses of improbable espionage and pornography.
Mrs. Macaulay was, of long experience, realistic about her
afternoon and had brought her knitting. She would sell any
historical romance she had to Mrs. Finch, anything with thighs
and breasts on the cover to Stuart Mott and have a terrible
time finding anything for the Unwins or the vicar who were
all obliged, by tradition, to make a purchase from every stall.
Beyond that, she would have plenty of time in her folding
chair beside the peony to negotiate the shawl collar of her
cardigan jacket.

As close to the house itself as they could get—and laughingly insisting that that was where they had been put—Gerry
and Rosie Barton set up what they called their community
stall. This had involved both of them visiting every cottage in
the village for a contribution, explaining, with unfading smiles,
that they wanted every person in Pitcombe to feel just a little
bit *involved*. Granny Crudwell, interrupted in a Saturday afternoon's wrestling on television, had told them to bugger off.
Other people had produced scraps from their gardens and jars
from their larders and, in Miss Pimm's case, two mustard cot-

ton crocheted dressing table mats, so that the community stall under its banner "Your Village Stall!" resembled the kind of nameless detritus people are thankful to leave behind when they move house. Rosie and Gerry were not attending to their stall; they had left their fat and despairing German au pair girl, whose sole aim in life appeared to be the meticulous correctness of her lifeless English, in charge. They themselves were flitting from stall to stall, smiling and encouraging the stallholders and indulging in the little jokes which inferred, no more, that *we*, the village, were somehow in cahoots, and superior cahoots at that, against the Big House, and all that it stood for. Sally Mott and Gwen admired Rosie Barton. At least she didn't give herself airs. There were some people round here, Sally said to Gwen as they filled the Mothers' Union tea urn, who needed to be reminded we were living in the twentieth century. When Rosie had started her Village Wives' group, Sally Mott had been the first to sign up. As she said, living with Stuart and old Fred made you desperate for some area of your life where you could be sure you'd never meet a man.

The tea stall was flanked on one side by Stuart Mott and his tombola, and on the other by the white elephant stall which Alice and Clodagh had taken real trouble over. Every bit of rubbish they had collected had been mended and washed and polished and Alice had made a huge banner to pin on poles above the stall on which a line of elephants, trunk to tail, was dancing. It had been an immense amount of work organizing the stall, and Alice had been grateful for it because it had given her something to do with Anthony. Anthony had been staying for over a week now, and he was beginning to get her down. He watched her, all the time, and spoke to her in words that were very affectionate, but neither his look nor his tone matched his words. Clodagh had stayed up at the Park far more while Anthony was around and when she did come to The Grey House, to help with things for the stall, she was sharp and aloof. Alice had tried to corner her to talk about what was happening, and twice she had tried to telephone secretly, but Clodagh had simply said, "Wait till he's gone, Alice, wait." But for Alice, who had at last woken up and who was full of appetite and gratitude, this was almost impossible. She resolved she would ask Martin to move Anthony out; after all, Martin didn't want him there, hadn't wanted him at all in the first place, it was *she,* with her overflowing heart, who had said come, do come, *I'll* be nice to you, I'm nice to everyone just now. But he'd brought something nasty with him and he had added to it since he came. Arranging a row of little cut-glass bottles on a piece of white cotton lace, Alice thought she would ask Martin *tonight* to ask Anthony to go. And at the idea her heart simply lifted and she turned to give Clodagh a smile of pure love.

Clodagh put a cardboard box of five-penny and ten-penny pieces into Michelle's hands.

"Run over to Martin with these, would you? It's his float. Twenty-five pence a go or five for a pound."

Michelle went off across the lawn in her new white stilettos.

"What a bloody week," Clodagh said. "I've missed you. I've never missed anyone so much. When is that bastard going?"

Alice looked quickly at Natasha who was piling their float money into neat categories.

"As soon as possible. I'll ask Martin—"

"He knows. Anthony knows. He knew at once."

"Knows?"

Mrs. Fanshawe was approaching with a paper plate of cupcakes.

"I don't care," Alice said. "I don't care if the whole world knows."

"I've brought these," Mrs. Fanshawe said, "because you stall ladies always get left out at teatime."

She put the plate down.

"*Thank* you," Alice said. A vast relief was bubbling up in her.

Mrs. Fanshawe looked quickly over the white elephants.

"Do you know, my grandmother had exactly that vase? I remember it distinctly. You helping Mummy with the change, dear? That's never your baby! He's grown so . . . Must fly, you know how they all fall up on the cake stall the moment they're let in. Must be at my post! Granny Crudwell's made one of her fruit cakes and to tell the truth you can almost smell the brandy from here . . ."

She backed away. Clodagh made her nervous. Alice said softly, "I'd like to tell *her*. I'd like to tell everyone."

Over by the pair of Union Jacks wedged in painted oil drums that marked the entrance, Shadwell blew on a whistle. At once a surge of thirty or forty people hurried into the circle of stalls and made purposefully for their particular objects. As the first two possible competitors, a couple of boys of about twelve, approached the game under the laburnum tree, Anthony said casually to Martin, apropos of nothing they had been saying before, "Of course, Clodagh Unwin is a lesbian."

Martin said, "What do you *mean*?" and then the bolder boy held out fifty pence and, when Martin began to explain the rules, said, "I know. I played it before."

Martin handed him a stack of plastic cups and set his stopwatch.

"Ready? Rubbish, Anthony. Anyway, how do you know—"

Anthony said nothing. He waited for the boy to score, and then for his shyer friend to score two higher and for their scores to be entered in a notebook, and then he said, "I know because she is having an affair with Alice."

There was a silence, and then Martin said with great distinctness, "Alice is my *wife*."

"Alice, your wife, and Clodagh Unwin are having an affair."

A small girl was being helped up towards Martin by her granny. She was holding twenty-five pence. Martin explained the game, very carefully, and between them the granny and the small girl slowly put six cups on the pegs in thirty seconds and then the stopwatch rang and the child began to cry. Her granny, promising treats, took her away with an accusing look at Martin.

He said to Anthony, "Don't talk such utter, bloody rubbish."

"It's true."

"It's a lie. It's a barefaced bloody lie. You've made it up because you're jealous."

"It's true," Anthony said. "You only have to watch and you'll see."

Sir Ralph, jovial in a Prince of Wales checked suit and a yellow rose in his buttonhole, came up and said he'd better make a fool of himself like everyone else. Martin said that it was jolly good of him, sir. He made a great thing of not understanding the rules and then attracted quite an audience when he actually played, with immense skill and swiftness, topping all three previous scores. He straightened up and clapped Martin on the shoulder.

"I like to outwit a legal brain when I can."

There was a ripple of polite laughter. Sir Ralph, saying he'd better buy an improper book from Mrs. Macaulay, took his small crowd with him. When he was out of earshot, Martin said, "I want you to go away. Now. Just go. Wherever you are you make trouble, and I don't want you making it here. Just get the hell out, will you, *now*—"

Anthony took a step away.

"You want me to go because then you think you won't have to face the fact that your wife is a dyke."

Martin fixed his eyes on Sir Ralph's checked back stooping over Mrs. Macaulay's bookstall.

"If I wasn't in the Unwins' garden, I'd smash your fucking face in."

Anthony sighed.

"Smash what you like. It doesn't change facts. No one but you could possibly have lived with such a set-up and not noticed. But then, you only ever *have* seen what you wanted to see."

Several people were approaching.

Anthony lingered for a second as if contemplating saying more, but then he said, "Bye," quite lightly and moved away towards the drive. Martin straightened up and looked at his customers. They seemed to him miles away. Then the first one, Sir Ralph's tractor driver, wearing a T-shirt which said "If you hate sun and sex . . . don't come to Greece" across the chest, said, "What do I have to get to beat the boss?"

"A great man," Martin said, in mild reproof. His voice sounded perfectly ordinary.

"Watch me, then," the tractor driver said. He held out a pound coin. "Watch me beat 'im then."

It was almost completely dark in the drawing room. They had been sitting there for hours while the light faded and the scent of the lilies John Murray-French had planted years before came pouring in through the open windows. There were just Alice and Martin. Clodagh had gone home after the children had been put to bed. She would not stay for supper, she said, they knew where she was if they needed her. They had been silent for ages now, quite silent since Martin had stifled a brief bout of weeping and declined to let Alice comfort him. He had been very polite. He had been polite all evening. Alice wondered if she had ever found him as lovable as she did now. She said to herself, "He is being wonderful," and was full of admiration.

"You can't comfort him," Clodagh said, before she left. "It's arrogant to think you can."

He had uttered one cry of reproach. He had turned to her in the half-dark and said, "How *could* you?" And she knew he meant not only how could you do this to me, but how could you fall for a woman, have sex with a *woman*? So she had leaned forward and said, trying to help him to see what was so crystal clear to her, "But you see, it wasn't because Clodagh was a woman. It was because Clodagh was Clodagh. Can't you see?"

He'd given a little grunt.

"I like everything I have better because of her," Alice said, and then, with the idiotic confidence of her happiness, in the midst of it all, added, "Even you. I like you better because of Clodagh."

That was when he had cried. Not for long, though. He had blown his nose with great decisiveness and after that they had stayed quiet in their chairs in the deepening darkness. Balloon had come in and made a few enquiring remarks and had jumped on Martin's knee and been thrown off, with quite unfamiliar fury, and so had stalked out again, aggrieved. At long last Martin said, "What about the children?"

She turned her head towards him.

"What about them?"

"Well—" He shifted in his chair. "You and Clodagh, influence and things. You know—"

"No!" she shouted. "I do *not* know. Clodagh adores them. So do I. We are two loving adults, not aggrieved minority group proselytizers—"

"Shh," he said, calming her. "Shh. Sorry. I didn't mean—I

mean, I thought—'' He stopped. Then he said more firmly, ''Do they know?''

''They know I love Clodagh and she loves me. They love Clodagh. They don't know about adult love because they are all under eight.''

There was another pause. Then Martin said, ''I could never reach you. Could I? Never. Just at the beginning a bit—''

''Please—''

''I remember thinking, taking you out to dinner once at some fearful joint in Marlow, I'll propose to her, and I was longing to, and then I suddenly realized I had the power to wait, so I did. I was so happy. I suppose it was the only time I had the upper hand.''

''I did love you,'' Alice said. ''I do. I do love you.''

''But not *in* love—''

There was a little silence.

''No,'' Alice said. ''Not *in* love. Never with anyone.''

''Till—now,'' he said painfully.

''Till now.''

He gave a little grunt. Then there was a thump and she realized, from where his voice came from, that he had stood up.

''I'm going to bed.''

''Martin—''

''Don't worry,'' he said, forcing a little bark of laughter. ''I'll do the decent thing. I'll sleep in the spare room.''

''You've been so—marvellous—''

''Long way to go yet—''

''Not tonight.''

''No,'' he said. ''Not tonight.'' And then he went softly across the dark room and opened the door and a faint gleam of light from the landing above illumined him in the doorway.

''Good night,'' Alice said. ''Try and sleep.''

''You too.''

The door closed. She put her head back. In a minute she would telephone Clodagh, but for now she would sit there with her eyes shut and think of Martin and of the affection and admiration he aroused in her, which led, inevitably, to her feelings for Clodagh which had made all this possible, all this joy and richness and sadness, all this *life*. Whatever was coming now, Alice told herself, she could manage. Every muscle of her emotions was in condition to comfort and cope and see some way forward. She stretched her arms out in the darkness and flexed her fingers. The bridge—such a bridge—was crossed.

TWELVE

$\diamond$

Anthony rang Cecily and told her he was going to Majorca for two weeks; a friend had lent him a villa.

"Where are you ringing from?"

"London."

"I thought you were at Pitcombe—"

"I was. I left on Saturday. You can have too much village life."

"Anthony," Cecily said. "What have you done?"

"Nothing—"

"Then why are you going to Majorca?"

"Because I'm a natural sponger, as you know, and I'm being given a fortnight's shelter in return for repainting a loggia. Luxury shelter, mind you."

"I don't doubt it. How was everyone at Pitcombe?"

"Fine," Anthony said heartily.

There was a pause, and then Cecily said, "Well, off you go. And mind you *do* paint the loggia."

"Trust me," Anthony said and put the receiver down.

Cecily went out into the garden. Her white border was looking spectacular; it had taken eight years to achieve. She had planned it, she remembered, to celebrate Natasha's arrival, her first grandchild. She went down the length of it, stooping and peering, whipping out the odd grass that had seeded itself among the lupin spires, but she wasn't really concentrating. She was thinking about Anthony. About Anthony and Alice and Anthony's going to Majorca. When she had left Vienna, she had thought she would never be caught up, heart and soul, in human things again. She had gone on feeling like that, all through the early years of her marriage, even through Anthony's and Martin's childhoods, and when gardening took her over, it seemed to her quite natural that it should, quite natural that something passionate but platonic should fill up the vacuum she had endured since she left Vienna. But ironically, the gardening had brought her back to a hunger for humanity; it seemed, quite simply, to have led that way. She told herself that it was far too late to reach Richard and that her sons were both, in their separate ways, alien to her—Anthony too unreliable and dangerous, Martin too conventional. And then came Alice, and because of Alice Cecily could make the connection, really make it, not just long to with Martin and Anthony—and she would have with Richard too, if he had allowed her anywhere near him. And now here she was, more than three times the age she had been when she left Vienna, as trapped in the intensity of family feeling as she had ever been in romantic and erotic love. Such feeling was, she discovered, pulling dead tufts off an artemesia, quite as intense and obsessive as her earlier passion had been. She could scarcely credit the number of wakeful nights and restless days that those very people she had resigned herself to being unsuited for—a natural accident, she would say—had caused her.

At the end of the white border there was a bower. It was made of golden hops trained around an arched trellis and it contained a stone seat with a back like an acanthus leaf. It had been photographed—twining gold-green fronds, lichened stone, clumps of grey-leaved, white-flowered rock rose—for a dozen books on English gardens. Even now, on a grey day without the brilliance of blue sky behind the brilliance of the hop leaves, it was a satisfaction to look at. Cecily stood in front of it for some time, and considered how long it was since she had had a really creative idea. It was almost as if you could pour your creativity into people or into your work but seldom into both. There simply wasn't *enough* for both. Men knew that. Men didn't even try to cover both. She could weep, she thought, standing there in front of her acanthus seat, she could simply weep at the frustration of this division, this unwanted intrusion into the wholeness of herself . . .

"Telephone!"

She turned. Dorothy was standing at the far end of the border flapping a duster. She began to walk quickly back.

"So sorry!" Dorothy said, "but it sounds urgent. The vicar from Pitcombe—he says—"

"The *vicar*—"

"Yes. A Mr. Morris—"

Cecily ran. In the hall, the telephone receiver lay beside a luminous white hydrangea in a Chinese bowl.

"Mr. Morris?"

"Ah," Peter said. "I'm so glad to speak to you. Nobody's hurt. You must understand that. All your family are unhurt. But I think you should come. I think they need you. I think your son would like you to come."

"What's happened?"

Peter Morris said carefully, "There has been an emotional upset."

"What sort? What do you mean?"

"Could you come? It would be easier to explain to you, if you came—"

It would not, really, and he knew it. It would never be easy to explain but it was always worse on the telephone, when one was unable to see the other person's face. He screwed his own face up at the reproduction on his study wall of Carpaccio's St. Jerome at his desk with the little dog badgering him silently from the floor nearby, and said, "Everybody is well and being cared for, but your family needs your support."

"I'll come," she said. "I'll be two hours."

"Come to the vicarage. Come to me first."

"Yes," she said. "Yes." And he could hear her voice falter.

He put the telephone down and looked at the chair where she would be sitting when he told her that her daughter-in-law and Clodagh Unwin had become lovers and appeared to have no intention of ceasing to be lovers. He would have to tell her how Alice had come to him the night before, in a very bad way indeed, and asserted that her husband had tried to rape her. Rape, she had said, over and over. "He tried to force me. He's mad, he's *mad*—"

He had sat her down in the rectory kitchen and made tea. Alice told him how good Martin had been initially, how accepting, and then how he had suddenly changed and come bellowing at her, accusing Clodagh of trying to fob him off with being the Unwins' lawyer as compensation for taking Alice, and how he had flung her on the floor and wrenched at her clothes and his own and been uncontrollably violent and savage, shouting all the time and weeping, and how James had come in and that of course had stopped things. Then Martin had locked himself in the spare room and could be heard sobbing there, and Alice had rung Clodagh who came down from the Park to help her comfort James, and she had left them together and come here because they needed a doctor, she thought, and more than a doctor probably, she didn't know, she could hardly think . . . The mug of tea in her hand was jerking uncontrollably and tea was splashing down on to her skirt, great hot splashes she hardly seemed to notice, so Peter took away the mug and sat and watched her until he thought she might be able to tell him again, more slowly, what had happened.

"He kept roaring," Alice said. "He kept roaring at me, 'You're a lesbian, do you hear me, you're a *lesbian*'—"

"But you are. If what you tell me of you and Clodagh is true, you are."

"And is that so wrong?"

"Yes," Peter Morris said. "It is very wrong."

She gazed at him. Her mass of hair was loose and wild.

"But it made everything better, happier—"

"No," Peter said. "That is an illusion. It was a selfish, short-term pleasure. There is nothing good in a pleasure which inevitably creates innocent victims."

"And if I was a victim before?"

"Free will," Peter said. "Always a choice, all your life."

"I'm not bad," Alice said, weeping suddenly, "I'm not a wicked woman."

"I know that. Goodness, essential goodness, does not guarantee anyone against wrongdoing."

"It isn't wrong! How can love be *wrong*?"

"In itself, it can't. It is what you do with it."

He had then telephoned the doctor at King's Harcourt and had walked Alice home through the Sunday twilight to The Grey House where there was silence behind the spare room door and in the kitchen a subdued, uneasy quiet while Clodagh read to James, and Natasha at the table filled in the diagrams in a dot-to-dot book. James was on Clodagh's knee, but when Peter and Alice came in she set him on the floor and came across to Alice and put her arm round her. Peter could not look at them. He went over to the table and admired what Natasha was doing.

"They don't, of course, look *real*," Natasha said, drawing on. "Because of all the corners."

James went across to Alice and Clodagh, his thumb in his mouth, and leaned against them. He was in his pyjamas. Alice stooped to lift him and he put his arms round her neck and stuck his bare foot sideways so that Clodagh could hold it.

"Dr. Milligan is coming," Alice said. "He will give Daddy something to help him sleep."

"When I had chicken pox," Clodagh said, "when I was little, Dr. Milligan gave me a biro and told me to draw round every spot I could find. It took a whole day."

James chuckled, his face in Alice's shoulder.

"I shall go upstairs," Peter said. "I shall go up and wait for the doctor."

Alice carried James back to the Aga and sat down with him on her knee. Clodagh stayed where she was.

"Alice—"

"Yes?"

"You're not wavering? What did Peter say to you—"

"That what we have is wrong."

Clodagh snorted.

"I hope you took no notice."

"I must take notice. But it does not mean, if I take notice, that my mind is changed."

Natasha looked up and watched Clodagh.

"And your heart?" Clodagh said. Her head was high. She was wearing a brief, pale grey dress and she stood upright in it, a narrow shaft under her cloud of hair.

"Of all people," Alice said, "you know about my heart."

Clodagh came forward suddenly and leaned on the table. She said urgently to Alice, "It's real you know. *Real*. It isn't just *pour épater la bourgeoisie*."

"I know."

Clodagh put her hand on Natasha's.

"It isn't selfish. It's giving. It folds in other people. It's what's best in women—"

"Clodagh," Alice said, "I know."

Tears were running down Clodagh's face. She took no notice of them and they dripped on to the table.

"You *must* know it," Clodagh said. "Everyone must. They must see that it is as strong and real as ordinary love. I never knew that before but now I do. Oh, *Alice*—"

They were all watching her. James had taken his thumb out. Alice stretched out a hand.

"Clodagh. Clodagh, why all this, why worry—"

"Because of the centre line," Clodagh cried out, letting go Natasha's hand and covering her wet face with her own. "Because of that. Because I'm afraid of it, because I'm afraid it will pull you back, it will, it *will*—"

Natasha got hurriedly off her chair and came to her mother. Alice took her hand. She sat upright in her chair, holding her children, and although her face was quite drained by fatigue, she said in a voice of great calm, "You needn't be afraid."

Clodagh took her hands away from her face and went over to the roll of kitchen paper on the dresser and tore off a strip and blew her nose ferociously.

"Alice. Oh my precious Alice. You are such an innocent—"

And then the doctor had come. He had gone upstairs with Peter Morris to Martin, who, bruised to his very depths by his own behaviour as well as by the bitter discoveries of the last twenty-four hours, had conducted himself with the passive courtesy of a well-brought-up schoolboy, and had been helped into pyjamas and into bed, and given an injection to help him to sleep. Outside on the landing, with a weary distaste, Peter Morris explained the circumstances to Dr. Milligan and then the two men went down to the kitchen and found that Clodagh had gone and that Alice was sitting at the table playing hang-man with her children.

Dr. Milligan said he would call again tomorrow but he thought Martin should be taken away for a while.

"So that," he said to Alice, "you can put your house in order."

Alice said nothing. She stared at the spot on the table where the hanging lamp made a neat circle of apricot light.

"It isn't 'F'," Natasha said. "Only four more wrong and I've hanged you."

Alice felt the two men looking down at her, big, grey-haired men in a late Sunday comfortableness of clothes. She heard Clodagh in her mind, Clodagh saying to her, laughingly, "Why should men despise you? Honestly, you're a walking stereotype. Do women despise gay men? Alice, Alice—"

She looked up with difficulty.

"I will ring your mother-in-law in the morning," Peter Morris said.

"Oh—"

"Yes," he said firmly.

Dr. Milligan moved away towards the door.

"I'd get those children to bed if I were you. And yourself." He opened the stable door. "Rain," he said, and went out into it.

Peter Morris came round the table and laid a brief passing hand on each child's head.

"You can always ring me—"

"Yes."

"Martin will sleep all night."

"Yes."

"Get to bed now."

When he had gone, Natasha said, sighing, "It was all Uncle Anthony, wasn't it?"

"Well, partly—"

"Will Daddy be better in the morning?"

"A bit better."

"Who's doing the school run?"

Alice thought.

"Mrs. Alleyne."

James's lip trembled.

"No—"

"It's her turn—"

"I want Clodagh—"

"Yes. Yes. I know."

She stood up and took James's hand.

"Come on. Bed."

He trailed after her, dragging on her hand. They went slowly up the stairs, past the eloquently closed spare room door, and along the passage to James's room where his bed awaited him under a fly-past of model aeroplanes. He looked very small and fragile in bed. The sight of the back of his neck filled Alice with panic. She kissed him quickly for fear she might cry before she was out of the room, and for once he did not beseech her to stay, but put his forbidden thumb in and turned docilely on his side.

In her room next door, Natasha was settling Princess Power into her pink plastic castle for the night. Without turning, she said, "Should I say goodnight to Daddy?"

"I think he is fast asleep. Have you put out your ballet things, for tomorrow?"

Natasha nodded. Tomorrow, Alice thought. Monday, ballet class, community shop, Clodagh to see to the children at tea-time, Martin awake again, Cecily coming, Gwen coming, everyone beginning to know. And before that, this night to get through. She went over to Natasha and kissed her.

"The moment she's organized, Tashie, you hop in. I'll come in later, when I've had a bath."

"I wish," Natasha said, "that I could have her Power Chariot too."

"Perhaps, for your birthday—"

Natasha began to talk, softly and intimately, into the pinkly mirrored throne room. Alice went out and closed the door. Then she listened at all the other doors, even, after a struggle, at the spare room door, and then she went along to her own bedroom and took her shoes off and lay down on her bed. She did not turn the light on. She simply lay there in the pale darkness and stared up into it, and outside, in the summer night, the rain pattered down on to the hard, dry ground.

"What are you telling me?" Cecily said, but she didn't really mean it. She knew.

Peter Morris said nothing more. He got up and went over to the window and looked out at his damp garden.

"And the doctor?"

"He went to The Grey House this morning. He thinks you should take Martin home with you for a few days. He needs looking after." He turned from the window. "The results of shock, you see. What might, a century ago, have been called a brainstorm."

Cecily had her eyes closed.

"This whole business is grotesque."

"But it is happening."

She opened her eyes and spread her arms out to his study walls.

"But here—"

"In Pitcombe?"

"Yes."

"Humanity is no different. It's just that the setting is prettier than, say, Solihull. And no crowds to hide in."

Cecily said with a kind of stiff shyness, "It must seem absurd to you, but I have never encountered such—such a—a situation before."

"Nor I," Peter said. "Men yes. But not women. It is quite different, with women."

Cecily shut her eyes again.

"No doubt—"

Peter Morris crossed the room and laid his hand on her arm. "We must go round to The Grey House."

"The children—"

"They are at school."

"Not the baby."

"The baby is where he should be," Peter said. "With his mother."

Cecily allowed herself to be helped from the chair and guided from the house. The village street was empty except for Stuart Mott trimming the two green moustaches of privet that separated Miss Pimm's harsh little front garden from the pavement. He looked up when he saw them coming and gave a tossing nod of his head to show that he couldn't possibly relinquish the handles of his shears to wave. He knew who Cecily was. It looked, from the way she was walking, as if she had some bad news to break at The Grey House. Perhaps Mr. Jordan's father had died or something had happened to that brother. Miss Pimm, dusting her dead mother's bureau in the front first-floor room, saw them too, and remembered that she had seen Peter Morris walking Alice along like that, as if sheltering an invalid, only the night before. Miss Pimm picked up her mother's inflexible photograph. The night of her mother's fatal stroke, she had gone straight to the rectory, just run there, even before she telephoned the surgery. It was the only time in her life she had ever tasted brandy.

"Is—is it known," Cecily said, "in the village?"

"Not yet."

"Must it be?"

"It can't be stopped—"

"Why should not Alice go," Cecily said, suddenly angry and turning upon Peter. "Why must it be poor Martin—"

"The children."

"Yes—"

"My feeling is that Martin and Alice must heal separately before they come together again to heal their marriage."

Cecily snorted.

"Their marriage! My dear Mr. Morris, that is surely over—"

"Not at all."

He gripped her arm to cross the street.

"Such a betrayal," Cecily said, thinking not solely of Martin.

"No worse, I think, than conventional adultery. Both are sins. Neither need destroy a marriage, given sufficient support."

In the lane leading to The Grey House they met first the milk float and then a pick-up truck bearing Martin's heavy-duty lawn mower away for repair. In the last cottage garden, a rubber sheet blew on the washing line beside several pairs of immense pyjamas. At the gateway, Peter Morris took Cecily's arm more firmly and led her across the front of the house and round to the stable door to the kitchen. The top half was open and inside, in jeans and a checked shirt, very pale and with extremely neat hair, Martin sat at the table with the newspaper before him.

He looked up when their figures darkened the doorway, and then stood up, and said, "Hello, Mother," and came over and opened the door and kissed her cheek. Then he said, "Good morning, Peter," and stood back, politely, as if there was nothing more he could do.

Cecily put her arms round him. He stood and allowed her

to. Then he said, "Would you like some coffee? I expect there is some."

"Darling," Cecily said. "Darling."

"Please," Martin said. He put her arms away.

"I've come to take you home, darling. I've come to take you home with me for a while—"

"I should like that," Martin said.

"My car is at the rectory—"

She looked round the room.

"Where is Alice?"

Martin said carefully, "Alice is taking Charlie for a walk in his pushchair. She would be glad for me to be at Dummeridge."

Cecily gave a savage little yelp.

"I am *sure* she would!"

Martin's face immediately creased with distress and Peter Morris came forward and took his arm.

"Of course she would. She wants to see you better. We all do."

"Heaven knows what Milligan gave me last night," Martin said. "I feel as if I'd been hit with a sledgehammer." He put his hand to his face. "I tried to ring the office. Alice said—"

Cecily put her arm around him.

"Don't worry about those things. Don't worry about anything. We'll take care of them."

"My bag," Martin said. "I packed my bag—"

Peter went upstairs to look for it. On the landing, he found Gwen, bundling sheets into a pillowcase for the laundry.

"That's his mother come then?"

"Yes—"

Gwen believed clergymen had a threefold social duty to baptise, marry and bury and no business to step beyond it.

"I suppose you got her to come?"

"I am looking for Mr. Jordan's bag—"

"If you'd wanted to be useful," Gwen said, pushing in sheets patterned with Paddington Bear, "you'd have sent Clodagh packing weeks ago." She jerked her head towards an open door. "You'll find Mr. Jordan's bag in there."

"Gwen. Gwen, I hope you'll stay. At least until Mr. Jordan gets back—"

"Depends," Gwen said, "on what I'm asked to do. Doesn't it."

Peter said with some asperity, "I don't seem to remember you having any moral difficulties with Major Murray-French's girlfriends."

Gwen gathered up the bursting pillowcase.

"That was different, wasn't it? That was *normal*." She moved towards the stairs. "If I stay, it'll be because of the kids. You can't despise the kids, can you?"

Alice, on the river path with Charlie, saw Cecily's car go down the village street, cross the bridge and climb easily up the opposite hill, southward. She could see two heads in it. When it had disappeared, she put Charlie into his pushchair with his drooping bunch of buttercups, and pushed him resolutely up the street, talking to him animatedly. Cathy Fanshawe, coming out of the shop, saw her and ran across to say breathlessly that the fête had made nine hundred and fifty-one pounds, would you believe it? Alice said how wonderful. Cathy thanked her profusely for her stall and ran back again to her car. Soon Cathy Fanshawe would know why Martin had been taken away by his mother.

In the kitchen at The Grey House, Clodagh was frying a sausage for Charlie's lunch. Gwen had pointedly gone home. Clodagh too had waited until Cecily's car had pulled away from the rectory. She had had nothing to do all morning but wait. She had meant to speak to her mother, but Margot had gone up to London early for a dental appointment and lunch at the Parrot Club. The speaking would have to happen that evening or else Margot would hear, distortedly, from the village, and Clodagh wished her to know that she, Clodagh, would be leaving quite soon, and taking Alice and the children with her, to Windover. She had said nothing of this to Alice. She was waiting until she and Alice were alone.

When Alice came in, she put Charlie into his highchair and then went over to Clodagh and held her. Neither of them said anything. Charlie, looking for something he could reach, found the telephone cable and pulled it, so that the receiver clattered off and Alice had to come to its rescue.

"Awful *boy*."

Charlie beamed.

"I am a coward," Alice said. "I couldn't face Cecily."

"There are quite a lot of cowards around here," Clodagh said, turning the sausage, "and you ain't one."

She put the sausage in Charlie's dish, with a chopped up tomato, took it over to him, and cut it up.

"Nah," Charlie said.

"It's all you're getting."

He blipped the pieces of sausage with his spoon. Clodagh put her hand on Alice's shoulder.

"Sandwich?"

"No thanks. Nothing. Not hungry."

"Alice," Clodagh said, "this is no moment to have the vapours. We are just beginning to get somewhere."

Alice smiled. She picked up Clodagh's hand and laid her cheek on it.

"It's not the vapours. It's lack of sleep and lots to think about. And anyway, I must go. Shop day."

Clodagh opened the door.

"I'll be here when you get back. We all will. Waiting for you."

They stood and looked at each other. Then Alice leaned forward and kissed her and went out into the garden towards the drive.

The Community Shop was standing as usual in the yard behind the post office. Also as usual, Mr. Finch was standing on some aluminum steps washing the windscreen with a plastic bucket in one hand and a sponge in the other. The back doors of the van were open, and what was not usual was that Mrs. Finch, in a frilled floral blouse, was inside stocking up the shelves. Mrs. Finch prided herself on having no manual part in the business though she kept an eagle eye on the books, and if she was minding the shop when a customer wanted potatoes she would pull on rubber gloves before she touched them and make it very plain, with deprecating remarks and smiles, how unaccustomed she was to this aspect of what she called the commercial world.

Alice went up the steps into the van.

"Hello, Mrs. Finch. No Michelle?"

Mrs. Finch paused, holding two bottles of vinegar.

"No, Mrs. Jordan. No Michelle."

"Is she ill? She was fine on Saturday—"

"She is quite well. She is serving in the shop."

"I see," said Alice, who didn't. "Well, let me do that. I know you don't like it—"

"Mrs. Jordan," said Mrs. Finch, clasping her bottles, "I am not one to flinch."

She took a breath. She had rehearsed this to herself several times, ever since Gwen's astonishing visit to the shop shortly after midday. She put the bottles in their allotted place and

turned towards Alice with her hands folded against her sunray
pleated skirt.

''Mrs. Jordan, I am sure you will not misunderstand me. I
am also sure you will understand why I must, out of delicacy,
say this to you, rather than allow Mr. Finch to. Michelle will
not be on the van with you this afternoon because her mother
has requested that she shall not be.''

Alice began to laugh.

''Don't be *idiotic*—''

Mrs. Finch watched her.

''I've lived a bit, Mrs. Jordan. There isn't much I haven't
seen. I'm not one to judge. But I'll tell you that in not judging,
I am very rare. Very rare indeed.''

THIRTEEN

"You will not," Sir Ralph said, banging his fist into his open palm, "stay here one more hour. You will not. You will leave Pitcombe."

His face was scarlet. Margot and Lettice Deverel, who had been summoned from a peaceable kitchen supper with the parrot, both endeavored to speak, but he brandished his arms at them, commanding them silence.

"I put all my faith in you. All my faith. And you have betrayed me and perverted all the decency of your upbring-ing—"

"Ralph," Margot cried. "Ralph. Don't be so exaggerated. It doesn't help. Clodagh is still Clodagh."

"Of all people," Sir Ralph said. "Of all my treasured peo-ple."

Clodagh was sitting very upright on a small sofa in her father's library. She had gone to her mother soon after her return from London about seven o'clock and it was now after ten. Mrs. Shadwell had as usual left a cold supper in the kitchen but nobody had been near it. It seemed, when she had begun upon it, that there was far more for Clodagh to tell her parents than she had supposed, particularly as she had had to repeat many things and explain many more. The separateness of her intimate life, which she had come to believe was inviolable, seemed not to be so; the purity of her independence was, before her eyes, being trodden all over by violent distress and abhorrence. Margot had not, whatever her feelings, said one unkind word. Her father had made it plain that her sexual tastes revolted and bemused him and that he was personally outraged that she should have sought to gratify them in Pitcombe. She had tried to explain about love, and it was his reaction to that that had sent her mother to the telephone for Lettice Deverel.

Sir Ralph had always been fond of Lettice. Privately he admired her brain and strength of personality, and publicly he called her, with affection, our jolly old bohemian. When Lettice came into the room, still in her gardening trousers, he held his hands out to her piteously and said, ''What are we to do? Oh, my dear, what is to become of us?''

Lettice had taken his hands and kissed him, and then gone over to kiss Clodagh, before saying, ''We are not going to lose our heads.''

''You don't understand—''

''My dear Ralph, I do. I understand you all.''

He had been calmer then, and while Lettice talked to him Clodagh had sat with her head bent and attempted to quiet her own storm of rage by thinking of Alice. No one should say a word against Alice, she was resolved upon that. But then her father did, he could not help himself; he cried out that Alice must have persuaded his daughter and Clodagh screamed with fury at him and then he said she must leave Pitcombe within the hour. It was melodramatic, crude, stupid, oh all those things and worse, but it was human and, most of all, it was *happening*.

''There is no end to the horror,'' Sir Ralph said. ''It will be round the village like wildfire, round the county. The reputation of centuries—"

"Ralph," Lettice said warningly.

"It *will*," he insisted.

"It will be a nine days' wonder. What *do* you suppose goes on inside some of your own cottages? In intimate matters," Lettice said, placing a hand on each of her trousered knees, "your tenants are infinitely more experienced than you."

He glared at her.

"How dare you."

She was unperturbed.

"It will be a nine days' wonder. Seven if Clodagh goes quickly."

Margot made a little mewing sound of misery.

"We are both going," Clodagh said. "Alice and me. We will go together."

"I hope not."

"Alice has *children*," Margot said.

"They come too."

"I hope not," Lettice said again. She looked at Clodagh. "That should not be the future. There *is* no future in that. The future lies in you using your able head for the first time in your life. It wouldn't hurt you—" She paused. "It wouldn't hurt you to learn to be alone."

Clodagh turned her head away.

"You may have been spoiled," Lettice said. "There's no call to spoil yourself."

Clodagh's teeth were clenched.

"I'm thinking of Alice."

"Are you? And her children no doubt. How will they fare, brought up as they have been, if you take them to Dorset and expect local society to accept you both as an ordinary couple? Rural society can't do it. Maybe city society can, though I doubt it does. I believe it to be thin, sham stuff. And what has their father done, beyond be a man? A dull man perhaps, an unexciting, inhibited man, but no brute. Just a man. Live with that, will you? World well lost for love, eh?'' Lettice leaned forward and prodded the air towards Clodagh. ''If Alice was a free woman, I'd say off with the pair of you and good luck to you. Shut up, Ralph. But she's not and I can't say it.''

Clodagh felt not only anger now but fear. She couldn't delude herself that Lettice was a conventional, orthodox, right-wing old puritan, however hard she tried, and if *Lettice* said they couldn't because of the children . . . She tossed her head. Nonsense. Of course they could. The battle would just be bloodier. She said so.

''I shall never have your children at my knee,'' Sir Ralph said suddenly, ignoring her remark.

Margot, even in the emotional state she was in, could not look at Lettice.

''If that's what's worrying you,'' Clodagh said brutally, ''I can easily bear a man for *that*—''

Sir Ralph gave a little cry. Margot got out of her chair and came across to slap Clodagh's hand.

''Behave yourself!''

''Bed,'' Lettice said, getting up.

''Well, certainly no more of *this*—''

Clodagh got up too and went swiftly over to the door. It was huge and panelled and painted white, and as she stood against it for a moment before she opened it she looked to Margot as she had looked before she was twelve, when the mischief of her childhood turned into the waywardness of her adolescence.

''You are *not*,'' said Lettice, watching Margot, ''going to start asking yourself where you went wrong.''

Clodagh went up the dim stairs without putting the lights on. The air was deep misty blue, but not dark. On the landing the enormous Chinese ginger jars that had come home with an adventuring eighteenth-century Unwin gleamed like fat-bellied barbaric gods. There were eight of them, on rosewood plinths, and as a child Clodagh had named each one. Now she went past them as if they were strangers, past the little Chippendale sofa where she had posed, every birthday, for a photograph, past the naïve painting of pigs she had always said she would *kill* Georgina for (and Georgina had half-believed her), past the icon of St. Nicholas she had once believed could see her conscience, past the cabinet of fans and the cabinet of snuff-boxes, past her mother's bedroom door and off the plushy broadloom overlaid with Afghan rugs of the main landing, on to the haircord of the old nursery passage and her bedroom which looked south towards the beeches, the beeches which hid Alice from her view.

She knelt on the window seat and looked hard down through the beeches. Alice was there. Alice, who needed her. Alice whom she had rescued. That had been the most exhilarating discovery of Clodagh's life, that discovery that Alice didn't believe, deep down, in her own value. When that became plain to Clodagh, when she saw that however different, however stylish Alice *looked*, she didn't have real faith in herself, she even doubted the worth of what she *was*, out here in the demanding conventionality of country life—then Clodagh had felt real intoxication coming on. *She* could wave the wand. She could do for Alice what Alice couldn't quite do for herself.

And she had done it. Alice was changed, but then, so was she. She laid her cheek against the smooth wood of the folded shutters. She needed Alice now. She hadn't meant to; in fact, having never needed anyone, only wanted them, briefly, it hadn't occurred to her that needing might happen. The thought of not having Alice made her want to scream and scream, hysterically, and break things. Nobody should make her bear such pain. Alice was *hers*. She would woo her again, a second time. She had wooed her to be hers, now she would woo her to be hers for ever, to come away with her.

She leaned forward so that her forehead rested on the windowpane. It was nearly as dark as it would get. If she went and stood in front of St. Nicholas now, and stared at his intractable dark Byzantine face, she would be able to look at him without a tremor. She had done a good thing. After a quarter of a century of doubtful goodness, Clodagh had no doubt that now she was on the right track. She had made an unhappy woman happy, and the happiness had spread all round her, to her children, to her friends, to the village. As for Martin—well, that was a slight casualty, but one outweighed by all the benefits. Clodagh's mind went rapidly over Martin, a small thing taken in proportion to the whole. In any case, he had, consciously or unconsciously, damaged Alice. And it was Clodagh who had healed her.

She left the window and went over to her bed and put on the lamp beside it. A moth with a pale furry head and black pin-dotted wings immediately began to bang senselessly about inside the shade. Clodagh watched it. Then she spread out her hands in the glow of the lamplight and looked at them. On the wedding finger, she wore the silver band Alice had given her. She had given Alice a ring too, a ring as fine as a thread, and Alice had slipped it on her own wedding finger, under the ring Martin had given her. They had not spoken at all during that little ceremony, just sat, touching hands, across Alice's kitchen table one afternoon while Charlie, on the floor, rattled a wooden spoon inside a plastic mug and shouted at it. That was how it had always been, so unstagey, so strong and unsentimental, so *real*. And that was how it would always be.

"I'm so sorry," Alice said, "I don't quite understand. Will you come in?"

Rosie Barton said she would love to. She followed Alice across the hall and into the kitchen and Alice could feel her eagerness at her back, like an electric fire.

"Coffee?" Alice said.

"I'd *love* it. What a morning!"

She sat herself down at the table which still bore the children's breakfast bowls and leaned on her folded arms and said with immense solicitousness, "How *are* you?"

Alice had her back to her, putting the kettle on the Aga. She said, "I'm all right, thank you."

Rosie said, "*Alice—*"

Alice turned. Rosie was not smiling but her whole face and attitude exuded sympathy.

"Look," Rosie said, spreading her hands on the table. "Look, I know we don't know each other very well, but I hope we can rapidly put that right." She smiled. "I'd like to. We'd like to. Alice, I've come to offer you our support, mine and Gerry's. I don't want you to be in any doubt about it."

Alice put her hands behind her back and gripped the Aga rail. God, why wasn't Clodagh here? But she was taking the school run into Salisbury, because she had said she would be better able to brazen it out with Sarah Alleyne than Alice.

"I'm afraid," Rosie Barton said, and her voice was very kind, "I'm afraid a place like Pitcombe has some very archaic attitudes. They can't be changed overnight, but we won't give up because of that, I can promise you. But Gerry and I were worried that you might feel quite isolated. We feel it is always such a help to know you are not alone."

Alice went over to the dresser and took down two mugs. Then she put coffee into the glass filter jug and poured boiling water on to it, and put it, and the mugs, on the table among the cereal boxes and jam jars.

"You don't have to say anything," Rosie said. "I can imagine how you feel."

Alice said as gently as she could that she didn't think so. Rosie took no notice of this but began to describe the many gay friends she and Gerry had, had always had, and how much they valued them and what sweet people they were. In fact, their youngest's godfather was gay and he was a wonderful person and had been in a stable relationship for years.

"Gerry and I," she said, "regard it as perfectly natural."

Alice pushed the plunger of the coffeepot down, very slowly.

"Then you are wrong. It isn't natural but it's as strong as if it were. For some people, it is stronger *and* preferable to what is natural."

"*Exactly*," said Rosie Barton.

Alice poured coffee.

"It's kind of you to want to help, but I don't think you can. And I don't think we want help—"

"But the village—"

"I know," Alice said. She had yet to brave the shop, but today Gwen had said that she would not come to the house if Alice and Clodagh were in it together. Alice had laughed at her absurdity and Gwen had become very huffy, and Alice had suddenly seen that she was about to cry, and that she was in a real confusion of prejudice and affection, and been sorry, and said so.

"I'm afraid," Rosie said, spooning brown sugar into her mug, "that people *are* talking."

"Of course they are. But they won't talk for long."

Rosie looked disappointed, but she said bravely, "Well, that's a wonderful attitude."

"Not really. It's more a sort of recognition."

"And your husband?"

Alice stared at her.

"This really is none of your business."

"I'm so sorry, I was only trying to help—"

"I've told you," Alice said, "you can't, and I don't want it."

Rosie stood up.

"Alice, I know you're upset. Who wouldn't be? I could kick myself, I've come far too soon. But I must tell you this. I do have experience of campaigns. A *lot* of experience. And you can't run them alone, it simply isn't possible. So in a week or two, just remember we are there. Anything we can do, anything—"

"I am not a campaign," Alice said. "We are not. We never will be. We are people."

"Yes, of *course*."

Rosie began to move towards the kitchen door. Her mind was already forming the profoundly understanding things she would say to Gerry about Alice. It was, of course, the fault of the village. The sheer weight of intolerance and narrow-mindedness was enough to drive anyone on to the defensive. From the doorway, she gave Alice a little smile and wave.

"We're always there. Don't forget."

"Give me the whole village baying for blood," Alice said later to Clodagh, "the whole of Wiltshire if you like. Anything, anybody, rather than one more minute of Rosie Barton's sympathetic understanding."

Then she made sick noises, and the children, who were eating tea in a desultory way, were enchanted by her and enthusiastically joined in.

Miss Payne was so fond of Alice. Doing the church flowers with Alice had been such fun after all those years of Cathy Fanshawe and her passion for silk flowers when there were lovely real things in the garden, even if they didn't last and shed petals three days after they were done. When Miss Payne heard about Alice and Clodagh she had been desperately upset and had had to take her angina pills again after not having to take them for seven months. Of course, Miss Pimm wouldn't speak of it at all but just went round the village looking like the spinster aunt in a Giles cartoon, the one in a permanent state of shock. Buntie Payne wasn't shocked so much as made utterly miserable. Every time she thought of Alice—and try as she might, she *kept* thinking of Alice—she thought of those little children and Alice being so sweet to her over some broken delphiniums, and all that Alice and Martin had done to the house, and the life of the village. That made her cry and then she had to put another tiny white tablet under her tongue, and *make* herself sit still.

But when she sat still she had even more time to think, and then she thought about love which, in her virgin state, was very much more interesting and real to her than sex had ever been. She had never really loved a man beyond members of her own family, but she had loved—did love—women all right. Feeling the tablet fizzing away beneath her tongue, she asked herself what on earth she would do without her sister Marjorie, even if she did live in Taunton, and her friend Phyllis who lived at King's Harcourt and whom she saw at least twice a week. She had said something of this to Lettice Deverel whom she had met on the field path that ran parallel to the village street behind the cottages, and Lettice had said, "It's one of the curses of our age. Sex has driven out friendship."

Buntie Payne had said, did she mean the sixties and the permissive society, and Lettice had said well, partly, but the rot had begun with the Bloomsbury Group, much earlier.

"The moment self-indulgence gets into the hands of the intellectuals," Lettice said, "society is in for sailing in a rudderless ship. It is now considered bourgeois to control yourself."

Buntie hadn't really known what she was talking about, but being seized by a sudden spasm of bewildered, unhappy sympathy for Alice, cried out, "They mustn't make it hard for her!"

And Lettice said that you couldn't stop them; all you could do was not join them.

"Hypocrisy being, as it is, a national pastime—"

Buntie didn't need telling that. She had heard Sally Mott and Janet Crudwell airing their opinion of Alice in the village shop only the day after Janet's two eldest had been brought back by the military police from Larkhill Camp at three in the morning. Buntie, choosing onions one by one, had been seized with indignation, and when Sally and Janet had left the shop and she had been handing her bag of onions to Mr. Finch she had heard herself demand, "So. A hunger for love or a greed for money. Where do *you* stand on that?"

But Mr. Finch, whose imaginative capacities had recently been so stretched he could summon up neither opinion nor poetry, had simply goggled at her, and said, "Pardon?"

"It's awful of me," Juliet Dunne said to Henry, holding her face in both hands, "but the whole thing absolutely turns me up."

Henry was filleting a kipper with extreme precision.

"I really don't want to talk about it—"

"No, darling, but you never *want* to talk about anything in the least personal. Looking back, I can't quite remember how you conveyed to me that you wanted to marry me. Did I set you a questionnaire?"

Henry buttered toast in silence.

"The thing is, I've simply got to talk to you because I have to get all this off my chest and you are all I have, by way of audience. *Please* stop crunching."

Henry put his toast down with an air of obliging martyrdom. "How can you *eat*?"

He looked at his forbidden toast.

"With great difficulty."

"*Henry*," Juliet said, and began to cry again.

She had cried quite a lot of the night, and the previous evening. It wasn't that Henry wasn't sorry for her, because he was, but he was having rather a bad time with his own feelings and until he had got to grips with them, he hadn't much energy to spare for Juliet.

"Aren't you revolted?" Juliet said between sobs.

Henry sneaked a morsel of kipper. He was revolted; less so than if Alice and Clodagh had been two men, but revolted all the same. And puzzled, intensely puzzled. And somehow let down, almost betrayed, almost—heavens, almost *humiliated*.

Juliet blew her nose.

"It's incredibly reactionary of me, I'm sure, but it's the truth. It turns everything upside down. It makes such a non-sense of everything we were brought up to. I *hate* it. I feel sick and I feel lost."

Henry picked up his toast again with one hand and reached out to pat Juliet with the other.

"I've known Clodagh all my life," Juliet said. "I can't *believe* it. All my life and she's been like this. And Alice. I *loved* Alice. There was no one else I could complain to like I could to Alice—"

"She isn't dead," Henry pointed out.

"How can *anything*," Juliet said, getting up to fetch the coffee percolator, "be the same again after this?"

"Not the *same*—"

"Trust goes," Juliet said. "Once that goes, you've had it. That's why I couldn't possibly stay married to you if you slept with anyone else. I'd never trust you again so we'd have noth-ing to build on any more."

Henry looked down at his plate and thought of Alice, and

how he felt about Alice. And now here was Juliet talking as if Alice had deceived her personally and in so doing had destroyed the vital trust in a friendship.

"Alice is your girlfriend," Henry said, "not your husband."

Juliet began to pour coffee, unsteadily, mopping at her nose with a tissue.

"She was special to me." She stopped pouring. "At the moment, I hate Clodagh. *Hate* her."

"Shouldn't do that—"

"Well I *do*."

Henry pushed his plate away.

"That's not going to help Alice."

"She doesn't *want* help—"

"How do you know?"

"Rosie Barton went to see her and got very short shrift—"

"And when did you and Rosie Barton ever see eye to eye about anything?"

Juliet hid her face behind her coffee mug.

"Henry. The truth is I don't know what I'd say to Alice because I don't know what I *feel*—"

"Why don't you just ring and say you're still friends?"

"But *are* we?" Juliet cried. "*Are* we? I mean, can we be after this?"

Henry stood up and began to rattle the change softly in his trouser pockets. He said, "I'm going to see Martin."

Juliet stared.

"What'll you *say* to him?"

"Dunno. Nothing probably, nothing much."

"*Poor* Martin—"

"Yes."

He went round the table to Juliet and she leaned tiredly against him.

"You're behaving much better than I am," Juliet said. "But then you always have. Haven't you."

He put his arms round her and stooped to kiss the top of her head.

"No," Henry said.

Martin had several visitors from Pitcombe besides Henry. Sir Ralph Unwin came, and so did John Murray-French and Peter Morris. Only Sir Ralph spoke of Alice and Clodagh directly, but that was more, Martin could see, because he was literally exploding with his own feelings than because he thought it best to be straightforward with Martin. Martin was thrown, but he didn't blame Sir Ralph for letting go any more than he blamed Henry or John or Peter for not letting go. He himself behaved with great control while they were there. Only when they were gone, and Cecily was safely in her study or in the garden, did he give way to the consuming and inarticulate rage that possessed him. At night it took the form of hideous dreams, dreams of violence and savagery and killing that sometimes had in them people he had not thought about for years like the prefect at school who had told him how pretty he was and who had then—because Martin had been afraid and disinclined to do what he wanted—instituted a campaign of brilliantly subtle mental cruelty.

The rage was more exhausting than anything Martin had ever known. It fed on everybody, everything, and it refused to subject itself to reason. It boiled in him like some seething, evil broth, and whether he controlled it or gave vent to it out on the cliffs with his mother's dogs, he felt no better. Sometimes he thought he would burst, and often he wished he would, trapped as he was in this boiling cauldron. Cecily would say to him sorrowfully that she wished he could let go.

If only she knew! He suspected that if he let go entirely, he would die, and most days, for a spell at least, he wished for that. He imagined the cool, quiet, dark state of nothingness because, when it came to the crunch of thinking about Heaven, he discovered that he didn't want to believe there was one. He could not bear the thought of any further existence, in whatever form. The most desirable state was nothingness, just not to be. That seemed to him the only state in which there could be no torment.

The only crumb of comfort—the smallest crumb—came from the oddest quarter, from his father. When Richard came home from a journey to Australia, Martin saw at once, and to his amazement, that Richard perceived his rage. Richard made much less fuss of him than Cecily but he was, for all that, much more tender. He made Martin feel that he was not a broken child but a fellow man. Martin heard him, one morning, saying to Cecily in a voice of great anger, "For God's sake, will you allow him his *dignity*?"

He could not hear Cecily's reply. He was sure she made one because she never let accusations just stand, she always had to defend herself. She looked old and tired just now. So, Martin thought, looking in the shaving mirror each morning, did he. He avoided looking at himself except for shaving because somehow the sight of his face made him desperate for his children, for Charlie particularly, in his cheerful baby simplicity. And he couldn't think of them because that led back to Alice, to himself and Alice, man and woman, and then, of course, the path of thought went downwards suddenly into the roaring cavern of his anguish and his rage.

Richard cancelled a follow-up trip to Australia because of Martin. Instead he told Martin they were going to pull down a stone shed that had once held a primitive pump engine, and use the stones to repair the wall at the far end of the famous potager. In the fields beyond, the fields that ran up between the woods towards the sea, they were harvesting, early. The huge combine, like a vast ship, went calmly up and down the golden slopes leaving behind it the shorn earth and the great rolled bales. At midday, there was always an hour of quiet and the odd bold rabbit would streak across the fields and vanish into the sanctuary of the woods. The air smelled of burned earth and dust because, although the sun rarely came out, it sailed imprisoned behind a steady veil of cloud which kept the land heavy and warm and quiet. Martin and Richard worked mostly in silence. Martin said once, "I'd forgotten how good you are at this sort of thing."

And Richard, turning a piece of stone in his hands to see how it would fit, said, "So had I. I sometimes think I've quite a lot of talents I didn't exercise. Usually through my own fault."

When the wall was finished, Martin said he wanted to return to work. Cecily grew very agitated and said how could he, where would he live, who would look after him, was he going to divorce Alice? He said he didn't know about divorce, in fact he didn't know about anything much, just now, except that he wanted to stop feeling an invalidish freak and go back to work. He would live, he said, with the Dunnes. Henry and Juliet had invited him for as long as he wanted.

"But I shall have nothing left," Cecily said later, fiercely, to Richard.

"There's me—"

"You! You need nobody. You never have."

"I am made up," Richard said, "of exactly the same human components of need as you."

And he went away then, and by some instinct went up to the old playroom in the attic and found Martin there, with a tumbler of whisky, weeping without restraint because he had thought nobody would hear him.

FOURTEEN

Most days one of the children asked when Martin would be better enough to come home. Usually Alice said, soon. Once a week Juliet came over and picked them up and took them home with her so that they could see Martin, and the night after these visits James usually wet his bed. It was the school holidays and the days yawned for occupation. Alice devised a list of duties, and Natasha's was to go down to the shop. She liked this because all down the street people stopped and talked to her and asked her how she was and Mrs. Finch would come out of the back part of the shop and give her sweets and sometimes a kiss pungent with Coty's "L'Aimant." The rest of the day she did not like so much. The feeling in the house was peculiar, without her father, and she missed school, and Sophie, who had been taken to Corfu by her family. She spent a lot of time in her bedroom, drawing a wardrobe for Princess Power, and she wrote a huge notice saying "Private—Keep Out" which she stuck on her door, four feet from the floor so that James could not possibly avoid seeing it. Behind the closed door, besides drawing, she spent a good deal of time painting her toenails with Clodagh's scarlet polish.

When Cecily telephoned to suggest that she and Martin and Dorothy take the children to Cornwall—as usual, she said with emphasis—Natasha thought it quite extraordinary that Alice wasn't coming. James, in floods of tears, said he wouldn't go without Alice. Natasha said why couldn't they *all* go, Alice and Martin and Clodagh and everybody, and Alice said it was difficult to explain but she was desperately tired in the complicated way that happened to grown-ups sometimes and she had to be by herself for a bit.

"So Clodagh can come," said Natasha.

"Well—"

"Clodagh isn't tired."

"Clodagh can't come. Clodagh has got something else to do that she can't *not* do."

"I'll ask her to come," Natasha said. "We can show her the witches' rock."

James's eyes bulged at the memory of it.

"I can't come," Clodagh said. "I'd love to. But I can't. I've got to plan my future, you see. I've got to find a job."

Natasha said then at least a holiday would make Daddy completely better and he could come home afterwards. Then she burst into tears. Alice, trying to hold her, said, "I do promise you that when you come back, everything will be sorted out."

But Natasha would not be held and shouted, "I *hate* you!" and rushed out into the garden and picked up Charlie's sandpit spade and hurled it so that it sailed up into the air, far further and harder than she had meant, and came down through the greenhouse roof. Then she stood and screamed with panic at what she had done. James, standing in the kitchen doorway and watching her, began to pee helplessly into his shorts.

Cecily came to collect the children herself. She thought Alice looked awful, but she would have been even angrier if Alice had not looked awful. Indeed, she looked so awful that Cecily would almost have liked to say or do something affectionate but Alice, though perfectly polite, made such a gesture quite impossible. Together, they put the children's bags into the boot of the car, and then strapped in Charlie's car seat, and Charlie into his car seat, and urged Natasha and James to get in beside him. Nobody was quite crying but everybody almost was.

"Bring me some shells," Alice said through the car window.

"Mummy—" James mouthed at her, not daring to speak for fear of letting out his sobs.

"You might find a starfish—"

Cecily put the car into gear.

"I'm sure we will. And James is old enough for the smallest surfboard now—"

"James! Isn't that lovely?"

The car slid forward. Three faces turned her way, crumpling, and Cecily's free hand waved from the driver's window. Alice made herself stand there and wave back until the car was gone between the hornbeams and then she turned and went back into the empty house.

"If we were city women," Alice said slowly, "we'd have a completely different life. It's being country women that makes it so difficult—"

She stopped. City or country made no difference to Clodagh. Clodagh was Clodagh wherever she was.

"Difficult for me, I mean. Even if I moved to a city, I'd still be a country woman now. I'd still feel visible."

"You're visible because you're you."

"I'm *too* visible just now—"

There had been a nasty little moment in the shop that morning, a moment when Cathy Fanshawe had ignored Alice's greeting and turned effusively to speak to Stuart Mott who was buying cigarettes and staring at Alice with a look of such repulsive interest that she had felt quite sick. When she came out of the shop, Michelle had darted up to her, out of the shop yard, and had clutched her convulsively and wordlessly, but it wasn't enough to undo the silent insults of Cathy Fanshawe and Stuart Mott. Going up the street, slowly, with her head as high as she could get it, she thought that even the cottage façades looked as if they had taken stands, were holding their breath until she was past.

"You must get away," Clodagh said.

They were lying in the orchard under the old Russet Egremont where Clodagh had suggested they plant a Paul's Himalayan Musk which would spread through the gnarled branches like a cascade of late blossom . . .

"No," Alice said slowly.

"Yes. *Yes!*"

Clodagh rolled on her side and propped her head on her hand. She put out her free hand and ran a forefinger down Alice's profile.

"Come with me. We'll go down to Windover. We'll start a new life there together, you and me and the children. I'll get a job. You'll paint. *Alice—*"

Alice turned her head to look at Clodagh.

"Windover will be just the same as here."

"No. *No.* Here everyone knew you as a married woman. There we'll arrive as two women, you and me, no past. We can do it. We can do anything we want." She pushed her face close to Alice's. "You don't need money. I've got that. You don't need anything, you just need to come. I love you. Do you hear me? I *love* you."

Alice just went on looking. After a long time, it seemed to Clodagh, she said, "And I love you. More than I think I have ever loved anyone."

"Then come, then *come*—"

Alice turned back to look at the sky. She pulled a long grass from its sheath beside her and put the juicy end between her teeth.

"Loving you makes all decisions much more difficult. Loving anybody does—"

Clodagh snorted.

"You sound like Lettice—"

Lettice had stopped Clodagh the other day, coming down from the Park, and had taken her by the shoulders and said, very fiercely indeed, "If you love Alice Jordan, my girl, you have to let her go." Clodagh had been amazed. She still was. She liked Lettice a lot but some of her opinions had got stuck in some kind of time warp. Throw away the best thing that had ever happened to her? Deliberately? Causing heartbreak all round? Honestly.

Alice was frowning.

"Alice," Clodagh said softly, to win back her attention.

"Mm?"

"Look at me—"

Alice turned.

"I'm looking—"

"Tell me why you love me."

Alice smiled, a slow, lazy smile.

"I love your gaiety. And your freedom of spirit. And your arrogance and strength and mad courage. And I love your love for me."

After some time, Clodagh said, "We don't have to go to

Windover. I can sell it. It's worth millions, I should think. We'll go abroad. We can go anywhere. What about the South of France?''

"Lovely," Alice said, but her mind had slipped into neutral once more.

"You have to come with me, you know. You'd only be half a person without me. Like I'd be, without you.''

"I know.''

"Then when shall we go?''

Alice sat up and pulled her plait over her shoulder and began to pick grass seeds out of it.

"You must go.''

"Shut up!" Clodagh shouted in panic, springing up.

"Calm down," Alice said. "I just mean for a bit. I must be absolutely alone, for a bit—''

Clodagh stooped to seize her shoulders.

"You won't go and see Martin, promise—''

"Martin is in Cornwall.''

"Or Juliet. Or my mother. Or—''

"*Clodagh*—''

"Promise!" Clodagh screamed.

Alice slapped her.

"Shut *up!*''

"Sorry," Clodagh said, crying. "Oh God, Alice. Oh my *God*!''

She fell on her knees beside Alice.

"I'll kill myself if you leave me.''

Alice put her hands over her face.

"Think what we've shared," Clodagh said. "Think what we do together. No one else can do that for you, no one. Only me. We'll go to France. We'll have a house in the sun, we'll all go naked in the sun. We'll have a garden with lavender and thyme and a terrace over a valley. We'll never have to be apart, nights and days together, days and nights. The children will be bilingual, brown as nuts and bilingual. We'll make love when we want to, quite free, in sunlight and moonlight, and you'll come so alive you'll wonder you ever called it life before—''

Alice's hands were shaking. From behind them she said, "Be fair."

"*Fair?*"

Alice put her hands in her lap and held them tightly.

"I expect you think I am deeply bourgeois but I can't come to paradise dishonestly—"

"Dishonest? What the hell's dishonest about us? It's being so bloody *honest* that's half-killing you!"

"Clodagh," Alice said. "Clodagh. I can't think while you're here."

"I'm terrified of your thinking—"

"What would *you* do," Alice said, "if you had three children?" She looked at Clodagh squarely. "And a husband."

"It's excuses," Clodagh said at once. "All excuses—"

"Call it whatever names you like. Nothing changes what *is,* what I have in my path that you don't have in yours."

Clodagh grew excited again.

"I see, I see. You're going to be the sacrificial lamb, nobly giving up the best happiness you'll ever be offered—"

"I didn't say anything about giving up anything. I have thought about sacrifice and I'll think some more. You could think about it too. You could think about a good deal, and stop shouting at me."

"Alice," Clodagh said, "I'm scared as hell."

Alice put out a hand and took Clodagh's.

"I remember the day you told me your lover in New York was a woman. We were down in the river meadow and the children had made a boat out of a log and you were wearing your wizard's cloak. I shan't ever forget that conversation. I shan't ever forget that I suddenly could see the powers and freedoms that might be mine. 'We all have a choice,' you told me. 'You, me, everyone.' Well, you had chosen, and then I did. Nobody made us, we chose. And now here we are with the results of our choice and we have to choose again—''

"I can't *believe* what I'm hearing!''

"Yes you can. You know it's true. 'If you can't stand the heat, stay out of the kitchen,' you said to me.''

Clodagh snatched her hand away.

"But you won't stay in the kitchen *with* me!''

"I didn't say that. I haven't decided anything. But we must be apart for a bit. I don't want it but I can't think at all while there are emotional demands all over me, yours, the children's, anyone's. It isn't just the *now*, you see, it's the future too. Things never stand still, do they.'' She looked at Clodagh. "You ought to think about your own future too. For your own sake.''

Clodagh stood up. She was wearing a peculiar patchwork skirt with long handkerchief points to the hem, which brushed against Alice's bare arm. Alice looked with love at the triangle of red and yellow cotton lying against her skin.

"Just a week,'' Alice said.

"I'll go to London.''

"Yes.''

"Who knows''—defiantly—''who I may meet?''

Alice said nothing. Clodagh moved away to lean on the apple tree trunk.

"Wouldn't you care?''

"Of course—''

"Would it make you angry?''

"No.''

"Sad?''

"Very.''

"Alice—Alice, why don't you resent anyone for anything, damn and blast you?''

"I do."

"You *don't*—"

"I do. I just can't resent anyone for something I've done—"

"Go to hell!" Clodagh shouted. She swirled from the tree in her gypsy rags. "Priggish, conventional, bloody bourgeois! I'm going, I'm *going* and you'll never know where!"

And then she ran from the orchard and across the lawn by the sandpit and Alice heard her car start up and roar furiously round the house and down the drive. Then Balloon came, dancing through the long grass, to remind Alice that, crisis or no crisis, a cat would like his supper.

When the Unwins heard that Clodagh was going to London, they both tried desperately to stop her.

"But you *wanted* me to go. In fact you *ordered* me—"

"Not to London."

"Why not to London, for God's sake?"

They could not answer her. They could not utter what they had newly learned about London. Clodagh watched them struggle for a while and then she said, "You mean that you think I'm going to London to cruise."

Even she was sorry. She looked at the *utter* misery on their faces, their self-confident, prosperous, genial faces, and was sorry.

"I'm not," she said, and her voice was softer. "I'm not interested. It's one of the things you don't understand. But I must get away from here, I must be somewhere anonymous. I might," she said, trying to make small amends, "I might see about a job."

Margot drove her to Salisbury station and they listened to the car radio on the way, to an adaptation of an Arnold Bennett

novel, and there was a scene between an overbearing mother
and a defiant daughter longing for independence, and neither
Margot nor Clodagh could turn it off for fear of tacitly ad-
mitting that it had any particular significance to either of them.
It was market day in Salisbury and it was trying to rain, warm,
thin, summer rain that made the roads feel greasy. The spire
of the cathedral rose imperturbably into the grey clouds and
tourists carrying National Trust carrier bags spilled off the narrow pavements in search of lavatories and Marks and Spencer
and Mompesson House. Margot gazed at their apparent ordi-
nariness with passionate envy and Clodagh with energetic
scorn. At the station, Clodagh bought a single ticket.

"Oh darling, not a return?"

"No," Clodagh said. "Not because I'm not coming back.
But because in my present mood I just wouldn't like the feeling."

They were ten minutes early for the train.

"Don't wait—"

"I want to."

"Ma," Clodagh said, "please don't wait."

"I can't bear to see you so unhappy," Margot said, her own
face ravaged by wretchedness.

"It's pretty hateful—"

"Oh, Clodagh—"

"*No,*" Clodagh said. "Don't start. If it makes it easier, just
pretend I'm in love with a man."

A flash of anger braced Margot.

"I will certainly *not* stay, to be spoken to like that."

Clodagh watched her go, upright in a summer dress of
cream linen, watched her stop to speak to an elderly porter
who had helped with Unwin school trunks for fifteen years,
watched her smile goodbye to him and go out past the folded
iron gates to the station yard, back to her car, back to Pitcombe, where Alice was.

When she got to London, she took a taxi to Highgate, to the flat of the woman writer who had been her first real lover. The writer had a new lover, another writer, and they made Clodagh extremely welcome and were most sympathetic about her pain and her fears. It was comforting to be in their flat, to be in a room where the atmosphere was full of acceptance and understanding. She talked far too much and they were very patient. During supper, one of them said, very gently, that she didn't think promiscuity would be the answer, and Clodagh said probably not and that was almost the worst part of it, not being able to *affect* Alice just now.

"I feel," she said, "that I'm the one that's given her the confidence to behave like this. So can you see why I feel so frantic?"

They could. They made her camomile tea and put her to bed in a little, comfortable back bedroom with a copy of *Sinister Wisdom* that one of them had brought back recently from America. Then they told her to try and sleep, and went out, and Clodagh could hear them moving about, clearing up, talking companionably to one another, and she looked at the room with its blue and white cotton curtains and its brass lamp and the rough white Greek rug on the floor, and she was so consumed with longing and envy that she turned her face into her pillow and cried and cried as if her heart would break.

In her kitchen, Juliet Dunne pretended to make watercress soup. She chopped shallots and made stock from a cube and hummed a bit but it wasn't any use. She'd only started because she'd met this very tired bunch of watercress lurking in the fridge behind the walnut oil and the Mister Men yoghurts, and she'd thought she'd just do something with it as a distraction from thinking of Martin and Alice sitting eight feet apart on her terrace supposedly having a talk. She had always happily regarded the roles of wife and mother as the absolute pits, but they were knocked into a cocked hat by the role of mediating friend. It was *awful*. Offer the participants a drink and they both say no, thank you, just Perrier, ask them where they'd like to sit and they say anywhere, it doesn't matter; say, trying to make a joke, look, I'll come and break it up in ten minutes and they look mortally offended. So you shove them out on to the terrace and say *do* look at my Whisky Mac rose, don't you think it's almost as disgusting as the drink, and they ignore you and sit down, sighing, a long way from one another as if they suspected a contagion. So you hop about a bit, being inane, and then you say oh my God something in the oven, and rush into the kitchen for another bloody cry and then you think, must *do* something, can't just sit here and wait, so you find some practically fossilized watercress and think, aha, I'll make *soup*. But all you really want to do is go on bawling, in between tiptoeing to the window and looking out at their unhappy, separate backs. I *hate* being fond of people, Juliet thought, stirring her dissolving stock cube with a knife handle, I simply hate it. I'd much rather loathe them, like I loathe Clodagh. At least you know where you are, with loathing.

After twenty minutes or so, Alice came and stood in the kitchen doorway.

"Martin's gone for a walk. It's so kind of you to have him."

Juliet had her back to Alice, stirring her soup.

"You know I'm not kind."

"And it was kind to have us both here—"

"Shut up," Juliet said. "Stop mouthing crappy platitudes at me." She turned round. "Did you get anywhere?"

"No." Alice paused and then she said, "He wants me to apologize, I think. He wants it to be all my fault."

Juliet said nothing. She took the soup off the cooker and peered at it.

"Henry'll never eat this. Looks like pond slime."

Alice said, "I'll go home now. But thank you."

Juliet banged her saucepan down.

"What the hell *do* you expect from him? What has he done, poor brute, except be the boring old Englishman he's always been—the one you married?"

"It isn't as simple as that—"

"Simple? You bet your life it isn't simple." She came across the kitchen, holding the wooden soup spoon. "Allie. Allie, how *could* you?"

Alice looked at her.

"How could you treat Martin like this? How could you be so absolutely normal all these years and then suddenly—God, Allie, have you fallen off your trolley?"

"In order to even begin to understand," Alice said, "you have to want to."

"And what about *you* trying to understand Martin?"

"I do."

"You *do*?"

"Understanding unfortunately doesn't mean I can wave a wand and put everything right, but it does mean that I'm trying to take everyone into account."

Juliet marched back to the cooker.

"*Too* good of you."

Alice left. As she went out of the Dunnes' house, she could see Juliet's little boys on a climbing frame across the lawn. She got into her car. On the floor there were bits of Lego, and a cassette tape of *Charlie and the Chocolate Factory* and a bangle of Clodagh's, purple and gold, that Natasha had borrowed to take to school and awe Sophie with. There were also rather a lot of sweet papers.

"I want you to be more slutty," Clodagh had said to her.

"My beautiful, sexy, slutty Alice. I want you to let your elastic go. Life to the senses, death to sense."

Alice started the car, and drove slowly down the drive to the lane. The heavy August green of the countryside weighted the land right down. Some days, when it was still, you felt the fields could not breathe. Gross weeds lined the lanes, tangling on the verges. Alice thought she felt like it looked, exhausted, weighed down, ripe for harvest. She put her hand up for her pigtail, and held it as she drove, one hand on it, the other on the steering wheel.

As she came into The Grey House the telephone was ringing. An immense happy certainty seized her. It would be Clodagh. Clodagh had been away a week and it would be so like her to ring now, in the early evening, so that Alice didn't have another whole night to get through, wondering where she was. She took her time, confidently, getting to the telephone, and when she picked up the receiver, she was smiling.

"Hello?"

"Alice," Richard said.

"*Richard*—"

"I won't ask how you are because you can't be other than awful."

"Yes."

"I'd like to see you."

She closed her eyes. Tearless for so long now, she could feel the floodgates weakening.

"Alice?"

"Yes. Yes, I'm here—"

"I'd like to see you. Would you like to see me?"

"*Yes.*"

"Come to London. I'd come to Pitcombe except that I don't want to be curtain-twitching fodder. Come before the children get back. Have you heard from them?"

"Postcards—"

"I'll see you on Tuesday," Richard said. "Come to the flat. We'll have lunch."

"Yes," Alice said, crying.

"Come on, love. Come on—"

"Don't be kind to me, it's hopeless—"

He laughed.

"I'll see you on Tuesday," he said.

It was mattins on Sunday morning. The sun was out, and the clumps of hollyhocks by the lych gate were jubilant with their papery trumpets. Mattins was preferred by the Protestant *habitués* of Pitcombe because the hour was civilized and there was no delicate dilemma as to whether one should eat, or not, before communion, and if *not,* in Miss Payne's case, risk the humiliation of breakfastless internal rumblings in all the quietest and most holy moments. Once she had been compelled to go out of the church entirely and suffer an agony of blushes by a table tomb in the churchyard.

August was usually a poor month for congregations because of holidays, but this particular Sunday seemed to fall between the end of Europe and the beginning of Scotland in the Pitcombe holiday calendar. The narrow nave, decorated with immense white phlox sent down from Pitcombe Park, intermingled with royal blue artificial delphiniums provided by Cathy Fanshawe—'Good God," Henry Dunne said, hunting for hassocks, "is it Life-boat week?'—filled satisfactorily with people, red-faced from harvest and Cornwall, brown-faced from Umbria and Tenerife. Miss Pimm, in a brown print, with tremulous bare arms, sat at the organ. The choir, a mixed bag of Motts and Crudwells and the reluctant Barton child who was required, by his parents, to *participate*, sat below her, picking their noses and whispering.

Rosie and Gerry Barton sat in the front pews on the right, opposite the Unwin pew. The Bartons were smiling, the Unwins were attempting to. Behind the Unwins, the Dunnes formed a loyal cohort, Henry in a blazer with his old regimental buttons, Juliet in a blue flowered frock, their boys—whom Henry intended to hold in half-nelsons for most of the service—in identical T-shirts and shorts. Buntie Payne sat across the aisle from them and smiled at the children, which emboldened them to make grisly faces. Down the rest of the aisle, scattered in twos and threes, sat the Fanshawes, a local farmer, John Murray-French with his cricket-watching panama on the pew beside him, several visitors, Michelle and her friend Carol, a new family who had modestly chosen a back pew, and old Fred Mott, in his wheelchair, wheeled up by Mr. Finch who believed him to be an absolute test case for the promise of universal redemption. He sat wheezing a little, fingering his trousers and loudly sucking on Fishermen's Friends.

Peter Morris came out of the vestry in the green stole of Trinity and looked pleasedly at the church. He went down the aisle greeting people, and then up to the choir to say a few admonishing words. He often thought he would have forgiven them a great deal if they had been able to sing at all. Then he went back into the vestry for a few private moments, moments in which he was always surprised at how easily and earnestly prayer came, and went back into the church and saw Alice Jordan, sitting alone and very upright two pews behind the Dunnes. She was staring straight ahead. Instead of embarking upon the bidding prayer, Peter went down the aisle to her and said, in the resounding silence, "How nice to see you, Alice," to which she said thank you. He then went back to the chancel step, opened his arms wide and began.

Alice, kneeling, sitting, rising, told herself she must get through it. She said the Lord's Prayer, but she did not say the General Confession or join in the hymns which everyone else seemed to sing with a kind of exaggerated gusto. It occurred to her that the atmosphere was like the one she imagined prevailing in doomed aircraft, tremendous stoicism tussling silently with incipient hysteria. Sir Ralph, as churchwarden and sidesman, came round with the collection bag during "Lead me, Heavenly Father, lead me" and Alice dropped in her coins without looking at him. During the sermon, the little Dunne boys, who had known her all their lives, twisted round to beam broadly at her, and were cuffed back into place by their father. It was only at the end that her courage faltered, and in the last hymn she slipped quickly out of her pew so that Buntie Payne, who had been planning to kiss her in front of everyone, turned eagerly to do so after the Peace and cried in a voice loud with disappointment "Oh, it's too bad! Really it is! She's gone!"

FIFTEEN

"I was going to take you out," Richard said, "but then I thought that the moment either of us managed to say something we really wanted to say there'd be a waiter asking if we wanted pepper on our salads. So I went to Selfridges Food Hall and got this."

Alice looked down at the coffee table in the little sitting room of Richard's flat. On it was a bottle of wine, a plastic envelope of smoked salmon, brown bread and a lemon.

She said, "Are you going to grill me?"

"Heavens no. Why should I do that?"

"Because you are Martin's father."

He picked up the bottle of wine and went to find a corkscrew.

"I'm a human being too. I'd have to be a pretty unpleasant one to drag you all the way to London just to tick you off."

He disappeared for a moment into the tiny kitchen, reappearing with wineglasses.

"You mustn't be defensive."

Alice threw her head up.

"I don't want to be. But I keep feeling driven into it."

It had been so lovely in the train, coming up, being nobody. And the Tube had been even better, jammed in with people, all strangers.

"London's a luxury," Alice said, accepting a glass of wine, "after Pitcombe."

"Yes," he said. "Yes, it would be."

He put a hand on her arm and steered her into an armchair. "Are you hungry?"

"Not terribly."

"Drink up then. We've got all day."

"But the office—"

"It can wait."

"Martin said you had built a wall together—"

"You *saw* him?"

"Yes," Alice said. "At Juliet's. It didn't really work."

"No," Richard said. "It wouldn't have. Poor boy."

Alice said nothing.

"Poor boy," Richard said again. "Poor boy. He's been misinformed, somehow, all his life. He wouldn't begin to understand. He's in a rage of not understanding."

"I don't blame him," Alice said. "I wouldn't have understood either. Before Clodagh."

"Talk to me," Richard said. He leaned forward and poured more wine into Alice's glass. "Talk to me."

"No—"

"Yes. I may be one of the few people who can help. I love Martin." He paused. "I love you. I think I understand Martin. I would like to understand you."

"I don't want this," Alice said. "I don't want my marriage kindly mended."

"I don't want to mend it."

"You *don't*?"

"No," Richard said. "But I want a resolution. For him, for

you, for my grandchildren." He looked at Alice. "Talk to me, about Clodagh."

"I can't—"

"Why not?"

"Because you're a man."

"Alice," Richard said, "I don't think you know very much about men, or you wouldn't say such a thing. Do you trust me?"

She thought.

"I don't know—"

"Pay me the compliment of knowing that I will believe you and probably understand what you tell me."

Alice got up. She walked round the little room fiddling with things: an ashtray on a sideboard, a marble egg on a wooden stand, a foolish adult toy made of a heap of magnetic paper clips on a black glass base. Then she came back to her chair and sat down.

"What makes it so difficult is that the love between women has *always* been belittled. Hasn't it? Down the ages. Treated as something at best foolish, like—like a kind of silly harmless hobby."

She put her wineglass down and picked up the lemon, rolling it in her hands and sniffing it.

"But what I feel—and I may never fall in love again—is that what Clodagh has given me has enriched me. It hasn't impoverished anything about me, hasn't taken anything *from* me, if you see what I mean. It's grown me up. It's enabled me to love everyone else in my life properly, and as far as I can see only another woman would do for that instructive kind of love because only another woman could see I needed it and could understand about the children and self and the permanent balancing act of motherhood and self. Only another woman," Alice said firmly, "could understand and—and *supply*."

Richard slid off his chair on to his knees beside the coffee table and began to make competent sandwiches.

"If you want to know," Alice said, rolling the lemon, "bed isn't the most significant thing. At least, after the beginning it wasn't. I think sex is more important for Clodagh than for me. If I'm honest. But what I love, what I'm terrified of doing without again, is the life force. A kind of elixir. Do you see?"

He nodded, peeling salmon off cellophane strips.

"You can't imagine how much fun we have. You can't conceive of how differently I see myself, because of her. It's a kind of revelation."

Richard took the lemon away from her, cut it and began to squeeze the juice on to his sandwiches.

"I was so lonely," Alice said. "I don't blame Martin. He didn't know what to do about me, and I didn't know what to do about me either. But Clodagh did. I woke up. When I looked back at getting married and honeymooning and then being married, I think I was simply asleep. I must have been. Twelve years, dawdling about in a kind of half-life."

Richard put two sandwiches on a plate and balanced it on her knee.

"Eat up."

Alice looked at the plate, then at him.

"Do I make sense to you?"

"Yes."

"Can you imagine what I mean?"

"Of course. I've felt something like it. But in my case it was for the opposite sex, rather than my own."

"Who was it?"

"Cecily, of course," Richard said.

"*Cecily!*"

"Yes."

Alice took an unenthusiastic bite of sandwich.

"You talk," she said. "You talk now."

There was a little pause, then Richard said, with great carefulness, "If you had had a confident, loving man make love to you, this would never have happened. You'll think that's just common or garden male arrogance. It isn't. There's a world of difference between making love and having sex. I was never able to make love to Cecily as I wished to because her mind was quite closed to me. The summit of her emotional life was Vienna and she would never allow anything to approach it in case it proved only an illusion and the giant, secret romance of her life crumbled to dust."

He stopped, and rose to fill Alice's glass. She waited, watching him.

"But I could have loved her, if she'd let me. At the risk of sounding incestuous, I could have loved you, because, like Clodagh, I know what you are like and what you like."

He looked at Alice.

"I'm not jealous of Clodagh. I'm only sorry that you should be put through this hoop for her, socially. I understand exactly what you say about loneliness. I've had a mistress for years—fifteen to be exact—because I'm a tender man and a passionate man and Cecily can't let herself allow me to be either. It doesn't suit her to acknowledge that I *like* women."

"Martin—" Alice said.

"Cecily never brought the boys up to like women. She didn't try. They are both afraid of women. I didn't try either. I didn't see until too late. In that respect, I am quite as much to blame as she is."

Alice reached over to take Richard's hand.

"So sad," Alice said. "So sad. You are actually exactly the right man for her."

He smiled.

"Oh, I know that. I've known that for forty years."

Alice bent her head.

"Forty years! The things people live with—"

"Sometimes you have to. If you don't at heart want anything else."

"But a *mistress*—"

"Would a string of call girls be better?"

Alice looked up.

"You mean—?"

"Yes."

"Jesus," Alice said, with Clodagh's intonation.

"I haven't been allowed to make love to Cecily for almost twenty years."

"But you *still*—"

"Yes, I still."

"Wouldn't you like to have stopped? Loving her, I mean—"

"Only very theoretically. And occasionally. Perhaps I'm just immensely pigheaded and won't admit to failure. Perhaps it's love."

Alice flung herself back in her chair.

"Love," she said.

Later, when he was driving her to Paddington, Richard said quite casually that he would like to buy her a little flat or house in Salisbury, to be near the children's school. He said it would be a secret between the two of them. He said it would have no strings. She could have it for a month or a year or however long she wanted it for. She felt quite bewildered by the offer and said, looking away from him "But why?" and he said for the children first and for her and Martin second.

"Martin?"

"If you have some independence, he won't feel so threatened or resentful. It will make the next step easier. He cannot bear the thought that the law will require him to give money to a woman he believes has betrayed him. If you don't need so much from him, that's one less battle. One less battle is good for the children."

"But you can't, why should you—"

"Mind your own business," Richard said. "Just let me know when you know."

In the train, tiredness fell upon Alice like a hammer blow. She put her head back on the orange tweed headrest with which British Rail sought to cosset its passengers, and closed her eyes. Through her mind a procession of people moved, Clodagh and her children and Martin, her parents, her parents-in-law, Clodagh's parents, all spinning slowly by, their faces seeming to wheel up out of a soft darkness and then melt away again into it. I am the link, Alice thought. All these people, through me, have their future. It's a horrible power, but it's real. And it's mine. Even if I don't want it, it's mine. Things aren't going to happen to me now because I have to make the next things happen. I have to choose. I am far beyond any point I ever was before and there's nothing to shield me now. I am in a high, bare, painful place . . .

"Excuse me," a voice said next to her, "but am I on the right train to make a connection for Didcot Parkway?"

Elizabeth Meadows opened the door of her sister's house in Colchester and found Richard Jordan there. She was so astonished that she almost shut the door again in fright. He said, smiling, "I wondered if you would have forgotten what I looked like."

"Yes," she said, "No—"

From the through sitting room where she was polishing the brass fire-irons, Elizabeth's sister Ann called, "Who is it? I wish you'd shut the door."

"Come in," Elizabeth said.

He followed her into the cream painted hall where a Swiss cheese-plant sat exactly in the centre of an otherwise empty table, and then into the sitting room. Ann Barlow was wearing cotton gloves to protect her hands from the brass cleaning wadding and a flowered pinafore with a big front pocket on which "Breakages!" was embroidered in royal blue stranded cotton. She scrambled to her feet, frowning. If there was one thing she hated more than an unexpected caller, it was an unexpected *man* caller.

"You remember Richard Jordan. Alice's father-in-law—"

In Ann Barlow's mind, the Jordans were entangled with the breakdown of her sister's marriage. She pulled off a glove and held out an indifferent hand, making ritual noises about coffee which Richard said untruthfully that he would love. He was directed towards a flowered armchair from which he could see a regimented garden and a white painted seat and a line of washing hung up in strict order of size. Elizabeth did not know what to do with him. She resented him fiercely both for coming and for looking so at ease now he was here. She sat opposite him and stared at his well-shod feet and resolved that she would not help him conversationally.

He did not seem to mind her unfriendliness. He told her that James had learned to swim in Cornwall, which she remained inflexible about since Alice hadn't seen fit to tell her they were going to Cornwall in the first place. He admired the delphiniums and said Cecily was opposed heart and soul to the notion of the new pink ones. He remarked on the beastliness of the A12, to which Elizabeth managed to reply that she didn't drive any more, and then Ann came in with a tray of coffee and there was the usual fuss—Elizabeth despised Ann's houseproudness as deeply suburban—with little tables and spoons and plates to catch biscuit crumbs. When the fuss had subsided, Richard began to talk very differently. He said he was here without Alice's knowledge or permission but she had enough to cope with just now and he had made a unilateral decision to come that he would probably be punished for. He then said, with a calm Elizabeth found horrible, that Alice and Martin had separated because Alice had had a love affair with a woman, and that Alice was at the moment trying to determine her future and Martin was trying to recover from a breakdown. He then said, unwisely, that he hoped they would not be too harsh on anyone. At this point, Ann Barlow put down her coffee cup and left the room.

"I hope," Richard said, "that I have not shocked your sister."

"Of course you have."

"And you? Have I shocked you?"

"Nothing," Elizabeth said angrily, "nothing really shocks me." She gave Richard the first proper look she had awarded him. "You are a meddler," she said. "And I doubt your motives."

He shrugged.

"I hoped to smooth Alice and Martin's path—"

She snorted.

"I'm not a fool. Prurient is the word that springs to mind. Prurient is how I should describe your action in coming here."

He lowered his head. She thought his colour was darkening.

"Heaven knows," Elizabeth said, "heaven knows what your motives are, what they have ever been."

He kept his head down.

"Could they not be," he said into his chest, "could they not be altruistic?"

"Impersonally, of course they could be. In your case, I doubt it. I resent your coming. I resent your crude translation of my daughter to me. I resent your possessive attitude to grandchildren who are as much mine as yours. I resent your patronage. I resent the divisions you have, as a family, made in mine."

He got up, abruptly, clumsily.

"I had better go."

She said nothing. He was beside himself with rage.

"I shall tell Alice of this—"

"You are wrong to suppose she will have any sympathy for you. Much less gratitude."

He wanted to shout at her that he saw exactly why Sam Meadows had left her, why Alice had seen in Cecily the mother Elizabeth had declined to be. He began, but she went past him to open the sitting room door and then the front door and he found himself outside, beside a bed of stout begonias, bellowing to himself in the quiet residential road, almost before he had said a quarter of it. There was nothing for it but to drive back to London.

Two days later, Alice received two letters at The Grey House. One was from her mother.

"I had a call from your father-in-law," Elizabeth wrote, "in the course of which I learned a great deal more about him than about you. Perhaps you will write. Perhaps you will even come and see me. Do not be afraid of coming, because I would not try to counsel you."

It was signed, "With love from your mother, Elizabeth." The other letter was no more than a postcard. It was undated and unsigned, and it simply said, in Clodagh's wild black writing, "Women need men like fish need bicycles."

That was all. The next day the children came home and Alice realized, holding them with great relief and love, that in the fortnight they had been away she had come to no decision at all.

"What are you doing?" James said. He was holding a plastic ray gun and half a biscuit.

"Writing to Grandpa."

"Can I too?"

"Yes, but not on this paper. On your own bit of paper."

James put the ray gun down on Alice's letter. He did that all the time now, putting his spoon on her plate, his book across her newspaper, his toothbrush into her mouth.

"*Jamie*—"

He put his hand on the gun. Silently he dared her to move it away.

"I can't write—"

He raised his other hand and pushed the bitten biscuit at her mouth.

"*Darling*. Don't—"

"Eat it!"

"No, Jamie, no, it's all licky—"

He jabbed it against her lower lip and it broke.

"You broke my biscuit."

"You broke it. Being silly. Move your gun so I can write."

He kept his hand on the gun and screwed his foot round on the piece of biscuit that had fallen on to the floor until it was a brown powder.

"*There.*"

Alice took no notice. He threw another bit down and did the same thing. Alice gripped the table edge and her pen and glared at what she had written.

"After thinking it over and over, I know I must decline your offer. The price—the price of having to rely on you—is too high. I can't do it. You are too protective, somehow, too *administering*. I couldn't breathe. I don't really know if I trust you."

She thought, I should be saying this, not writing it, but if I say it he will argue with me and try to persuade me otherwise.

And I may say, like last time, all kinds of things that I should not have said.

"Gun," said James loudly. "Gun, gun, *gun*."

He pushed it roughly into her pen-holding hand and hurt her. She held the hurt hand in the other, tense with pain and fury, and he watched her.

"Gun," he said again, but with less confidence.

"Go away," Alice said. "Go away until I have written my letter. Go and play with Tashie."

He shook his head, but he was chastened by the red mark on her hand. He crept under the table and lay down and put his cheek on Alice's foot, and after a while she could feel tears running into her sandal. She moved her toes, so that he could feel them, and with an immense effort picked up her pen again.

"I can't," she wrote to Richard, "be the cure-all for your frustrations. I don't want that ever again, the prison of grate-fulness. I *am* grateful, but I'd rather be it from a distance, on equal terms."

She felt James's hand on her other foot.

"Jamie? You're a bit tickly—"

He giggled, faintly.

"You trapped me," Alice wrote, "didn't you. You trapped me into talking. I'd rather not think why you wanted to do that and I'd rather not think why you want to help me. But what has happened to me has moved me out of the objective case into the subjective case so that I am not available for anyone else's plans just now."

She signed the letter, "With love from Alice." When it was licked up and stamped, by James, they put Charlie into his pushchair and found Natasha, who was arranging her Cornish shells into an interminable exhibition all around the upstairs windowsills, and went down to the post. On the way they met Lettice Deverel who was very kind and ordinary and invited them to tea to meet the parrot. When they got home, Alice made cheese sandwiches for lunch and they ate them in the garden while the children talked about all the things they would do when Daddy and Clodagh came home again.

⁂

"Have you seen her?" Clodagh demanded.

Lettice held the telephone at a little distance from her ear.

"Yes. Yes, I have."

"And? *And*?"

"We didn't speak of you, if that's what you mean."

"How did she look?"

"A little tired. That's all."

"Lettice," Clodagh shouted. "Lettice. How can you be so awful to me?"

There was a little silence. The parrot, across the kitchen, clucked approvingly at a grape it held.

"I used to think," Lettice said, "I used to think that you had promise and originality. And courage. Now I don't know. I'm more depressed by this episode than I can tell you. You seem to me like some kind of Hedda Gabler, all style and shallow selfishness."

In London, sitting on her fortunate friends' sofa, Clodagh began to cry.

"Except you have a heart," Lettice went on. "I know that because I can see it's been touched. Oh, Clodagh dear, I do beg you to *make* something of your life."

"No!" said the parrot. "No. No. No. *Not* pretty."

It threw the grape stalk out of its cage.

"I can't give this up," Clodagh said. "I can't. I'll die."

"On the contrary, you will live much better."

"Is she missing me? Does she look as if she's missing me?"

"Don't ask me idiotic questions. Ask me how your poor parents are."

"Well?"

"Much in need of hearing from you. You should have rung them, not me."

"I couldn't ask them about Alice."

"You shouldn't be asking anyone."

"What about the children then? Did they mention me?"

"No. We only spoke of the parrot."

"Oh, *parrot*," said the parrot. "Dear parrot. Dear me."

Clodagh's voice grew small.

"I *long* to come down."

"I dare say—"

"But I'm not crawling to *anyone*—"

"If you don't get off your bottom, Clodagh Unwin," Lettice said, "and make an independent decision, you'll find that Alice will probably have made them all for you."

"What d'you mean? What's going on? What did Alice—"

"I mean nothing, except that Alice has three children and no money of her own and can't fiddle-faddle around like you can."

"Has Martin been around?"

"No. He's living with a friend in Salisbury."

"I'm coming down, damn what everyone thinks—"

"Think!" Lettice cried. "Think! *You* try a little thinking."

The parrot hooked its beak into the wires of its cage and began to haul itself up to the top. When it got there, it hung upside down for a bit and then it said, with great calm, "Damn *and* blast." Lettice began to laugh. Delighted, it joined in, and Clodagh, hearing what appeared to be a roomful of merriment in Pitcombe, put the telephone down, in despair.

Martin was just waiting. He had stopped talking to anyone about Alice, particularly to Cecily. He had a very comfortable room in a friend's house on the edge of the Close in Salisbury, and he was working hard, and seeing his children once a week when Alice left them for him at The Grey House and went out, and he was making sure he played tennis a good deal and golf a bit, and he had accepted an invitation to stalk in Sutherland in October. He was making quiet plans to sell The Grey House. Whatever happened next, they couldn't possibly stay there.

Cornwall had restored him in some measure, certainly as to how he stood with his children. He liked being with them but was amazed at how much they needed done for them, how insatiable and helpless they were. Except for the brief time over Charlie's birth, he had never been responsible for them, a thing he didn't like but was perfectly prepared to do, if he had to. He felt perfectly prepared for a lot of things. That was the trouble, really, feeling like that. Nothing seemed violently upsetting any more or impossible to face or to be worth very much angst of any kind. When he tried to think what really *mattered* now, he couldn't. So he thought he would just get on with each day, as unremarkably and pleasantly as he could, and wait. In any case, if he waited, in the end it would be Alice who had to do something. And that would be only just. Wouldn't it?

SIXTEEN

On Friday nights, Sam Meadows went to Sainsbury's. He had grown rather to like the expedition because the store was full of people who had just finished work and who were full of a pre-weekend relief and excitement. As the years of his lone living went on, he found to his amusement that he was making sure he had no teaching commitments early on Friday evenings to get in the way of going to Sainsbury's. He also noticed how he was beginning to buy the same things, whisky and white bread and black cherry jam and pasta and jars of *pesto,* and how he would make for the same check-out because there was such a dear little woman on the till, who ducked her head at him, bursting with half-hidden smiles.

Since he had left Elizabeth, a good many women had tried quite hard to live with him. He had let two of them begin but they had both had over-clear ideas about how life should be lived, and had been unable to keep those ideas to themselves. The only woman he had wanted, in ten years, to come and do whatever she liked with his life as long as she came, hadn't wanted to. She liked his bed, but preferred her own life outside it. Because of this, Sam had continued to love her and had stopped collecting his pupils like an array of Barbie dolls. They still flirted with him, particularly if essays were late, but these days he could just let them. In any case, the university now had a ferocious female Committee Against Sexual Harassment.

Sam had five years to go before he retired. When he retired, he thought he would go and live in Wales, preferably in a fishing community, and write a book on the power of language that would become an indispensable textbook in schools. When he had done that, he would write fools' guides to the Bible and classical literature because he was still so exasperated, after thirty years of teaching, to find that clever modern students of literature were so ignorant of both that they couldn't get through a line of Milton without having to look up the references. After that, he thought he would probably die, and be buried in an austere Welsh hillside under the wheeling gulls. He didn't really want a headstone but he did want something to indicate that he had meant to be a poet, so that posterity should know that inside his apparently phlegmatic, idle, pleasure-seeking bulk, quite a lot of striving had gone on.

Standing in the Sainsbury's queue one August Friday, he was offered most of a very small, very wet dolly mixture by a gregarious baby in the child seat of the next trolley. He accepted it gratefully and ate it. It tasted of scented soap and reminded him of the sweets of his childhood. The baby reminded him of Charlie. Or rather, not of how Charlie looked, because Sam had only seen him once when he was too new to look like anything, but more that Charlie existed, that Sam *had* a baby grandson. In the early spring, Alice had sent Sam photographs of The Grey House and had said that it would all be ready for him, when he came for his annual summer visit. After that, he had heard nothing. He hadn't minded or noticed much, because he presumed that she had been too busy, and because he had been busy himself, but now, standing in the queue and smiling at the strange baby (it was not a pretty baby, it had a high domed forehead and its chin was glossy with dribble, but the gift of the dolly mixture had been true generosity in one so young), he thought that perhaps Alice's silence was beginning to have a flavour of oddness. Half the summer vacation had gone and she had not even telephoned. No more had he, he wasn't blaming her, but now that he thought about her, he found that he wanted to see her and his grandchildren. By the time he had got his groceries to the car, he wanted to see them very much indeed.

When he got home, he put the grocery boxes on the kitchen table beside the remains of a very good lunch of Scotch eggs and Guinness, and went to the telephone. Alice answered it with a kind of breathless eagerness, but when she heard who it was she became constrained.

"What's up?" Sam said.

There was a silence.

"Come on," Sam said. "Come on, Allie. Is something wrong?"

"A great deal has happened—"

"Are you all right?"

"Oh yes. Perfectly."

"And the children?"

"Fine. Absolutely fine."

"Don't fool around with me," Sam said. "I am your non-interfering father. I also smell a rat."

"Martin isn't here any more—"

"Allie—"

"I fell in love with someone. Martin's living Salisbury." Sam pressed the receiver against his skull until it hurt, and closed his eyes.

"I'll come—"

"Please. You don't have to. I really am managing. There's

a lot to be decided, but I'm doing it, bit by bit.''

"Where's this other fellow? Is he with you?''

"It isn't a fellow,'' Alice said. "She's a girl.''

Slowly Sam raised a clenched fist and knocked his knuckles on his forehead, bang, bang, rhythmically.

"A girl.''

"Yes.''

A kind of groan.

"Allie—''

"I can't possibly explain over the telephone. Nor can I convince you how all right I am. Sad, of course, but all right.''

"The children, how are the children—''

"They miss Martin and they miss Clodagh—that's her name, Clodagh—but we are getting by, getting on—''

"You thought I was Clodagh, telephoning—''

"Yes,'' Alice said. "I did. We haven't communicated at all for three weeks.''

"I'll come down tomorrow.''

There was a little pause and then Alice said, "I'd like that.''

"Hold on there,'' Sam said. "Hold on.''

He was close to tears.

"I'm holding,'' Alice said. "I promise you I'm not going to fall off anything.''

"I'll be with you by teatime. No, earlier, lunchtime. I'll be with you by lunchtime.''

He put the telephone down. It was quite silent in his kitchen except for a bluebottle that had got into one of the grocery cartons and was fizzing about noisily against the cellophane packets of pasta. Sam went over to the box, pulled out his new bottle of whisky and took it into his bedroom, holding it against him with both arms. Then he lay down on his bed, still holding the bottle, and began to cry and cry, like a baby.

Mr. Finch was unpacking New Zealand apples from nests of blue tissue paper. It was the sort of job Michelle should have done, but Michelle had handed in her notice because she said she didn't like his attitude to Mrs. Jordan. She must have said something similar to her mother, because she had then left Pitcombe and gone to live with her married sister in Poole, and Gwen was buying twice as many Silk Cut as usual and wearing a face like a boot. One of the Crudwells, Heather, who wore black stonewashed jeans so tight you wondered how she had got her feet through, had offered to come and help instead. But Mr. Finch was frightened both of her sexuality and her light-fingeredness, and had declined. So she had brought two friends into the shop to laugh at him with her, and he had been very miserable. Even Mrs. Finch, whose sympathy for him had run out long ago on account of his want of style, had been sorry for him.

"It's Alice Jordan's fault. Without all that business, this would never have happened."

She said that a lot now, in between reminding him that she had never, being a woman of experience, been one to judge. In Mr. Finch's view, almost everyone judged. It seemed to him that he was probably the only person who didn't, and that was not because he had no opinion but because he was so entirely bewildered. The *strangeness* of the affair paralyzed him, he had never come across anything like it. The element that really shook Mr. Finch was the combination of emotional and sexual unorthodoxy and—you could see this plainly on Alice Jordan's face—the *reality* of it. The thing was actual *and* stupefying. However much of a good face Alice put upon things, it was all too evident that with Clodagh away she was suffering real pain, the pain of having new, vital, tender roots ripped up at just the moment they began to take hold and grow. It frequently occurred to Mr. Finch that he understood far more about poetry than about life, because life was often just too peculiar to take in.

A very few people felt as he did. He knew that because of the things they were doing. He'd heard that Mrs. Macaulay had been up to The Grey House to offer Alice a puppy, a free puppy. Gwen had told him that, contemptuous of Mrs. Macaulay and disgusted with Alice, who had declined the puppy and then gone into the downstairs lavatory and cried her eyes out. Buntie Payne, though prone to immediate distress if Alice's name was mentioned in the shop, had flown like an enraged kitten at Sally Mott who had remarked, for Mrs. Finch's benefit, that villages were too small to cope with bad influences.

"Don't you use the word bad of Alice Jordan!" Miss Payne had cried.

Sally Mott had banged out of the shop and Miss Payne had had to sit down to weep and be given a glass of water and to explain, over and over again, how strongly she felt but how she couldn't quite describe what it was that she felt so strongly about.

The pub, where Mr. Finch allowed himself a weekly pint, was simpler in its approach, perhaps because fewer women went to it. In the lounge bar the subject was hardly mentioned, and in the public, led by Stuart Mott, there was briefly considerable crudity and then, with the football season starting up, loss of interest. As for the church—well, here Mr. Finch's frail faith, born out of a love of ritual and a powerful wish that something, some day, might come out of regular church attendance, was very disappointed. He had hoped for a sermon on sin, full of words like evil and phrases like wrong-doing, not because he wished to see Alice condemned, but because he wanted a stout moral rail upon which to put his own hand. What he had got was a sermon on St. Barnabas and another on inner city renewal. The strange part, thought Mr. Finch, gazing fixedly at a single apple he held in his hand, was that a business like this, an upset like this Alice Jordan–Clodagh Unwin thing, was that it drove you in on yourself for hours and hours of self-examination. The firm ground you thought you stood on suddenly began to heave and shudder and give way. Mr. Finch put the apple on the rack with its fellows and frowned at it.

Behind him, Sam cleared his throat.

"I was wondering if you could direct me to The Grey House?"

Mr. Finch turned slowly. Sam was wearing a crumpled blue shirt and a red spotted handkerchief knotted round his throat, and had an air of comfortable bohemianism that filled Mr. Finch with envy. He hoped it was not immediately visible that his own trousers were made of polyester.

"I shall be only too pleased—"

He took Sam out on to the pavement and pointed up the hill.

"Go straight up until you come to the cottage with the well in the garden—the well is purely ornamental—and turn right there. The gates of The Grey House are directly ahead."

He waited for Sam to tell him who he was and why he was going to The Grey House, but Sam merely said thank you and climbed back into his car—the interior, Mr. Finch noted with admiration, was chaos—and drove off as he had been directed. Forlornly, Mr. Finch went back into the shop, reflecting that it was the lot of those who worked in service industries to be, for the most part, entirely invisible to those they served.

Alice, who had never been a demonstrative child in the least, seemed to want Sam to hold her; so he did. He held her for a long time in her bright kitchen while she neither cried nor said much beyond that she was pleased to see him and that she had had no idea that coming alive would be so hard. For the rest of the time she just had her arms round his solid trunk and her cheek on his chest. He was deeply touched by this. After many minutes she sighed and withdrew slowly and went to fetch a bottle of cider from the larder. While she was away, he leaned on the bottom half of the stable door and watched a pram under an apple tree which was rocking violently and intermittently. There was washing hanging out and a half-grown cat asleep in the sun and a trug of lettuces beside it. One of the things about humankind that had never ceased to amaze Sam was that in most cases, whatever the drama, life went on. Emotions and psyches were torn to ribbons, healths and minds were broken, lives were crushed, but on, on, went the relentless business of keeping the machine going, meal after meal, washing and sweeping and going to bed. Perhaps, he thought, turning to accept his glass of cider, it was the treadmill that stopped you going mad. Perhaps the need to do the laundry saved your sanity.

"Maybe I should have told you," Alice said, sitting on the corner of the table, "but I didn't tell anyone. I didn't want to. I felt so free. You know, there's been *years* of ought to's and have to's and suddenly there was pure, clear, strong *want* to. It was such a relief. There simply was no choice."

She looked at Sam.

"Society isn't necessarily right about what's good for you."

He drank.

"It's right," he said, "about what's good for most people. But not for everyone. It's the majority that makes the rules and then we call it society. A woman colleague of mine says she resents society for making divorce so easy. That's a circular resentment. She ends up, most likely, with herself."

"You always do, don't you. That's the great battle, learning to live with yourself—"

"I don't think," Sam said, looking at her, "that it's a battle that ought ever to be won."

"I hurt," Alice said. "I hurt all over. I don't think that there's an inch of me that doesn't hurt, inside or out. Every tiny bit of feeling hurts, loving most of all, which is the one thing I want to do, must do—"

Sam stopped leaning on the door and went across to Alice and held her pigtail at the base of her neck. She leaned her head back against his hand for a moment, and then she leaned it against him.

"I'm going to quote you something."

"Poetry?"

"George Eliot."

"I only ever," Alice said mournfully, "read *The Mill on the Floss*."

"This is *Adam Bede*."

She turned her face into his shirt front.

"Tell me."

" 'We get accustomed,' " Sam said into the space of kitchen above her head, " 'to mental as well as bodily pain, without, for all that, losing our sensibility to it: It becomes a habit of our lives and we cease to imagine a condition of perfect ease as possible for us. Desire is chastened into submission, and we are contented with our day when we have been able to bear our grief in silence and act as if we were not suffering. For it is at such periods that the sense of our lives having visible and invisible relations beyond any of which our present or prospective self is the centre, grows like a muscle that we are obliged to lean on and exert.' "

Then it was quiet. It was quiet for a long time and neither of them moved until a small commotion could be heard in the hall, and then the kitchen door opened and there, with James squealing joyously in her arms, stood Clodagh.

"You know why I've come back," Clodagh said later while they were getting supper. "Don't you?"

"Yes."

"I think I'll remind you all the same. I've come back to collect you. You and the children. I'm selling everything. We can go anywhere."

Alice went on slicing mushrooms. Upstairs Sam was reading *Winnie-the-Pooh* to Natasha and James, giving Australian accents to Kanga and Roo. It was a great success. Shrieks of pleasure filtered occasionally downstairs. Charlie, in his sleeping suit, was in his highchair in the kitchen eating raspberries with his fingers. Balloon, replete with supper, slept against the Aga. Outside the open stable door, the late summer countryside lazed in a syrupy sunset.

"Don't stonewall me," Clodagh said. "That's what you did when I went away. You said you must think. I've been away nearly a month and it's been a nightmare. Have you had a nightmare?"

"Yes," Alice said. She slid the mushrooms into a casserole. "I was silly to think I'd find any peace. There was no one but it was rampageously unpeaceful. I felt that I was in one of those little mechanical revolving machines used for stone polishing. Except that I seemed to be the one stone that wouldn't polish."

"You needed me," Clodagh said.

There was a little pause and then Alice said, "I *wanted* you."

"*Needed.*"

"I looked need up in the dictionary," Alice said. "It said it was a state that required relief. That seemed rather feeble."

Clodagh put her hands on Alice's shoulders and turned her.

"If you don't have me, you'll stop living."

"So you keep saying."

Clodagh's eyes were bright with tears.

"Alice. Oh, Alice, have a little *pity*—"

She took her hands away.

"You can't imagine what it was like in London. Eleanor and Ruth were so kind but they have each other. Ma and Pa are trying to be kind, even Pa, but they haven't a clue. Loving you has stopped me belonging anywhere because I'm not fit for anyone else but you. You've ruined me for other people. I don't want anything any more but to make you happy. And your children. I'd do anything for your children."

She looked across at Charlie who had fitted a raspberry on his finger like a thimble and was regarding it with wonder.

"I adore Charlie," Clodagh said.

She sat down on a kitchen chair and bent herself round her knees.

"I hate whining like this. But it's so important. I want to *give* to you and the children. I know I'll be better if I do, a better person. I thought, while I was in London, that I'd like to work for you all. I was so happy when I thought of that."

Alice came to sit next to her. She put a hand out and stroked her wild head, and thought, as she had thought before, that when Clodagh was distressed she became like an exotic broken bird with tattered, gorgeous plumage and splintered frail bones showing through.

"Clodagh."

There was silence.

"Clodagh, I didn't want to say this now but we seem to have got to the point where I have to because there isn't anything else we can say with this between us. I'm not coming away with you. If it's any comfort, I'm not going back to Martin either. I expect you'll accuse me of being pompous, but I've made those decisions because it wouldn't be honest to live with either of you. Desire doesn't come into it. What does come into it is all the emotional leftovers I'd have to tow into either relationship and which I'd never be free of. It's no good blaming anyone and it would be worse to lug blame around with me.''

After some time, Clodagh raised her face and glared at Alice.

''I sometimes wonder if you even *have* a heart—''

Alice got up and went over to Charlie, lifting him out of his highchair. She said over her shoulder, ''I can't keep saying I love you. It loses value if I keep saying it, like some silly jingle. But I do. If you're in the pain you say you're in, you should be able to imagine how I feel too. I'm scared stiff of being without you. But I have to be.'' She put her face briefly into Charlie's neck. ''I'm not telling you the way I wanted to but I suppose that's inevitable. I'll probably make an awful mess of telling Martin too.''

Clodagh was crying. Seeing her, Charlie's face began to crumple up.

''You see,'' Alice said, ''we've got to stop this. We've got to stop all this not sleeping, and crying, and giving each other such agony—''

''*Your* way!'' Clodagh shrieked. ''*Your* bloody way!''

Alice had a sudden spurt of temper.

''How you hate it, don't you, when you can't have yours!''

Charlie began to wail. Clucking at him, Alice took him out of the kitchen and up the stairs. From Natasha's room came the sound of Rabbit explaining something officiously to Tigger who wasn't listening. Alice carried Charlie into his cot where he settled at once into the private oblivious contentment that lived there. She pulled the string of his musical box which began to play ''Edelweiss'' unevenly. Suppose, she thought, bending over Charlie while he sucked ferociously on his fingers, suppose that instead of coming down and attempting to storm her way to success, Clodagh had come to tell Alice that it was over and that she, Clodagh, had found someone new? What then? Would that have been easier? She straightened up. Easier, but worse. Once you had stopped letting things happen and started to make them happen, you couldn't go back ... Clodagh had known that all her life, which was why she was in such anguish now, powerless, rudderless.

In a sudden rush of pity, Alice ran back downstairs to the kitchen, but of course Clodagh was gone, leaving all the knives and forks on the table crossed over one another in a childish gesture of love and anger.

"So you want a divorce," Martin said.

"Yes."

"I ought to tell you that I feel pretty bitter."

"Yes. I know."

"I'm not to blame."

"It all," Alice said, "goes too deep for blame. Or apology."

"I don't see it that way."

"I know. I know you don't. You think that if I were to grovel and apologize abjectly you would suddenly feel better, everything would be all right. Well it wouldn't and nor would you because *nothing's* that simple and this particularly isn't."

Martin had taken a flat overlooking the river. He had been most insistent that Alice should meet him there, whether to assert his independence, or to demonstrate the sad impersonality of his life now, she could not guess. It was a sunny flat, on the first floor of a substantial Regency house, furnished inappropriately in early Habitat. They sat in two foam-filled chairs covered in chocolate-brown corduroy and watched the river and a family of swans with three beige, black-beaked, adolescent cygnets.

"You can't get away from the fact that I'm the victim," Martin said.

"You speak as if I set out to hurt you. To *punish* you. As if I acted out of malice—"

"You did," Martin said. "I bored you. I disappointed you."

Alice said nothing.

"I expect you wished you had never married me."

Still she said nothing.

"You shouldn't have married anyone, anyway," he went on, goading. "Should you. You have to face that now, whatever else you refuse to see."

She looked steadfastly at the swans.

"I don't expect a judge will be very keen on giving you care and control of the children."

Alice said, "Why must you insist that I am your enemy?"

"You are. You humiliated me the worst way a woman could humiliate a man. It's your doing."

"Would you have preferred me to have slept with another man, thereby showing you up as an inadequate lover?"

"Yes," Martin said. "No," and put his head in his hands.

"Stop thinking about sex. It isn't really about sex. At least, sex is only a part."

"I can't—"

"I don't want a divorce so that I can live with Clodagh. I want a divorce because I'm not going to live with anyone. If you think you'll feel better by making it all difficult, I can't stop you. You have heaps of people on your side. But I'm not going to help make it a battle. I'd rather be your friend than your enemy. I'd rather be—Clodagh's friend than her enemy. But I won't for all that pretend I regret what has happened because it wouldn't be true."

"You must be mad."

"I expect it's easier to think that."

"Easier!"

"If you tell everyone I'm mad then you don't have to consider what I am or what I've done seriously. You don't have to acknowledge that I'm part of the human pattern. You don't even have to begin to look for anything good."

She stood up.

"I must go. I'm lecturing. I seem to have an awful tendency to lecture at the moment."

He gazed at her. He didn't want her to go and did not know how to make her stay.

"I'll see the children on Saturday—"

"Of course."

"How much do they know?"

"What you would expect," Alice said, "at their age. They just want everything to be normal again."

"And whose fault is that?" Martin cried out, unable to stop himself. "Whose fault is that, that it isn't?"

When Alice had gone, he went to his bathroom at the back of the flat and watched her walk across what had been the old kitchen yard of the house, to her car. Well, his car really; he'd bought it, after all. She was wearing a huge, fell, long denim skirt and a red shirt and a suede waistcoat and her plait fell down her back as straight as an arrow. He leaned his forehead on the glass. She opened the car door and climbed in, folding her skirt in after her, and shut the door. Martin closed his eyes. A sense of loss, a terrifying, savage sense of no longer having something that had been his alone, engulfed him in a black flood of bereavement.

Sam, sitting in the garden of The Grey House with a copy of the *Times Literary Supplement*, was half-supervising his grandchildren. This occupation struck him as being rather like invigilating public examinations, except that the children did not fix him with the anguished, reproachful stares of candidates immobilised by exam nerves or inadequate revision. Instead they seemed absorbed in some extraordinary ritual under a car rug hung between kitchen chairs and only came out intermittently to make him solemn offerings of daisy heads on a tiny plate which Charlie seemed eager to eat. Sam let him. The Elizabethan kitchen, after all, had made excellent use of violets and marigolds.

His presence in the house for the last few days had given it a solidity. Rituals had formed at once around him, as grandfather and as man, little tendrils of the instinct for security reaching out to cling to him. He liked it. He thought he liked it a great deal more than he remembered liking fatherhood, which had come at a time in his life when he wasn't ready for it. His grandchildren interested him a lot; he was struck by the dignity of Charlie's babyhood. He was sorry to think that his children had not interested him very much, a sign, he thought now, of his immaturity then. He saw the realistic female certainties in Natasha and the romantic male agonies in James and he now saw in his daughter, Alice, a mixture of both, as he supposed they ought to exist, in adults who were adults. He also saw, to his delight, that he had a role. The family came to him. They came, Alice had said—and she had said this sadly—in a way they had not come to Martin.

"He is too young," Sam had said. "Just as I was. He is still too full of self."

She had been determined to go and see Martin. Sam had said it would achieve nothing and she replied that it wouldn't *now*, but that it might make some little difference, later. When she came back, Sam had a plan to put to her. They would all live together. With whatever her share of the proceeds of The Grey House came to and whatever he could get for his flat, they would put together and buy a house near Reading, for the five of them. He envisaged a ménage of security and individual freedom. If, when the dust had settled, Clodagh wanted to visit them, well, he wasn't going to object. And Martin could of course come and go as he wished.

Charlie came crawling over the grass and hauled himself upright on Sam's trouser leg.

"Hello, old man."

Charlie beamed. Sam thought of his journeys to Sainsbury's and how in future he would put Charlie in the child seat of the trolley. He lifted Charlie on to his knee.

"How about living with your grandfather then?"

Charlie examined a shirt button intently.

"We could have a dog."

From the drive came the sound of Alice's horn, announcing her arrival home. Holding Charlie, Sam stood up and, calling the children to him, led them all round to the garage to greet her.

SEVENTEEN

The cottage was undeniably ugly. It was built of yellowish brick under a blue slate roof and stood in a long garden that ran down to the lane, a tangled garden with aggressive great clumps of delphinium and hollyhock and ornamental sea kale. There was also an apple tree groaning with fruit; it was clearly in the habit of being so prolific because one long, low, laden branch was propped up on a stout wooden stake driven into the ground.

The cottage was uncompromising as well as ugly. It had four rooms upstairs and two downstairs, and in a narrow wing running out at the back, a bathroom above a depressing kitchen. The previous owners had believed very much in hardboard. It was nailed over fireplaces and panelled doors and banisters and beams, and had then been painted in either mauve or apricot emulsion to blend in with the surrounding walls. In the sitting room there was a fireplace of faintly iridescent tiles and below every tap in the house stains spread in green and brown tongues.

Two miles further up the valley there had been a pretty cottage for sale. It was built of stone and the interior was beamed and friendly. There had been great pressure on Alice to choose it because even if many of those exerting pressure didn't much, at the moment, care where she lived, they wanted the children to live somewhere attractive. But Alice had been adamant. She had been adamant about a lot of things and choosing East Cottage rather than the pretty stone one was one of them. The others were that she would live alone and that she would not, because of the children and their schools, leave the Salisbury area. She would move to the other side of the city, but she and Martin would have to risk meeting by mistake now and then. She was also adamant that he and the children should see a great deal of each other.

Natasha was disgusted with East Cottage. Her bedroom was the size of a cupboard and smelled of mushrooms. The walls were papered with fawn bobbly stuff and there was a grey bit on the ceiling that looked squashy. Alice said the room would be absolutely transformed, just you wait, but Natasha didn't want to wait, any more than she had wanted to leave Pitcombe. She told Alice quite often that she hated her and was confused and miserable to find that she felt no better after saying it, so she said it again, louder, to see if that worked. Even school didn't seem the same, with no Grey House to go home to, and Sophie wouldn't be friends this term, so Natasha turned to Charlotte Chambers who was slow and charmless but who had a swimming pool at home and a huge drawing room with a white carpet. The sitting room at East Cottage had no carpet at all, just a piece of rush matting. Alice said that room was going to be wonderful too, just you wait, so Natasha had gone to stay for a whole weekend with Charlotte Chambers, to punish Alice. But the punishment had gone wrong because Natasha had been so homesick. She came home on Monday night, after school, and she shouted, "I hate this house!" and then cried and cried and clung to Alice. Alice said to her, "I know it's hard to feel it, but every day we are going forward."

"But I want to go *back*."

"That's the saddest thing to do. Nothing is ever as good as you thought it was. Because *you* change. You see the old things with changed eyes and they *aren't* the same."

Lettice Deverel came to tea. She came bumping up their stony drive in her old car with the parrot in its cage on the backseat. It was not a good passenger and had screamed most of the way but was pleased to be stationary and accepted a slice of apple with goodish grace. Lettice said that it would probably live for about sixty years more than she would, and that she must find a very kind, interesting person who would look after it when she was dead. James, mesmerized by the parrot's self-possession and humour and little grey blue claw holding the apple, went into a fantasy of being considered sufficiently kind and interesting. He gazed ardently at Lettice, to make her notice.

"Margot Unwin would like to see you," Lettice said to Alice.

"Lord—"

"She needs to. It's very pathetic to see someone so capable so sad and confused. And of course she cannot talk to Ralph because she *wants* to understand and he cannot bring himself to."

"Do you mean she wants me to *explain*—"

"I think so."

"Lord," Alice said again.

"She wants you to go to the Park." Lettice looked at Alice. "I'm afraid Clodagh is going back to America."

Alice said in a low voice, "I thought she would."

"I hope it's just a passing impulse."

"To be made a fuss of, do you mean, to be comforted?"

"She has never been hurt before, you see."

Alice looked at her children.

"I think it's worse to leave being first hurt until you are grown up."

"You never know," Lettice said. "You never know in life, which is good experience and which is damage. Do you?"

After tea, they went out of the cottage to the long shed where Alice was making a studio. Her easel was already set up and there was a trestle table with a workmanlike array of paints and bottles and jam jars of brushes.

"I shall keep myself," Alice said. "Martin is keeping the children, but I shall keep myself. And about time too, I can't help thinking." She picked up a drawing. "Peter Morris has commissioned a painting of Pitcombe Church. The interior. So I'll have to sneak back to do that."

"Don't you *sneak* anywhere," Lettice said. She took the sketch and looked at it. "What is this horrible cottage for? A hair shirt?"

"It isn't horrible. It's real. You wait until I've finished with it. You see—oddly enough—it's easier to bear things here. It feels *mine*. Partly because it isn't what's expected of me, I suppose. That isn't defiance, just the best way to go forward—"

She stopped. Lettice eyed her.

"Will you be lonely?"

"No," Alice said. She took the sketch from Lettice and propped it on the easel. "Are you?"

"No."

"Then you see—"

"Yes," Lettice said, thinking of the sufficiency she had made for herself. "Yes. Of course I see."

⚬∽

Sam came most weekends. He was an enormous asset, not only emotionally, but also because he proved to be very capable with tools. He was delighted with himself, over this.

"If you'd told me, ten years ago, to re-hang a door, I'd have gone *straight* to the pub. But look at this. Go on, push it. See? Smooth as silk. Come on, Jamie, pick up my hammer. What use is an apprentice if he won't even carry my clobber?"

He was entirely unresentful that Alice had declined to set up house with him, and as the weeks wore on he came to think that she had been quite right and that he very much liked his new double life, single in Reading, family at East Cottage. He began, too, to feel first pity and then affection for Clodagh. Without Clodagh, he would not have had these enriching and complementing roles. He made a list of winter projects for East Cottage—"Replace gutters where necessary—Clear wilderness behind shed—Start log pile—Replace all lavatory glass with plain, etc. etc."—which he tacked up in the kitchen so that Elizabeth, who came, astonishingly, for two nights, was drawn back and back to it, to read it over and over as if she couldn't believe her eyes.

The children thought her peculiar, but peaceful, because she did not attempt to be affectionate. She seemed to like East Cottage and professed herself quite prepared to paint window frames, which she then did patiently for forty-eight hours. She declined, to Alice's relief, to have any kind of conversation even approaching a heart-to-heart, and only said, while they were washing up once and the kitchen was noisy with the children, "Well, you've taken a very long time to work yourself through all that nonsense, and you chose a very strange way out, but you've done it. And that's a great deal."

When she left, she said she was going to work for the Citizens' Advice Bureau and had taken a flat in central Colchester.

"I should have done it ten years ago. Ann is a very enervating companion. But I'm doing it now, just in time. Don't come and see me, it's a dreadful journey. I shall come and see you.''

When she had gone, James said, ''Was that really a granny?''

''Yes!''

''Oh,'' he said, ''I thought she was a school lady.''

From Cecily and Richard, Alice heard nothing. Cecily saw the children when they were with Martin, and they would return to East Cottage with new jerseys and bars of chocolate and books. This enraged Alice.

''It shouldn't,'' Sam said. ''They are just the sad symbols of frustrated power.''

''I loved her so much,'' Alice said. ''And now I can hardly bear to think of her. She wanted to eat me up.''

''Didn't Clodagh?''

Alice looked deeply distressed.

''Oh,'' she said, ''Don't—''

Sam was sorry.

''I didn't mean they were the same. In any way. Oh, Allie—''

But she wouldn't speak of it any more and after a while Sam heard her, in her bedroom, crying.

''Why is Mummy crying?'' Natasha said.

''Because she is missing Clodagh.''

Natasha nodded.

''Sometimes,'' she said, ''that makes me cry, too.''

East Cottage was half a mile out of a village. It was an odd village, without a shop or a pub, and the church only had a service every three weeks. The priest, a young, cadaverous, scowling man, who was deeply frustrated to find himself with five rural churches instead of the inner city parish he had wanted, came to see Alice and sat drinking mug after mug of tea while he told her how useless he felt. He'd had some sort of breakdown—he would not, mysteriously, be precise—and this living was supposed to be his stepping stone back to his *real* calling. He was called Mark Murphy. Alice liked him. On his second visit—he came for supper and ate as voraciously as he had drunk tea—she told him, as a kind of test, about Clodagh, and he said, "Love's terrifyingly hard to come by, isn't it? You have to grab it when you get the chance."

His vicarage was a small, unappealing modern house in a neighbouring village which he said had the soul of a shoebox. He took to coming on Saturdays sometimes, to help Sam with clearing the garden, and when Sam asked him if he shouldn't be at home with his family, he said there wasn't one to be at home with because his wife had left him two years ago and had gone home to Newcastle with their baby.

"I'm sorry," Sam said.

"Yes," Mark Murphy said, and sighed. "So am I. She said she had no idea that the other woman in a priest's life might turn out to be God."

Sometimes, in the lane going down to the main road to Salisbury, Alice passed a fair girl driving a dented Citroën with the back full of children. They had passed each other indifferently several times and then, by mutual consent, began to smile and wave. The girl left a note in the wooden mail box at Alice's gate.

"I'm Priscilla Mayne," the note said. "I live half a mile the other side of the village in the Victorian ruin that looks like a squat. No telephone yet. Come and see me when you feel like it."

Alice thought she would feel like it very soon. When a

postcard came from Anthony—she put it in the Rayburn at once—and one from John Murray-French which said, "The new Grey House people are decent and dull. Don't lose touch," she felt in some peculiar way that the possibilities in the as yet unknown Priscilla Mayne had somehow much more reality than her past, known though it was. Sam told her that this was the stuff of freedom, and that she must learn to drink whisky.

"Why?" she said laughing.

"Robert Burns. 'Freedom and whisky gang together.' Actually, freedom is headier than whisky but why not celebrate one with the other?"

It was almost Christmas before Juliet came to East Cottage. She came on a wet day when the cottage, still in a state of raw upheaval, presented its most lowering aspect, and Alice came upon her standing by her car and staring at the mountainous, sodden bonfire of Sam's clearance schemes.

"*Allie*—"

Alice seized her arm.

"Come in. Come in out of the rain. I've just made some unsuccessful bread."

In the kitchen, Juliet burst into tears.

"Allie, it's all so *awful*—"

"No. No, it isn't. I like it here."

"I don't *mean* here. I mean life in Pitcombe."

"Don't be silly. We can't have left that big a hole—"

Juliet said, sniffing, "You've left *heaps* of holes. Great black ones. People are falling in all over the place. I've been in one for *months*. That's why I didn't come."

"Isn't everyone making rather a meal of it?"

"Of course they are. Villages just do. Martin's seeing someone called Sophie. I cannot *tell* you how suitable she is. She drives a Mini and has a King Charles spaniel. Allie, I really hate you.''

"Yes," Alice said.

"I do. How could you leave us all in the lurch like this? Henry's got so pompous I think I'll have to knife him. It's only kind. I'm calling him Eustace in the meantime so I expect he'll knife me first. Allie," Juliet said, bursting into fresh tears, "it's such a relief to see you even if I think your behaviour so detestable that I can't think how it *can* be."

Alice poured them both a glass of wine.

"I'm doing the school run," Juliet said. "I really shouldn't. Blubbing and booze makes me quite incapable of anything except *more* blubbing and booze. Are you pleased to see me?"

"Tremendously."

"Have you got new friends?"

"One. And I'm planning another."

"Don't like them too much—"

"That's not very kind."

"I don't want to be kind," Juliet said, "I want to punish you like mad."

Alice took Juliet all over the cottage and explained what she was going to do with it. Juliet said it hardly seemed worth it.

"It isn't just a cottage," Alice said.

Juliet said too right, it wasn't. They got Charlie up from his rest and took him down to the kitchen, and he sat in his high-chair, damp with sleep, and yawned at his lunch. Alice gave Juliet more wine and made omelettes and they talked about Cecily and Martin and the Unwins, and when Juliet said she really must go, really, truly, she came and put her arms round Alice and kissed her, a thing she had almost never done, and then she drove away in the rain, waving and waving.

When she had gone, Alice took Charlie into the sitting room

and put him on the floor with his cars and the garage she had made him out of a grocery carton. Then she brought in coal and wood and newspapers to light a fire before the children came back from school, and knelt by Charlie, blowing at the kindling. When it had flared up comfortably, she sat back on her heels and watched the flames and Charlie crawled into her lap and offered her a police car. She put her arms round him and laid her cheek on his warm head. Even as she sat there, holding Charlie, Clodagh was somewhere above her, above those relentless grey clouds, flying alone to New York. Alice shut her eyes. Clodagh. To be remembered always with pain and thankfulness.

A Conversation with Joanna Trollope

1. In an interview you stated, "All my novels focus on what making a choice really means. I think sacrifice through choice is something that happens to everybody." What significant choices and sacrifices has life brought you? Did they factor into your writing in any way?

   Everything that has happened to me infuses my writing—it's called experience. And, like all human beings, the significant choices and sacrifices are those made relating to other people, to relationships.

2. What is a typical writing day like for you? Do you ever suffer from writer's block?

   Very dull and disciplined—5 hours in a long morning after which I am sandbagged with exhaustion. I do get stuck, but have learned to do something else—cook, garden—to release the flow again.

3. You almost always set your books in small towns and villages. Why is this? Will a city ever provide the backdrop for a Joanna Trollope novel?

   For visibility. Even dramatic, personal situations lose their edge in big city settings. I want my moral/emotional dilemmas to be seen in high relief.

4. Is your writing ever compared by reviewers to that of your great-great-great-great-great uncle, Anthony Trollope? Do you see any similarities between your writing and his?

No and nor should it be. He was great, I am merely good. Only, I would like to think, a benevolence about humankind. And perhaps a mutual sympathy about describing what he called "those little daily lacerations upon the spirit."

5. How important is it to have strong women characters in your novels? Are there any women in your life who served as role models?

   I think most women are pretty strong, certainly by their forties. The responsibility they take for other people, at home and at work, sees to that. No one woman is my heroine—it's more that I admire the flexibility, stoicism, capability, fun, and generosity that the best women of any age (and any period of history) seem to display.

6. Is there a universal theme that runs throughout your novels?

   Maybe my belief that we do have free will to choose, but that we must then bear the responsibility for the consequences of those choices. Also that happiness may be all very well, but it's something much less interesting and enriching than a bit of the reverse.

7. What words of advice would you give to aspiring fiction writers?

   Don't start too young. Watch people obsessively, and notice. Remember less words make for more meaning. Never forget jokes.

From: Joanna Trollope

Dear Reader –
  I am so pleased –
and grateful! – that you
have bought one of my
novels. I do hope you
enjoy it.
  I'd also like to tell
you that I have a new
book out which is – at
last – set largely in America.
I chose Charleston – surely
one of your most beautiful
cities – where I had a
fascinating time, doing
research.
  See what you think!
          Joanna Trollope